Dana

Best wishes

David..

DAVID E.C. READ

Salt in the Blood

A Young Man's Obsession with the Sea

PECRead.

iUniverse, Inc.
New York Bloomington

iUniverse books may be ordered through booksellers or by contacting:

iUniverse
1663 Liberty Drive
Bloomington, IN 47403
www.iuniverse.com
1-800-Authors (1-800-288-4677)

ISBN: 978-1-4502-6267-5 (sc)
ISBN: 978-1-4502-6265-1 (hc)
ISBN: 978-1-4502-6266-8 (ebook)

Cover photographs taken by the Author

Printed in the United States of America

iUniverse rev. date: 11/16/2010

Acknowledgements

I should like to thank my family for their encouragement in writing this novel particularly my eldest son, Nigel, for his comments and suggestions. Above all I wish to express gratitude to my wife Christine, for her understanding and help during the months of writing.

Dedication

To my father R.E. Read without whom my life at sea, as a Navigating Officer, would not have been possible. Also to Mum, Margaret and Phyllis.

~ A ship in harbor is safe, but that's not what ships are for. ~

Prologue

A wave shipped onboard and ripped across the deck. Edward, walking on the outside of the AB, George, was caught off guard. Unable to grab onto anything, he was swept off his feet. George was able to grab onto one of the flying bridge supports with one hand, and reached out with the other to grab Edward, but missed.

Edward was swept across the deck on his side like a rag doll, ending up at the side railings on the ships starboard side. On the way across he had hit a rail at a tank lid, an ullage plug, and some piping, but had been unable to grab onto anything. With the breath knocked out of him he hit a stanchion of the side rails, grabbed it, and hung on for dear life, literally. His legs were dragged under the bottom rail as the sea poured back over the side. The ship rolled to port, away from the sea on his side and he pulled his legs back inboard.

He was about to get up when he heard George yell, "Hang on!" The roll to port had shipped another wave that was now racing across the deck towards him. Edward held a rail with his left hand and wrapped his right arm around the stanchion and grabbed onto the left shoulder of his jacket. He swung his legs up wrapping them round the rail, interlocking his ankles and feet. He looked wide-eyed at the water hissing across the deck towards him, took a deep breath, closed his eyes, tucked in his chin, and held on with all his strength.

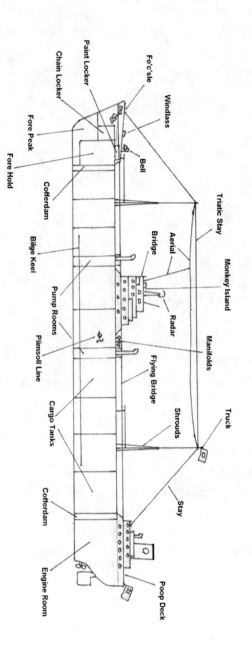

M.V. Combia

Drawing by author - not to scale

Paint Locker
Chain Locker
Fore Peak
Fore Hold
Fo'c'sle
Windlass
Bell
Cofferdam
Bilge Keel
Pump Rooms
Plimsoll Line
Cargo Tanks
Cofferdam
Engine Room
Poop Deck
Stay
Truck
Shrouds
Flying Bridge
Manifolds
Monkey Island
Triatic Stay
Aerial
Bridge
Radar

1

It was the only time he had seen his father cry. What was more upsetting was that his mother, standing beside his father, was also crying.

Edward Paige's parents, Roland and Mary, were on the platform of Grimsby's railway station. As he leaned out of the train's window, the cool breeze ruffled the blond hair atop his lean, six foot frame. They had said their goodbyes on the platform; a hug and kiss from his mum, a handshake from his father. Finally, the train started moving away from the station, but he continued to look back. His mother's brimmed hat was slightly askew atop her shoulder length hair, and her arms held her coat tight against her slim body. She had a damp linen handkerchief scrunched up in her hand which she lifted to give a final wave. His father, cap over his short-cropped dark graying hair, arms straight down at his sides, stood motionless close by her side, watching.

Edward returned the wave, pulled up the window by its thick leather strap until the latch slipped under its lower edge, and then settled down in his seat. In one way he was thankful that the uncomfortable goodbyes were over. He was also a little fearful of the fact that he was now alone on his way south, to London.

His destination in London was the office of The Anglo Saxon Petroleum Company, soon to become Shell International Petroleum Company, at Ibex House in The Mineries. There, he was to pick up travel documents for his journey to the south of France to join his first ship, a Shell Tanker, as a Deck Apprentice. It was early December, 1955. The weather was grey and cold, which fit quite well with how he felt inside. He was sixteen years old.

He soon brightened up, however, at the prospect of the four hour journey south that, for Edward, was an adventure in itself. He had not done much traveling, and had only ever been to London twice. He had never left England before, and now here he was on his way to Marseilles in the south of France; quite an adventure! As the familiar houses and streets of his home town slipped by, the landscape soon opened up to reveal the beautiful Lincolnshire countryside. He wondered when he would see his home and his Mum and Dad again.

As he sat looking out the train's window he had mixed emotions coursing through his body; excitement, loneliness, freedom, and fear of the unknown, and his thoughts drifted off to the events that had brought him to this point.

2

He'd left school the previous year at the minimum age of fifteen, which was a time that hadn't come soon enough for Edward; he had not enjoyed school at all, although he had done rather well in class. His father had found him a job down the fish docks, at a fish house just around the corner from where he himself worked. He had loved the atmosphere of the docks; the fishing boats, the sea, the constant bustle, and the honest, hard working, and friendly people. The work was tough, but he enjoyed the physical activity and went at it with the vigor of youth. Over his old working clothes he wore an oilskin apron with bib, and leather clogs on his feet that had wooden soles with metal 'horse shoes' nailed to the soles and heels. You sure couldn't creep up on anyone and surprise them wearing those! Wrapped round his legs, overlapping his clogs to keep his feet dry, were oilskin gaiters tied with string below the knees. He was just a young version of everyone around him, but more gangly and clumsy.

His first job in the mornings was scrubbing the wooden fish boxes and lids that were used to ship the fish off to their various destinations across the country, which was accomplished mainly by train. The washing was done by having the box on the ground next to a fifty gallon drum of fresh water, and slopping the water out with a hard bristled broom into the box, then scrubbing all interior surfaces like a maniac. Each box held about fifty pound of fish when filled, and after cleaning they were stacked upside down to dry, with the lids leaning against them. This took an hour or so depending on the estimated amount needed for at least that day, to supply the four workers who would be filleting the fish and filling the boxes. It was busy all day. Ray, the foreman, was of medium height, and always wore a tie with his work shirt, as did Edward's father. The tie was held in place by a short sleeveless pullover, and his dark hair was combed down with Brylcream. Like most men that worked down here, he was as strong as a horse, and kept everything flowing with quiet authority. He seemed to work harder than anyone. He laughed and joked with everyone, making Edward feel right at home; he was a great person to work with, his authority never questioned.

Next was the job he really liked, because it got him out-and-about among the throng of workers in this bustling, busy port. He had initially accompanied one of the experienced hands, pushing a large wheel barrow to pick up kits of fish from the various pontoons. After a few weeks he had been sent off alone, and he went about his work with great enthusiasm. Unknowingly at the time, he had inherited a great work ethic from his father. An ethic that ensured you worked hard for the person that gave you your pay check, and remained faithful to them. The philosophy - if you don't like the job, go work somewhere else; simple really.

The fish were purchased at early morning auction by the company buyer, who worked in the office above the fish house. After purchase, five or six labels were slapped on the top surface of each kit of fish, which bore the initials of the merchant, in this case J.C.S., and a note was made of their location. The buyer would then move on to the next auction. There could be cod, haddock, turbot, plaice, sole, halibut or hake, the latter having sharp fin spines and large sharp teeth, dictating care in handling. Not all merchants dealt with all the fish types - some specialized in hake, catfish, salmon, rock salmon or roughy, for the London market.

"Aye, son! Grab the barra and pick up kits from the East, North and West walls, thar's ten in all," yelled Ray.

Edward propped his broom up against the wall, pulled off his oilskin apron, put on his jacket, and off he went. The barra (barrow) was some seven feet long with big curving handles. It had a flat bed with a metal loop at the end some two and a half feet tall against which the kits of fish were stacked, and two ten inch tires near the front end. It also had two large metal loops that served as legs at the handle end to allow the barrow to sit level while loading or unloading. A kit weighs ten stone or one hundred and forty pounds, which was about the same weight as Edward. The barrow would often be stacked with twelve to fourteen kits, but when balanced correctly, the handles could be lifted with one hand, and held quite easily at a forty five degree angle. It was the pulling and pushing that became the challenge. It was always prudent to check that the tires were properly inflated before use.

To get back to the fish house, ramps up and down the various pontoons, cobbled roads and railway lines had to be navigated. When he had a full load it was quite a struggle to get back. Getting up enough steam to make the up-ramps was nigh on impossible for him and a cry for help would always result in one or two workers laughingly helping to push the barrow to the level pontoon, with its smooth concrete surface. This was easy pushing, but always at a slow steady pace as it was a devil to stop the barrow once it was in motion.

He liked to stop for a few minutes and watch the various activities going on around him. One of his favorites was two guys stood side by side, each skinning catfish. This was done by means of a hook on the end of a long chain, which was attached to the girder of the roof above. The large fish, some three feet long, were hooked through the eye sockets on the end of the chain. The men would start with a cut across the fish behind the head. Grabbing the cut edge with the knife blade and strong fingers, they took a step back and pulled down hard towards the tail of their respective fish. This brought the one side of skin off in one piece. As the skin came off, the fish swung away from them, sometimes in unison, which was quite a sight! Each of the skinners had two forty gallon metal drums beside him, and the skin was thrown into one of them. The fish swung back and they skinned the other side, again letting go and throwing the skin into the barrel. As the fish swung back again, the skinner would grab the fish by the tail and detach the head from the body with a powerful swing of his broad bladed knife, which actually resembled a small machete. Once again the chain swung away, and the beheaded fish was dropped into a metal kit at the foot of the barrels. When the chain came back from its final swing of the cycle, the head was taken off the hook, thrown into the second barrel, and replaced with another fish. Then the whole process started again. The men worked fast, with very little chatter.

The men didn't have to gut the catfish, as all fish landed at the docks were already gutted. This was done by the fishermen at sea, right after the catch, after which the fish are washed with a hose before being stowed below in the pounds, (divisions in the hold for the storage of fish), on layers of ice. This ensured that the fish would be fresh and clean when landed for market. During the process of gutting cod, the livers were collected and later boiled to extract the valuable oil.

Time to move on, he lifted the handles and leaned into the barrow to get it moving, *I wonder what they taste like*, he thought to himself of the catfish. Growing up within his happy family it was never a case of, 'I wonder if we're having fish for dinner today?' It was always, 'I wonder what *kind* of fish we're having for dinner today?'

Later, when he asked about the taste of catfish, his dad had pulled a face, saying, "They're no good, they're just junk fish."

He took his father at his word and dismissed catfish from any future menus. All of his family, including his two sisters, loved fish and strangely enough always would. His father only brought home what he called the premium fish; haddock and cod, (both fresh and smoked), plaice, Dover sole, halibut, turbot and kippers! The latter were smoked herring which, unlike all the other fish caught by trawling, were caught by drifters with gill nets. Trawlers use a net called the Trawl, which is cone-shaped and dragged along the sea bed. It captures everything that enters the open mouth; except the very small fish that can swim through the mesh, while a gill net is hung vertically in the water just below the surface like a long sheet. The openings in the mesh of a gill net are sized so that when herring try to pass through the mesh they're easily able to get their head through, but the opening is too small for the rest of their body. When they try to back out, the mesh gets caught behind their gill covers, hence the name 'gill net'. Smaller fish, again, are able to easily pass through the mesh, while fish larger than herring can't get through at all, so only the desired size herring are caught. Large fleets of these vessels followed the fish along the east coast of England and Scotland.

Edward lost control of the wheel barrow going down one of the ramps, hit the railway lines at the bottom, and tipped his load over the dirty road. *Stop dreaming boy!* he admonished himself. Many hands sprang forward to help; they righted the wheel barrow, dumped a wooden barrel of ice on to the road alongside the scattered fish, wiped all the fish on the ice, put them back in the kits, and put the kits back on the barrow. Soon he was on his way again as if nothing had happened. *A great bunch of guys!.*

He finally got back to the fish house, and sat on the handles of the barrow while his workmates unloaded the kits, taking them inside for filleting. "Good job lad!" came with a pat on the shoulder.

He didn't respond, but as he put the wheel barrow to one side, out of the way he thought. *Do I really want to do this for the rest of my life…? Hell, No! I have to do something better than this.*

On this trip he had picked up (literally) haddock, cod, and plaice. The haddock averaged about three pounds in weight and the cod seven. The plaice were about a foot long and were usually shipped with just the head removed, on the bone with skin on. When these were cooked at Edward's home, just the dark, rough, skin was removed while the soft white skin of the underside was left on. This helped to keep the fish together when cooking and was also quite edible.

He loved to watch the guys as they went about their job of filleting. Quick, deft movements of the razor sharp knives soon separated flesh from bone, and if not careful would do the same to their hands. The filleting table was a six foot trough, with water, in which the fish were dumped. On either side, was a one and a half inch thick wooden board for putting the fish on while filleting. There were two filleters per table, facing each other. It was a cold job that gave them cold, wet, swollen hands. They constantly stopped to sharpen their knives with a metal steel, pressing one end of it into the wooden filleting surface, or held away from them like crossed swords, while the knife was slashed up and down on both sides. If ever a knife slipped, all reaction at the table was to jump back with hands in the air.

"Never try to stop a knife from falling, or anything else around here for that matter. Just get out of the way and let it fall," he was advised. It was good advice that he would always remember.

The fillets were placed carefully to one side for weighing and packing later. Haddock bones with head still attached were thrown into a barrel. With the cod, however, the head was detached from the long bones and thrown into boxes to one side. Later these large heads were dealt with by removing two delicacies - the cheeks and the tongues. These were carefully separated into different containers.

All the barrels of waste bones, heads and skins were put outside the main doors and collected daily for shipping to fertilizer and fish meal factories. *Holy smokes, I have to get out of here. I can't do this for the rest of my life,* was Edward's repetitive thought.

3

Edward had had a yearning to go to sea for as long as he could remember. His father had spent twenty years on Trawlers and Drifters as a deep sea fisherman. He had spoken to his dad about going to sea and was told what a hard, dangerous life it was, and not very adventurous.

"If you want to go to sea you should go in the Merchant Navy; far better and safer and you will see a lot more of the world." This really gave Edward food for thought, and visions of plying the world's oceans filled his mind.

His father had worked through the ranks until he earned his Skipper's ticket, which was a Certificate of Competence obtained through written and oral exams. This Certificate confirmed him as qualified to command a fishing vessel, which he did on trawlers that traveled as far as the Grand Banks of Newfoundland. Because of this, Edward's thoughts became constantly focused on being an officer rather than a deckhand. This seemed much more romantic. How to go about achieving this was the next step. He was to get great encouragement from his fellow workers when he mentioned it to them.

"Go for it lad, get the'self outa this mess and go and see sum'in o' the world!"

Enquiries had led Edward and his father to the Hull Trinity House Navigation School, located across the Humber River from Grimsby, in Hull, Yorkshire. Hull was a place he had been to on a few occasions with his father, who had to make the trip in order to supervise shipments of fish down to London, for his company in Grimsby. He never did understand the logic of this; going from one fishing port to another to ship fish somewhere! However, he had always enjoyed the trips and the hard working people, and their lives on the fish docks. Sitting in the cafes with them drinking big mugs of thick, strong tea he'd felt like a grownup, yet was still small and fragile among these large, strong, energetic men.

It was on one of these trips to Hull that Edward had watched a freezer lorry being loaded with boxes of fish. The load was kept cool by cylindrical shaped ice blocks of solid carbon dioxide called Cardice. After the brown paper wrapping was ripped open, the Cardice was thrown in among the boxes, and the large fridge type doors were closed and padlocked.

The driver, Bill, a friend of his fathers, had said; "Aye Rolly, why don't yer let the lad come down to London wi' me? It's a good trip and he can see the ships in Tilbury, and I'd enjoy the company."

"What do you think son?" his father asked.

"Yes, Yes, Yes!" was Edward's enthusiastic response.

So, an hour later he was sitting in the cab of the lorry bubbling with excitement at the prospect of the long drive, especially considering the fact that it was the first time he'd ever been in a lorry. Also, he'd only been to London once before, on a school bus trip, where they had gone on a site-seeing tour. The lorry ride was quite an adventure. They headed west out of Hull and eventually picked up the A1 highway and headed south. The A1 had originally been a Roman road and was very straight and took them right to London.

On this trip they saw very little of London itself, just going directly to the docks in Tilbury. Seeing the big oceangoing ships up close was a real thrill for Edward and just intensified his yearning to go to sea. While Edward watched the unloading of the boxes of fish into the refrigerated unit of a warehouse, pieces of the Cardice fell onto the dockside. The large pieces were picked up, with gloved hands or by the torn paper wrapping, and thrown into the dock which caused the water to bubble ferociously, as if boiling.

"Watch this Edward," Bill called. He took a penny from his pocket and stood it on edge on a wedge shaped piece of Cardice lying on the ground. The heat of the coin caused it to sink into the ice, and as it did so the coin began to vibrate and ring like an electric bell.

"That's incredible!" was Edward's response. Bill picked up the coin and put it into Edward's hand, he immediately jumped back and let it fall to the ground, much to the delight of the guys unloading the lorry. The penny had become as cold as the ice itself.

On the way back north at a small restaurant and store, Bill gave Edward a few shillings so he could buy his mother a present - a hair brush, mirror and comb set. He dropped Edward off near the railway station in Grimsby where he could get a bus home, and then continued on his way back around the Humber River to Hull. There had been no communications to home as Edward's parents did not have a telephone, but Bill had called Roland's workplace from London to let him know that all was OK, and when to expect his son home.

As always, Edward was greeted warmly by his mother when he arrived home. She made a pot of tea and they sat down at the small kitchen table where she opened her present and excitedly gave him a hug and kiss. They sat sipping the hot tea, and as he told her about his trip she had listened intently and smiled. Edward did not realize it at the time, but these quiet moments with his Mum, and those in the future, would become very precious to him.

4

The visit to Trinity House that summer was both exciting and nerve racking. Trinity House, which held the finest maritime traditions in Britain, sits alongside Prince's Dock in the heart of downtown Hull. Two storey brick buildings, shops and offices lined the street facing the dock, and it was through these buildings that a large gated archway led to the cobbled courtyard of the school. This was on the north and east ends of the property, with the high brick wall of a warehouse to the south. At the west end of the courtyard stood a white painted flag staff with a red ensign, the Merchant Navy flag, fluttering in the breeze. It was this end of the courtyard that held the entrance that led to the Principal's office.

Edward and his father sat down with the Headmaster, Mr. Eddan, who was a tall, dark haired man in a suit that hung loosely on his thin frame. He was a good friendly man that quickly put them both at ease and made them feel comfortable. His father proudly showed Mr. Eddan his Skipper's Ticket, and it was handed back with a nod of approval. After many questions back and forth between the three of them it was decided that Edward should return the following month to sit an entrance exam for the term beginning the sixth of September. If successful, consideration would have to be given to accommodation, and the Merchant Navy Hotel was recommended to them. There was also the necessary purchase of a merchant navy/school uniform, which could be obtained just round the corner from the school. After about an hour they left the school grounds through the archway, onto the dockside where they paused for a moment to survey the area.

"You alright son?" his father asked.

"Yes Dad, I'm fine. Glad that's over with though." His father gave a wry smile.

The end of the dock they now faced led off to Victoria Square to the right, as well as Queen's Gardens, which at one time had also been a dock. Whitefriargate, the main shopping street, was in the same direction, running to the East, at the end of which was a little street called 'The Land of Green Ginger'. So if you're ever asked, 'Where is The Land of Green Ginger?' it's in Hull, Yorkshire.

The city of Hull was built on the banks of the River Hull, which is obviously where it derived its common name. The true name of the city is actually Kingston-Upon-Hull; Hull for short or as the locals call it, 'ull. Jokingly it was said that the city should have been called Kingston-Upon-Mud, as when the tide's out there is virtually no water left in the river. There's just a trickle in the centre of the channel with large mud flats on each side. Any barges moored in the river would sit at crazy angles on this mud, held by their taut mooring lines.

They set off towards an old warehouse district, turning left, then left again onto Posterngate. They passed the small uniform shop which they would be visiting in the near future to purchase Edward's uniforms and other sea gear. To their right, on the corner of Dagger Lane, was the 'Mission to Seamen'. These Missions were built all over the world in sea ports to offer a safe haven for seamen to gather whilst ashore, and were very popular. They also provided a place, for those so inclined, to attend church service and/or to pray. The popularity of these Missions would, sadly, decline over the years and this particular one would become a pub – The Mission.

Their short, pleasant walk took them down a narrow cobbled street and through to the market place. Just a few yards away was the wall and railings that enclosed the beautiful Holy Trinity Church, which Edward would see much more of in the following twelve months.

In a large tent just outside the entrance to the indoor marketplace there was a fish and chip shop, where they stopped for lunch. Sawdust covered the floor area, and there was a counter with salt, pepper, malt vinegar and a bowl of mint sauce. They sat on one of the wooden benches that lined three of the walls. The fish and chips along with mushy peas, a Yorkshire delicacy, and a slice of bread and butter were really good, and they both ate ravenously with very little conversation.

Actually, there had never been a lot of conversation between the two of them. Edward's father was a strict disciplinarian. He was very fair, never getting really angry, and his discipline was always vocal, never physical. He generally kept himself to himself, and any attempt to engage him in conversation was usually difficult, so they were just content to be in each other's company, and left it at that.

After lunch they walked alongside the church wall and turned right, stopping at the wonderful bronze statue of King William, known as 'King Billy'. After a brief look at this great work of art, they went down the steps to the public toilets below the guarding statue. *What an ignoble place for the King to guard!* Edward thought as they crossed the street and headed for the river.

They were now on their way to Wilberforce House, on the banks of the River Hull. As a history buff, it was Edward's father's favorite place to visit. At the north-east side of Queen's Gardens is a tall monument, similar to Nelson's column in Trafalgar Square in London, dedicated to William Wilberforce. Wilberforce was a Hull resident that was largely responsible, after decades of fighting in Parliament, for the abolition of the slave trade in the British Empire in 1807, and the abolition of slavery in the British Empire in 1833. It wasn't until thirty years later, in 1863, that President Lincoln abolished slavery in the United States.

Wilberforce House is a modest Georgian style home enclosed by a seven foot brick wall. A wrought iron gate opens onto a small courtyard lined with large trees, the back of which overlooks the river. Edward thought the inside of the house was quite dismal, but the books, manuscripts and artifacts were interesting, and comprehensively illustrated a shameful past history of, as famed Scots poet Robbie Burns put it, "man's inhumanity to man". That particular inclination, however, was not a new one to Britain, nor to a great portion of the rest of the world for that matter..

While Edward's father had a great interest and memory for historic events, Edward, in his youth, didn't spend a great deal of time pondering such things. As he grew older though, his understanding and abhorrence of such unspeakable injustices grew substantially, and he became a bit of a history buff himself.

They left Wilberforce House and walked down to Corporation Pier to catch the ferry back across the River Humber. Perhaps 'walked' is not the most accurate description; Edward had to almost trot to keep up with his father's long, purposeful stride. The ferry would take about twenty-five minutes to cross the Humber, docking at New Holland in Lincolnshire. Again there was little conversation. Edward looked affectionately at the quiet, almost secretive man by his side, whose sole purpose on this trip to Hull had been nurturing Edward's future. He wanted to hug his father but knew that it would not go down well at all; he was not the hugging type.

In spite of this, the ferry ride back across the Humber was something that Edward really enjoyed. He imagined himself at sea and stood at the bow, in command of the vessel's crossing. The ferry, the Lincoln Castle, whose sister ship was the Thornton Abbey, was a paddle steamer with large paddle wheels on either side. She had small glass ports that you could look through to see the paddle wheels going round. The steam engine was powered by a boiler fueled with coal, and could likewise be viewed from a window in the fore and aft alleyways, which ran along either side of the engine room casing. On the deck further aft was a manhole cover, where the coal was loaded into the bunkers below. The after deck was for cars, about eight in all, and it was rarely full. There weren't many cars around in those days.

The ferry rides always seemed so adventurous and invariably, they were over too quickly. From the ferry, it was a long walk up the ramp that rose and fell with the tide, then to the railway station at New Holland. From there it was less than an hour train ride to Grimsby and home. He looked forward to seeing his Mum, whom he could always chat with, and telling her of the day's events as she bustled about the kitchen preparing tea (supper). He loved this lady dearly, for that is what she was; a lady.

5

Edward's father worked hard at a fish merchant's on the docks, in charge of the large cold storage unit. The fish docks were four miles from their home, and he walked to work every morning. He rose between 4:30 and 5:00 a.m., cooked breakfast for himself, which was often boiled kippers and bread, made a sandwich for his lunch, and was at work by 7:00 a.m. to start at 7:30. He was never late for work, as that would have been sorely against his principles. He worked until 5:00 p.m. and usually walked home to their house on Huddlestone Road, though he was occasionally known to take the bus, which stopped five streets away from their house. He worked five and a half days a week, often did overtime, and usually slept in on Sunday morning until ten or eleven a.m. As Edward was only fifteen years old he started work later, and finished earlier than his father, so they rarely traveled together.

Occasionally, before lunch on a Sunday, the two of them would walk down to the fish docks to see the trawlers leaving through the lock gates and into the river to ply and fight the sea for another haul of fish. On a few occasions a fisherman would toss up a silver coin from the deck, and Edward would scramble to catch it.

"Why do they do that?" he asked his Dad.

"Some fishermen don't like to have money in their pocket while at sea, they think its bad luck". Sailors are a superstitious lot.

Other ships were coming in to get ready for market early the next morning, unloading their haul in the hopes that the market was good and their shared pay would be worthwhile. They led a tough life and the rewards could be small, but after a few days ashore they would be off again. There are areas in Hull, Grimsby, and Lowestoft, (Edward's father's home town), that fishermen live where one, or more, family on every street have lost men at sea in their fight against the elements;

the mother sea and all her moods. This was probably true for all major fishing ports, and all in an effort to bring her bounty to market.

….

The entrance exam date had arrived and Edward made the trip back to Hull, this time on his own. The exam was not particularly difficult and fitted in well with his secondary modern education. There had been no complicated mathematics; he'd be learning this soon enough. It was a proud and exciting moment when he learnt that he had passed. His father, he knew, was also very proud but just nodded at the news. Edward would start at the beginning of the new term. *Hopefully, the first step to a bright future ahead*, he thought to himself.

6

Classes at Trinity House were to begin on the sixth of September. Edward and his father had revisited Hull and purchased his uniform from the little shop across from the Mission to Seamen. They'd also been to the Merchant Navy Hotel on Anlaby Road, which is a short walk from Trinity House. There they'd sat down with the manager, Mr. Gates, and made arrangements for Edward's year long stay, beginning Sunday, the fifth of September. The rules of the hotel were explained in detail, and Mr. Gates actually became like a second father to Edward while he was under the hotel's roof. It turned out that he was just as strict as Edward's father, and an absolute gentleman.

It had been a proud moment when, dressed in his uniform, he stood in front of his parents. They were all very proud, his mum cheerfully tearful. They all knew then that they were going to miss each other, and even though Edward's mother was from a seafaring family and was used to the men going off to sea, it would not make their parting any easier.

Edward had given no thought to the expense of all this, plus pocket money every week. It was to be much later that he really came to appreciate the sacrifice his father had made to do this for him. They were, after all, just a middle class working family. The hotel was very reasonable as there was some arrangement through Trinity House. This did not belittle, however, his father's investment in his future.

There were to be a number of other cadets staying at the hotel, so there would be company for Edward, thank goodness.

The Sunday finally arrived, and after more tearful goodbyes from his mum, he set off for his journey by train and ferry. Across the river once more, Edward made the short walk to the hotel lugging all his gear. It was mid afternoon on a beautiful September day. He signed in at the hotel and was given directions to his room. Up the wide three-tiered staircase, along the hall as far as you could go, and through a small passageway into 'The Extension'.

The Extension was exactly that; attached to the south end of the hotel and protruding out some fifteen feet to the east, separated outside by a narrow passageway from the kitchen, which was on the bottom level of the hotel. There were three levels and it was very utilitarian. Three flights of concrete stairs with iron handrails went down at the one end, tiled floors, creamy colored painted walls, and two bathrooms on the stair landings at level one and two. Rooms were on one side of the four foot wide hallways and there were no windows. *Hell, it's like a prison block,* Edward thought, not knowing what a prison block looked like anyway.

The way in and out was the stairs at the one end, which were quite dark even with the lights on; without them it would be pitch black. Edward secretly hoped the lights would stay on. His room was on the second level, one of four doors on the left hand side, with a single door across the end. He unlocked and opened the door to his room, the third one down. As it swung open to just past the ninety degrees, it hit the single bed. There was a small desk with drawers, a chair, a small mirror on the wall above the desk, and in the corner a single wardrobe with one shelf and a hanging rod. The window had two panes, with one side that opened vertically that was big enough to climb out of, onto the fire escape. He had a lovely view of the brick wall of the hotel four feet away. The windows were dirty and were hard to see through. In front of the window was a small baseboard heater.

"Well, you couldn't swing the proverbial cat in this place," he said out loud. He sat down on the bed, at least it was clean with crisp white linen sheets, a brown woolen bedspread, and a folded blanket at the foot. He was feeling a little dejected and out of place. Not one to sit and mope, however, he unpacked his gear and slid the suitcase under the bed, then set off to explore what was to be his home for the next twelve months or so.

The rest of the hotel was in sharp contrast to the extension, with wide, brightly lit hallways, fancy moldings, bright paintwork, and lush carpeting on the floors and staircases. At the top of the stairs leading down to the lobby there was a large lounge with tables and chairs, sofas, and armchairs, and a piano in the corner near the large bay windows, which overlooked the street below. The ceilings were high with ornate moldings round the top of the walls, and thick carpeting on the floor. This was to be a wonderful study room, quiet and peaceful and, as it turned out, not used very much by other patrons of the hotel who favored the identical room directly below this one, on the main level. Also on the main level was a long hallway leading to a set of double doors, which opened onto the large dining room. On one wall were large, bright bay windows. At the far end there was a small stage against the wall, and it was the outside of this wall that provided the view from Edward's room. Alongside the dining room was the serving kitchen with doors to both the dining room and the hallway. Below this was the kitchen itself, with food being hauled up from below via the 'dumb waiter,' at the far end there were also stairs down to the kitchen. It was dinner time so he entered and found a table to one side, feeling rather self-conscious among all the other guests, with the feeling that everyone was watching him. This was also a new experience, and alone at the table he was nervous. The waitress, Mary, a peppy little blonde with a frilly apron round her slim waist, was very friendly and put him at ease, he showed her his room key, as his stay here included three meals a day.

"Trinity House cadet?" she asked.

"Yes, I'm Edward."

Mary nodded and made her way back to the serving kitchen. He had soup, roast beef and Yorkshire pudding, a typical Sunday dinner, and rice pudding for dessert. He ate quickly, not having realized how hungry he'd been.

On his way back to the lobby, walking past the bar where three sailors sat having a pint, he met the manager, Mr. Gates.

"Are you settling in alright, Edward?"

"Yes thank you, sir!" he replied, impressed that his name had been remembered.

"Don't be late for school tomorrow, eight thirty sharp." Mr. Gates sounded like his father.

"No sir."

Back in The Extension, as it was always called, other doors were open and he could hear voices. These came from the first room down the hallway and belonged to two guys his age. He stopped in the doorway and they both fell silent and looked at him enquiringly. Edward stepped into the room.

"Hi! You guys going to Trinity House?" asked Edward.

"Yes" they answered in unison.

They all shook hands and introduced themselves. "Edward, I'm from Grimsby."

"John, Whitby."

Whitby, Edward knew, was north along the coast in Yorkshire. John was tall and slim, although not as tall as Edwards's six feet, with short straight black hair. He was well dressed in blazer and flannels; *college type*, thought Edward.

"Tony, I'm from Boston, a fellow Lincolnshire yeller-belly," he said, smiling as he shook Edward's hand vigorously. Tony was about five foot six, with short, fair, unkempt hair, broad shoulders, and strong, judging by his grip. He looked like a boxer, and reminded Edward of James Cagney. He had on a loose fitting grey suit.

Edward liked them both instantly and felt less alone and, in fact, more secure in the knowledge he had friends and neighbors on the same floor. He felt a camaraderie with these two already, and the prospect of arriving at school the following morning was less daunting because of them. Things got better though, when they heard a fourth person bumping down the hallway, struggling with a large suitcase. Edward poked his head out of the doorway, "Here, let me help you with that!" he called out, springing forward to help the newcomer, who gladly put the suitcase down and looked up with a tired smile.

"Hi," said Edward holding out his hand, "Edward."

"Mike." His hand felt small in Edward's but the grip was firm.

Mike was shoulder height to Edward, slight build, sad looking brown eyes, and tousled short brown hair. Edward bent and picked up the suitcase with ease although it was quite heavy. *This must have been a struggle for this guy,* thought Edward; *all the way from the lobby to here!* His time down the fish docks had made Edward quite strong; something that would stand him in good stead in the future. Mike opened his room door, motioning for Edward to enter, which he did and threw the suitcase on the bed.

"Thanks."

"Where you from?" asked Edward by way of conversation.

"Leeds," Mike smiled, as he slumped down on the bed, hands between his knees as he let out a long sigh.

Edward liked him already, "I'm from Grimsby."

"Ah! The other side of the river," Mike said smiling.

Edward smiled back, "Yep!"

There is a long standing friendly rivalry between Yorkshire and Lincolnshire, which are separated by the Humber River. Each side claims that they come from the 'right side' of the river. This friendly banter was because of the two fishing ports of Grimsby and Hull each claiming that they were the largest fishing port in the world at that time. It was pretty close but, of course, it was obvious who Edward would be voting for if it ever came to that.

They were joined by John and Tony and they all chatted for a while. Then they decided to go 'downstairs' and hang out for a while. It was actually up the extension stairs, along the long corridor to the lobby stairs, and then down to the main lounge. They chatted and jostled one another on the way, like they had known each other for years, although Mike hung back a little.

Edward looked back; "Come on Mike, let's go!" Mike quickened his pace and caught up with the others.

Down in the lounge there were a few patrons sitting around, smoking, reading, and chatting. The four of them bustled in and were barely given a glance by the occupants. Sitting in an armchair near the large bay window that overlooked Anlaby Road, was a blond, strongly built lad of their own age looking at them questioningly. They all went over and slumped down on the large couch filling up the bay under the window.

"You going to Trinity House?" asked Tony, the James Cagney look alike.

"Yes," was the reply, and everyone introduced themselves to Dave who, as it turned out was from York.

Tony looked at Ed and smilingly said, "Looks like we're really outnumbered," and burst out laughing, referring to the Yorkshire/Lincolnshire rivalry.

They chatted away for a while and discovered that they were all on the one year course for Trinity House starting the next day. Except for John, the Whitby lad, they were all unsure of what to expect.

Sounding bored, John stated, "It will be just like any other school."

Well as far as Edward was concerned it would turn out to be anything but that. But there again, he had only ever been to one school. That had been Carr Lane Secondary Modern School, which had been divided into two parts, Primary - five years to eleven, and Senior eleven to fifteen. They had in fact built a separate primary school in what was known as 'the buttercup field', that in summer was totally yellow with this wild flower. The primary students were moved to this new school the year that Edward moved to the seniors, which then took over the whole of the building. So his ten years of schooling had all been at the one place.

7

The next morning, the five of them all dressed in their new doe-skin naval uniforms with their bright shiny brass buttons and polished black shoes, made their way downstairs. They had breakfast together feeling as conspicuous, and vulnerable, as a blackbird in the centre of a snow covered garden, with a hunting cat prowling at the edge.

After breakfast they donned their caps, which had the Trinity House school badge on the front in gold braid. It depicted an anchor upside down, lying at rest under the stars. Edward put his on straight, others at different angles, left side, right side, Mike (Cagney) put his on the back of his head, hair sticking out under the brim. They all decided not to wear their Burberry raincoats as they didn't want to hide their uniforms, and anyway it was a lovely sunny day. They left the hotel and waved to the manager, Mr. Gates, who stood at the window of his office smiling at them, and waved back.

They walked proudly down the street passing Victoria Square, with its statue of Queen Victoria standing in the centre with a staid expression on her face, as if admonishing them to behave.

It was here that they came across a smartly dressed individual, probably in his sixties, with flowing open raincoat, highly polished shoes, dark colored suit, with a silk cravat around his neck under a crisp white shirt, a Tyrolean-type hat, complete with a pheasant feather, atop his long dark hair, and a walking stick that he swung backwards and forwards as he walked briskly towards them.

"Good morning young fellows" he said as they passed, with a wave of the walking stick.

"Good morning" they replied in unison as they turned laughing to watch this colorful character walking happily on his way. They later learnt that this was Roland who was known by all, an apparently wealthy eccentric that lived somewhere in Hull. He became part of the scenery on their daily walks to and from school.

They went round the Prince's Dock and through the archway into the school, to be confronted by a courtyard full of cadets from twelve to fifteen years of age. A few were wearing the same type of uniform as them, which turned out to be the fifteen/sixteen year olds on the one year course. The others were the three year students, whose uniforms were more of the Nelson midshipman's uniform; short monkey jackets with a stiff white collar, open at the front, and brass buttons curving across the chest. Some had up to four vertical pieces of gold braid on the bottom of their sleeves with a small brass button on the top of each. These were the cadet officers, and it would be these cadets that would get this rabble to order and lined up in the class groups. They would then be addressed by the headmaster and marched into the school and the classrooms. *Fun, wow!*

There were four groups in total; the youngsters in the junior group who were new to the school; the intermediate group, who had moved up from junior the year before; and the senior group, which were the previous year's intermediates. Then there was the group to which Edward and his new mates belonged. There were just fourteen in this group and they stood out from the others because of their age and uniform, but at this time it was by appearance only, and certainly not by ability.

The headmaster's address was brief, touching on everyone's desire to be officers in the Merchant Navy. He wished the best of luck to those who had graduated. He welcomed those who were just starting.

He spoke of the commitment it took to "study and learn your craft from the best; your instructors." He also described how "all of you will be ambassadors for Great Britain when you travel the world as Merchant Sailors – Navigators. Be sure that you represent her well."

Edward was inspired. All the cadets, who faced the school building, were brought to attention, right turn, and the red ensign was hauled up the mast while the officers saluted. They were then marched into the school by rows and group, and into the classrooms. This would be the regular morning drill, with the speech being replaced by any special announcements.

And so it begins!

....

Edward's group settled into their classroom and Edward sat next to the person that would become his best friend for many years to come. In-fact, they considered themselves twins, although they looked nothing like each other, as they had the same birth date. His name was Peter Ford. Peter was a swarthy, swashbuckling type with thick wavy hair and an infectious toothy smile. Slightly bow-legged, he jaunted along with his cap always on one side, and was regularly told to straighten it when on parade. He already looked like a vintage sailor. He was from Hull.

The first morning went quickly and easily, with introductions all round by each of the attendees. The class instructor, Mr. Foster, was a tall, strongly built man in his early thirties, with black wavy hair straight across a narrow brow, and brown piercing eyes that only had to look at you to make you pay attention. He handed each of the class a print-out, that had been neatly done by hand, of the agenda, which was a monthly repeated activity. They were going to be busy. Edward had never liked school, the boring repetition of it all, but here there was going to be one major difference - a tangible reason for it all at the end of the year.

The following section is a little technical, but details and illustrates the subjects and hard studies of ship's officers in the British Merchant Navy. The year's activities would include:

Algebra. This, for Edward, was hard to understand at first. What possible practical use, with all its formulas, did this subject have? He would soon find out, and actually grew to enjoy it.

Trigonometry. (right angle) Here was another one, but its practical use was enjoyable. What was the rhyme? On A Train One Has Such A Happy Company

Opposite over Adjacent = Tangent

Opposite over Hypotenuse = Sine

Adjacent over Hypotenuse = Cosine

Opposite way round for Cotangents, Secants and Cosecants. *'Huh?!'*

The book most widely used for the solving of mathematical problems by use of logarithms, was Nories Tables, the bible for navigation at this time. At sea, when they owned their own copy of this book, it would be identified with the owner's name written along the outside edges of the pages, as the book was closed. This made it easily recognizable as their own, which was important, as each owner had their own notations and inserts taped inside.

Geometry. Edward had always liked technical drawing at school; he liked the precision and necessary accuracy and neatness of it. Being able to calculate areas and volumes would have practical use in the loading of a ship's cargo, areas of decks, volumes of ship's holds and tanks etc.

In one class the instructor asked, "What's a frustum?"

No one answered.

"It's a truncated cone, or a cone with the pointed section cut off, which gives you a frustum. Or, if you like, one of those things that an elephant frigs around on at the circus," the teacher informed them. This caused great laughter. Who would ever forget what a frustum was again?!

Navigation. Spherical Trigonometry - This was 'great' stuff, pun intended. This was all about triangles again, but this time the triangles are made up of the arcs of three 'great circles'. A great circle being a circle on a sphere whose plane passes through its centre. This then makes all the meridians of longitude great circles. However, only one parallel of latitude, the equator, is a great circle; other parallels of latitude being small circles.

Here was taught the use and makeup of the Sextant, that funny looking instrument used for obtaining the altitude of heavenly bodies; and what sailor *wouldn't* want to take the altitude of a heavenly body? A sextant is the sixth part, or arc, of a circle that is held vertically, the small telescope on its arm being pointed towards the horizon which is observed through a half mirror. The arm swings through the arc that has the degrees marked along its length. On this arm is also a mirror. This mirror reflects the heavenly body being observed to the half mirror alongside which the horizon is seen. The altitude, along with the exact time from the ship's chronometer, is noted. Although a sixth of a circle is just sixty degrees, because the angle of reflection is twice the angle of incidence, the sextant will measure angles up to one hundred and twenty degrees.

"What did you do at school today?" the cadet's mother asked.

"They taught us how to use our sextants," the cadet replied.

"Really!" the mother puffed, *"What will they teach you next!"*

<u>Chart work.</u> A subject Edward always looked forward to. The information given on a chart appeared endless. Issued by the Admiralty Hydrographic Office, they gave the depth of water in the place indicated, or if the numbers were on the land – heights above sea level. A compass rose with all three hundred and sixty degrees marked was always present, usually in a nice open area of the chart where there was little other information. This was used for the laying of courses and bearings using a parallel ruler. The chart also gave the information on variation and whether the depths were indicated in feet or fathoms; most were in fathoms; one fathom equals six feet. This always had to be checked on every chart, as some obtained in other countries might indicate depths in meters. You don't want to get these mixed up. Around the coasts these depths were separated by contour lines, very helpful to coastal navigation, so you would have five, ten, twenty and thirty fathom lines and so on. Five being a line indicated by a series of five dots, ten by one dot followed by a dash, twenty being two dots and a dash, and so on. Lighthouses, with their flash sequences, were indicated by a red mark. Abbreviations identified other navigational points of interest, for example, CGFS alongside a dot would indicate a Coast Guard Flag Staff, which could be used the same as other landmarks to take bearings, in order to obtain the ship's position through triangulation.

Ships usually carried one global gnomonic chart where all the meridians of longitude curved and met at the poles. On these charts, a great circle track, or course, showed as a straight line. However, all charts used for navigation were of the Mercator projection; Mercator being a sixteenth century Flemish geographer. Mercator charts were much easier to use, as the lines of latitude and longitude are shown as parallel lines. The lines of longitude are of equal distance apart, whereas the distance between the parallel's of latitude increase with their distance away from the equator. A great circle course on these charts shows as a curve, arcing towards the nearest pole. A straight line on these charts is known as a rhumb line. So, on these charts, the shortest distance between two points is not a straight line, it is a curve - the great circle. An airplane, for example, flying from the UK to the western United States will fly over Newfoundland in Eastern Canada, way north of where you think the aircraft should be, but it is following a great circle route.

Magnetism and Electricity. Algebra is used here in problem solving. Magnetism was very interesting. In particular, the effect an iron ship, which in itself is a large magnet, has on the ship's magnetic compass, for all its different headings. This is deviation, which together with variation, indicated on all charts inside the compass rose, is applied to the ship's magnetic heading in order to steer a true course.

The deviation chart for a vessel would have to be recalibrated after being in dry dock, for example, because the ship's magnetic effect changes due to lying in the same direction for a month or so and being surrounded by steel structures, such as a crane. This recalibration was usually done outside the harbor during sea-trials. It should be noted here that most ships of the time had gyro compasses that indicated true headings. In other words, it always pointed to true north rather than magnetic north. The magnetic compass was there as a standby should the gyro fail, which it would if its electrical power supply was cut. Then it would often take hours to 'settle-down' again to its true heading; its one downfall. There is a method known as precession that can be used to speed up this 'settling-down' period.

Ship Construction and Stability. Here was, to Edward, the most interesting subject other than navigation, and where Edward's love of technical drawing came into its own. Drawing cross sections through various parts of a ship's construction to show where it got its strength from. The reasons for various parts such as brackets where decks met accommodation, and their use to compensate for loss of continuity were of great interest to Edward and he loved this subject. Stability is the science of loading cargos, or ballast, in order to ensure that no undue stress is put on the ship. Simply put, loading the cargo evenly throughout the ship's length in her holds or tanks. A vessel running through a rough sea with its crests and troughs would be put under a lot of stress and she would be built to withstand this. Loading a cargo incorrectly could aggravate these stresses and cause problems. It was uncommon for ships to break in half but it did happen. A pivotal part of this (no pun intended) was the vessels GM. G being the centre of gravity and M being the metacenter. The smaller the GM the more unstable a floating vessel will be, she will roll very easily and the rolling will be difficult to stop. A large GM will make the vessel very stiff, and she will be difficult to make roll. If she does roll, however, she will come back to the vertical very sharply; not very desirable or very comfortable for those onboard. The center of gravity, G, will move towards a weight placed in or on the vessel. Therefore, if a weight is put on upper decks G will move up towards it. IF G moves above M, a negative GM will occur and the ship will capsize. An example of this occurred, when The Empress of Canada, a passenger vessel alongside in Liverpool, caught on fire. The water poured onto her by firefighters was retained in her upper decks, G moved up towards this extra weight, GM became negative and the vessel capsized right alongside the wharf. When at the seaside resort of Cleethorpes, right next to Grimsby, Edward would often see timber vessels with large deck cargos going up the Humber River listed over to one side. This, he now found out, was caused by the extra weight of sea water on the weather side being absorbed by the timber on deck, G moving towards this extra weight causing the list. This could usually be compensated for by moving ballast to bring the vessel upright. These cargos were usually from Scandinavia so it didn't take long, just a trip across the North Sea, for this problem to occur. It was known for vessels to lose their deck cargos at sea in rough weather because of this problem. There is another center, B, which is the center of buoyancy which also comes into play in the stability of a vessel.

<u>Seamanship</u>. While working down the fish docks, on the recommendation of his father Edward had gone to the Fisherman's School in Grimsby to learn rope work. Therefore, the knots and splices part of this subject, were a breeze for Edward; *thanks Dad*! The Rules Of The Road also had to be learned. These covered all aspects of the meeting of vessels at sea and who had the right of way and who was the giving way vessel. Maneuvering a vessel through a buoyed channel, the landfall (the approach of a vessel to the coast) and boating. The latter was fun as the school had a boat at a dock alongside the River Humber and once a month, weather permitting, the class group would march to the dock, launch the boat, and row around the dock in a very precise and orderly manner. If the lock gate was open they would row out into the river, which was much more of a challenge as the tidal current had to be dealt with. This gave the practical knowledge of launching a boat, no different really than doing it from a ship's deck except that the dock side was not moving.

Other subjects taught, like Science, English, Gym, First Aid and Hygiene, Swimming and Church are all pretty self explanatory. The latter being the whole school, about one hundred, marching from the School courtyard, where there was an inspection done, round the block to Holy Trinity Church. It was a proud moment as spectators along the way stood and watched as this smart bunch of naval Cadets marched by. This was done on a monthly basis to ensure that all cadets attended.

....

Trinity House had a yacht called the 'Patricia' that was used to patrol the coast of Britain to check and maintain all navigational aids, lighthouses, beacons, buoys etc. It took the vessel three years to 'sail' round the coastline once. It happened to be in Hull while Edward was attending the school and along with his classmates were taken onboard to visit with the Captain and crew. It was a beautiful schooner and had on the deck a channel buoy that they were repairing. The cadets were amazed at the size of this buoy as they looked so much smaller when in the water; kind of like an iceberg with a great part of it submerged under the water. The tour also included the engine room which was as shiny as a new pin with two engines side by side. It was a memorable visit and one they all felt very privileged to have taken.

....

This then, had been the repetitive activities of the year at Trinity House. It had been strictly business and one hell of a learning-curve for Edward.

8

The stay at Merchant Navy Hotel had also been mainly business due to all the homework that had to be done, and many weekends Edward had stayed in Hull in order to rewrite notes, study, and get caught up for the following Monday. There had been lots of fun though. The Cadets had been a mischievous lot and got up to some crazy stunts. The manager, Mr. Gates, had strict rules for them; no smoking, no running, no fighting, the bar out of bounds, etc. etc. And the number one rule - back inside the hotel by nine o'clock every night. The cadets rebelled against this one, not vocally to Mr. Gates though. They had devised so many ways of getting in and out of the hotel unseen, or so they thought, that 'Colditz' didn't have a look in, only there were no tunnels here! They went out windows, down fire escapes, through the kitchen, and through the service/loading area. The best and sneakiest way though, was to walk right out through the front door! They did discover that going down the fire escape of the extension was a real hazard, as unbeknown to them at the time it was overlooked by Mr. Gates flat (apartment) on the top floor of the hotel, and three of them were observed one evening scrambling down it. They were banned, all of them, from even going out onto the fire escape, never mind climbing down it. All of the cadets had regular visits to Mr. Gates' office, often in groups, standing to attention while being given a bollocking (lecture), much to the amusement of other guests of the hotel. His office was behind the reception desk and had large windows overlooking both reception and the stairs going down to the street.

Guests, seafarers staying at the Hotel, would often ask with a smile, "So what have you lads been up to now?" not really expecting a reply, but it was usually a shrug of the shoulders with a down turn of the mouth.

Other activities included sitting on the upstairs lounge windowsill on a Saturday morning, with feet hanging down towards the street waving to all the girls going by. Mr. Gates was married to the prettiest, slim, vivacious, sparkling young woman that you could ever meet; Susan, and she was on the side of the cadets; an ally that stuck up for them without offending Mr. Gates. They had no children of their own so the cadets were a great substitute.

"I knew it was you lot, when I saw all the girls waving," she said as she came bounding into the lounge, her long blonde hair falling over one shoulder. "You had better get back in before Mr. Gates sees you."

Mr. Gates was always the manner in which she referred to her husband. They all climbed back in and closed the windows, never wanting to offend her. She smiled and gave them all a cigarette knowing they all smoked when they could cadge one, since they didn't know any better at the time. Edward was part of this group even though no one in his family smoked, including his father… oh well!

"Don't tell Mr. Gates I gave them to you, and don't smoke them here." They all went joyfully shoving and pushing, back to the extension, where they congregated in one room and lit up their cigarettes, opening wide the window. It probably looked like the place was on fire from the outside.

Another activity they became infamous for was going from the lowest floor of the extension to the landing above the reception area without touching the floor. They used skirting boards, hand rails, picture rails -hanging on by finger tips, heaters, anything. In the extension itself they could put their backs against one wall, their feet on the other, and shuffle their way along the corridor to the stairways. Except for Mike, who was by now always referred to as Cagney; he could put a foot on each wall and together with his hands actually run along the walls to the end, he was like a monkey. It was the footprints on the walls, however, that gave them all away on this one. They had thought about sliding down the wooden banister of the stairway to the reception area but this was far too visible and would really be pushing their luck. They would certainly have had a message delivered by the porter, Len, with the dreaded words, "Mr. Gates would like to see you in his office."

Every Wednesday night was dance night at the hotel with a three piece band on stage, which was a whole lot of fun. They were allowed to attend and although, initially, none of them were great dancers they soon learnt, and would often be taken for a spin by some young women, much to the delight of others. They also stocked up on cigarettes that they were given by the sailors and also from part packs left on tables from when they helped clean up at the end of the dance. This was one of the conditions for being allowed to attend. Edward had been to dances before, at his church hall; the biggest dance being at Christmas. He was a proficient dancer but still a little clumsy. The waltz was his favourite, and the foxtrot and the quickstep made up his main repertoire. He could also jive but it was not really his thing. Encouraged by his two sisters, he had also gone to dances in Cleethorpes, at the Pier and the Winter Gardens. So he could hold his own on the dance floor but for some reason, probably his age, was always self conscious, especially with strangers.

....

One Saturday morning Mike's father came down to Hull from Leeds and Edward was invited to his first rugby game; Hunslip was playing Hull. Edward enjoyed the game but didn't understand the rules; his game, after all, was football. It was a lot of fun, and much to the delight of Mike's father Hunslip won.

Another weekend Edward went with Dave to his home in York; this was a good visit and his mother, like Edward's, was a great cook. Both in uniform, they went for a visit to Rowntree's chocolate factory and with their guide, a young attractive redhead, were shown the process of making and packing chocolates. The chocolates were put into little brown cups in the boxes, by hand, by four hundred girls in a room. They were on piece-work, so they worked very fast; an amazing sight. The two smart naval cadets did, however, cause a little distraction. Another room was for Smarties, which were all separated by color in one section and were put into what look liked cement mixers to polish them up. They were then mixed and poured into large metal troughs where they were scooped into tubes, by hand, and weighed on a shadow scale before moving on to boxing and shipping. At the end of the tour they were each given a sample box of all the chocolates that Rowntree made.

"So what did you think of all the girls that work here?" their guide asked mischievously.

"Don't know," replied Edward, "I was looking at the chocolates!"

They left there happily laughing and walked around York; what a fabulous place! They went to The Shambles, a narrow cobbled street that had some of the finest medieval architecture in Europe, named after the mixture of meat products (a real shambles) displayed on shelves by all the butchers. Here they went into a small coffee shop, The Five T's, named for five family members that owned it. They both had to duck under the ceiling beams and stand between them, they were so low. They had a wonderful cup of coffee, then left to do more wandering around. No visit to York would be complete without going to The Minster, which they did, and spent an hour looking at this incredible cathedral. Edwards favorite was still, however, Lincoln Cathedral, with its famous Lincoln Imp.

One of Edward's favorite Saturdays was on a visit back to Grimsby when, in uniform, he'd gone to visit the lads down the fish docks. He didn't know who was the proudest, himself or his former work mates. They made a great fuss over him, so pleased that he had got out of the life that they had to cope with. He would later reflect, while on a storm tossed ocean being battered by heavy seas, what a peaceful life they must be having.

9

The 'one year Cadets' returned to Trinity House at the start of the
following school year, where the results of their final exams were
discussed. All the Merchant Navy Hotel cadets, because of these
results, earned six months remission of sea service that was deducted
from the required four year apprenticeship. The school, which had no
new one-year wonders for this term, helped with the decisions and made
their recommendations in contacting chosen shipping companies where
their apprenticeships at sea would be served. Edward, along with his
friend Peter, had chosen Shell Tankers, which were highly recommended
by the school. So after all the backwards and forwards of this rigmarole,
it was arranged that they would go down to London, to the Shell office
at Ibex House, and sit an entrance examination. It was hard for either
of them to understand why this was necessary after spending a year at
one of the finest navigation schools in the country, but it was procedure
and there was no way round it. So, after all the travel arrangements were
made, off they went to London. It was September again, and it would
be an enjoyable trip if nothing else. Two good friends on an adventure;
they were glad of each other's company.

The train journey was uneventful with the two of them just talking
and laughing, and quiet periods looking out at the countryside racing
by, with only the noise of the train's wheels on the track accompanying
their scattered thoughts. Upon arrival at King's Cross they made their
way to the tube station. This was the first time that either of them had
been on the underground trains and it took their breath away. It was like
a main line station underground. There were five train lines to choose
from; Victoria, Northern, Piccadilly, Central and Circle. They found
the Piccadilly Line and made sure they were on the train going in the
right direction, and were whisked off towards their destination with a

crazy speed that made the train rock from side to side. The screeching of brakes as they approached a station was nerve racking to say the least, especially when they really had no idea where they were going. Looking once more at the sheet of instructions they had received with details of how to get to their destination, they followed their progress on the overhead map displayed on the curve of the train car's roof.

It was not a long trip to their station, where they squeezed and bumped their way off the train and made their way up to the street. What a relief! They found The Minories and made their way south to Ibex House. Mounting the wide entrance stairs and walking up to the second floor, they made their presence known and waited nervously in a small, cool, waiting room. They hadn't given this exam much thought as they had no idea what to expect.

The pair were finally shown into small, separate meeting rooms by a Mr. Meredith; a rotund, grey haired man of medium height, who gave them each the two hour exam and left them to it. It turned out to be half math and half general navigation and seamanship knowledge; not too bad at all. The required pass mark was seventy percent. After the two hours Mr. Meredith collected the completed exams, and Edward and Peter met in the hallway. They were thanked for attending and told they would be contacted with regard to the results. They left the office and were on their way once again.

"How did you do?" Peter asked.

"Not bad at all; certainly should have passed," was Edward's response. Upon discussing the exam it was found that they'd had the same one.

"What the hell was that one about the logs?" Peter asked.

"That one took me a while; <u>given the log of 3 and the log of 7, find the log of 441 without the use of logarithm tables?</u>"

"Yep that's the one."

"It's the magic number nine; 3 x 3 is 9, 7 x 7 is 49 so the 9 x 49 = 441," replied Edward.

"Shit!" was the disgusted response from Peter.

(Adding the logs of numbers is multiplying those two numbers, so the two logs of 3 are added together which gives the log of 9, add the two logs of 7 together and you get the log of 49, now add these two logs of 9 and 49, and the resulting number is the logarithm of 441; 9x49 = 441)

They got back to King's Cross and while waiting for the train sat in the station café and had a sandwich.

"Look," Peter said, "a British Railway sandwich. It's curled up at the edges so you don't have to open it to see what's inside."

They both laughed ate the dry sandwiches, drank their cups of strong tea, and sat for a while before walking down the platform to board the train, which was already waiting for their journey back to Hull. They were both to go to Trinity House the next day to discuss the Shell exam and then Edward would be on his way home to Grimsby.

It turned out that they both passed the exam, and now had to wait for assignment to a ship. In this regard Edward and Peter went their separate ways in Shell, and it would be four years before they met again. This occurred, again at Trinity House, after their apprenticeships were completed.

In the meantime, with letters from Shell, various documents had to be acquired. A Passport had to be applied for; also, from the shipping office, a Discharge Book and Identity Card had to be obtained, with photographs having to be taken for these three documents. The Identity Card was a small fold-out document with a photograph, description, and finger prints of the holder. A few years later this document was done away with as a requirement for Merchant Sailors; something to do with privacy and the fingerprints. The Discharge Book was to be a record keeper of all the ships that the holder sailed on, with the respective dates, and, as well as the photograph, also had a description of the holder, together with Income tax numbers and any certificates of competency achieved. This was a sailor's most important document, without which he could not sign-on to a ship. Inoculations had to be received for Smallpox, Typhoid, and the likes, which were recorded in a vaccine certificate booklet that was always kept with the passport, as many Countries required these documents before a person was allowed to enter.

Indentures also had to be signed. This document is a contract, an ownership, of the person named in them by the company issuing them. They could not be broken and spelled out the salary that would be paid to the apprentice. In this case it was for five hundred pounds sterling over the indentured period. The first year was for just one hundred pounds!

The indentures had to be signed and sealed by three people and in Edward's case it was himself, his father, and witnessed by their local shop keeper. Upon signing in the appropriate place, their thumbs had to be pressed on to the red seal alongside their signatures and the document sent back to Shell. Signed, sealed and delivered.

10

So… here he was on the train, on his way back to London. This time Edward had a large suitcase, which was in the baggage compartment with all his sea gear and uniforms in, and he carried a small overnight bag. At King's Cross he got a taxi to Ibex House where he met the Marine Superintendent, Mr. Murdock, who sat down with him, congratulated him on his exam marks, and told him of the journey down to the south of France. A train to Dover, ferry to Calais, train to Paris, then on to Marseilles, where a company agent would take him to his ship, the 'Combia', in Port de Bouc. It was mid afternoon and he would be staying in London overnight and leave from the office the next morning where he would meet his travel companions. That was good news. Leaving his large suitcase at the office he left carrying his small overnight bag and got a taxi to Sussex Gardens, where he would be staying at a bed and breakfast. He was shown to his room by the owner; a kind matronly woman who really made him feel at home. His room was small with a double bed, and shiny as a new pin. A small hand basin was in one corner, the toilet was down the hall. He dropped his bag on the bed and decided to go for a walk and see what this big city had to offer. It was noisy and smelly; *they don't call this place 'The Big Smoke' for nothing,* thought Edward, then smiled to himself because it was 5th November – bonfire night. Or 'Guy Fawkes night' as it is also known. Guy Fawkes was captured on November 5th 1605 whilst trying to blow up the Houses of Parliament in London. This occasion is commemorated in Britain every year on this date by burning an effigy of him on the top a bonfire. Along with fireworks it is a great evening.

Edward found a sit-in fish and chip shop and ate two pieces of haddock and a pile of chips with bread and butter and a cup of tea, then set off on his wanderings once more. It was early evening and beautiful weather. He happened upon Leicester Square, which he found was the home of the famous Odeon Cinema. The film playing was 'The Cockleshell Heroes' and starred Dirk Bogard. It wasn't out yet in the rest of the country, so he decided to go in and see it. It was about the Second World War, and he really enjoyed the film. As he walked back to the bed and breakfast though, his thoughts were of those awful years. The earliest recollections of his young life were of his mother carrying him downstairs to the sound of air-raid sirens. Down to the air-raid shelter, where he and his two sisters had sat shivering, listening to bombs whistling down. The whistling was followed by a short period of silence and then the sound of distant explosions, thank goodness for them - but not for other poor souls. They'd sat huddled together, waiting for the all-clear siren to be given. He shook himself, disturbed at the memory.

He arrived back at the B & B and went to bed, requesting a 7am wake up call. He slept like a log, and it really did turn out to be a bed and breakfast; at 7am the next morning, after a polite knock on the door, the landlady walked cheerfully into his room carrying a breakfast tray. Edward sat up as she placed the tray on his lap, then she left with a cheerful wave and closed the door. Wow, bed and breakfast - breakfast in bed. Edward thought nothing of it at the time but there were no locks on the doors, it really was like being at home. He polished off the breakfast, put the tray on the bedside table, and sprang out of bed to get ready for the exciting day ahead. There was no bill to pay as it was all looked after by Shell; he said his goodbyes and set off for the office, where he arrived at 8.45am.

It was here that he met a fellow apprentice and traveling companion, John Summers. John was almost as tall as Edward; slim, with short dark hair. This was to be John's second ship. Travelling with them was Mrs. Landy, the wife of the ship's Captain. Mrs. Landy was about five foot three with short graying hair; trim, in a matronly sort of way, in her middle thirties. She wore a snug fitting brown tweed suit and sturdy brown shoes, dressed for comfort and travel. She would turn out to be a warm, motherly and caring person and treated them like her sons. *Everywhere I go I get more parents!* - thought Edward. *Life's good.*

They loaded their luggage into one of London's famous taxis, a Hansom Cab, and were on their way to Waterloo Station for their train down to Dover. On the way Edward thought of the old joke;

Call me a Cab - You're a Cab. - Now call me a Hansom Cab. He smiled to himself.

Edward loved the trip across the English Channel. From Dover to Calais the Channel was a little choppy, with rather a fresh breeze. It was very busy, with ships crossing their path going east and west. He reveled in the experience with warm thoughts that this was now going to be his life; plying the oceans of the world. He would turn out to be a good sailor and was never seasick much to the chagrin of Mrs. Landy, whom he would find out was not a good sailor, particularly when the seas got rough. The ferry ride was over far too soon for Edward, and on arrival at Calais they disembarked and boarded the train that would take them on the next leg of their journey, down to Paris. In Paris they changed to the train that would take them to Marseilles, via Lyon. They ate in the dining car on the way south; it was a fixed meal, and not very large. Like the rest of his family, Edward was a meat and potatoes person…or should that be a fish and chips person?… he was used to good, wholesome meals. He wasn't sure what it was they were given, but he ate it, as he was as hungry as a horse. It was quite tasty and he enjoyed it; it *was* food after all. He would soon come to learn that his pragmatic attitude towards food would stand him in good stead during his life at sea. The trip was largely uneventful, with reading and watching the scenery, that was, in-fact, not much different than England with its rolling farmlands and stands of trees, and dozing off to the clickety-clack clickety-clack of the train wheels over the expansion joints in the rails.

Upon arrival in Marseilles they were met by a ship's agent. They loaded their luggage into his estate car (station wagon) while Mrs. Landy got into the front seat. John and Edward climbed into the back. Not seeing much of this famous city except its clutter of buildings, they were whisked off westward, twenty miles or so around the bay to Port-de-Bouc. Edward getting his first glimpse of the Mediterranean, not the bright blue he had expected but rather a somber grey in the early December air.

11

So here she is, the 'Combia' 465ft length, 59ft beam (across), 8,929 gross tons, and built in 1945 by Harland & Wolff Ltd., Belfast. She was tied up starboard-to the dock. The first impression of the ship was not a good one. It was a mess. They walked up the gangway to a dirty, cluttered, slippery, black-tarred deck, where a wire mooring line had to be stepped over to get to the steps that gave access to the 'flying bridge'. The flying bridge on a tanker is an elevated walkway that runs fore and aft, between the aft and the midships accommodation, and from there forward to the forecastle, pronounced fo'c'sle. As Edward reached the wire he turned and held out his hand palm-up towards the Captain's wife, which she took gratefully as she stepped over the wire.

"Thank you Edward."

"My pleasure," was his response.

After climbing up the steps they turned right, past the towering ventilators of a pump room, which had an open skylight. The thump, thump, thump of pumps could be heard from far below, pumping the ship's cargo ashore. They were met at the midships accommodation by the Officer of the Watch, the Chief Officer (First Mate), who had been expecting them.

"Welcome aboard Mrs. Landy, I'll take you to The Captain".

He nodded to Edward and John giving them just a cursory glance and turned to a young man standing off to the side.

"Thompson! Help your new shipmates here to get the luggage on board."

"Yes Sir," was Thompson's quiet reply.

The time was 1615hrs (4:15pm). Thompson, dressed in oily working gear of denim trousers and jacket over a check shirt, was a stocky, broad shouldered individual with a pleasant smile, a bronzed, clear complexion, and dark hair; the picture of health. It turned out he was also a deck apprentice and in this case the senior one, having been at sea for a little over two years, and on this ship for the past two months.

"I'm Doug," he said with a big smile while shaking hands with the two of them, who in turn introduced themselves.

"Let's go get your gear onboard," he said, and they followed him as he scrambled down to the jetty where their bags waited. A crew member followed them and took care of Mrs. Landy's luggage. The three deck apprentices grabbed the remaining gear and dragged it onboard, again back to the midships accommodation, where Doug took them to a cabin on the starboard side, on the same level as the flying bridge.

"That's my cabin there," said Doug pointing to a door one forward of where they were standing. "This one," he said as he pushed the door open and motioned them in, "is yours."

The cabin had two single bunks; one on the passageway bulkhead and the other on the outer bulkhead under the cabin's single brass porthole. Each of the bunks had two large drawers underneath. In between them on the forward bulkhead was a bench seat, in front of which was a table with a single chair. At the foot of the inboard bunk, opposite the porthole, was a single sized wardrobe and at the foot of the other was a set of four drawers, and then a second single wardrobe in the corner opposite the door. The picture was completed with a small wash-hand basin with mirror, at the after bulkhead near the door.

"Home sweet home!" quipped Doug.

Edward, knowing that he was the first tripper and therefore the junior of the three politely asked, "Which bunk do you prefer, John?"

"I'll take that one Edward," he replied pointing to the inboard bunk.

Edward swung his suitcase up onto the bunk under the porthole, and sat down next to the bunk on the bench seat. He was happy because this bunk would have been his first choice anyway.

"Looks good, John, what do you think?"

"Good. Hope you don't snore!" They all laughed.

"Well, I have to get back on watch," sighed Doug, "or The Mate will be wondering where I am. John, you'll be on the 12 to 4 watch with the Second Mate, and Ed, you will be on the 8 to 12 with the Third Mate; both are good guys. Ed, get on your working gear and come on deck with me at seven, and I'll show you what's going on before your watch starts. Dinner is at 5pm; you should change into uniform. See you later, good to have you both aboard" and he was gone.

Neatly folded at the foot of each bunk were two white sheets, two pillow cases, a bed spread, one bath towel, one hand towel and on top of these a bar of toilet soap and a large green bar of 'Fairy' laundry soap. Someone else had expected them; this turned out to be the amidships steward, Ray. Edward was impressed. He would later find that they would get a change of linen for their bunks each week; one sheet and one pillow case. The bottom sheet was replaced by the used top sheet that is, in turn, replaced by the new clean sheet; the new pillow case replacing the one that needed it the most. They unpacked their gear into the drawers and wardrobes. Edward put his working gear on the bench seat next to his bunk for later. He had been sent a list of required sea gear by Shell, which his father had purchased. Some of this gear would never be used; for example, the very formal number tens, which were white tropical gear with long white pants and a high collared, brass buttoned jacket. Edward would later wonder who the hell had made up this list of gear. Someone that had never been to sea, no doubt!

They changed into uniform; their blues. A small brass button atop a vertical two inch gold stripe on each lapel denoted their lowly apprenticeship rank. Hanging their civvies in the wardrobe they were ready for dinner. Well, at least Edward did not feel out of place in his newly pressed uniform and polished shoes after his year at Trinity House.

Stepping out into the corridor they turned forward. The corridor was U shaped, running forward from their cabin on the starboard side, across to port, and then round again to the outside deck. Edward and John left the cabin and walked around to the dining room that faced forward, overlooking the foredeck and the flying bridge that ran on the same level forward to the fo'c'sle. At the entrance they were met by the amidships steward, Ray, a young man in his early twenties, who led them to their seats. There were just two tables running fore and aft, large enough for all the Deck and Engineer Officers - a table for each. They were shown to the port side table where they sat down. These were to be their permanent places, as it turned out for the next eight and a half months. The meal was vegetable soup, roast beef and vegetables, with jelly for dessert.

Naturally, Captain Landy sat at the head of the table, with Mrs. Landy sitting on his right; the opposite side of the table from where Edward and John were sitting. The Captain was of medium height; rotund, in his early forties, with short grey hair. He was clean shaven, with thick jowls, and his jacket displayed the four gold stripes on the sleeve that indicated his rank.

"How are you boys doing?" Mrs. Landy asked smiling, "are you getting settled in alright?"

"Yes, thank you," they replied in unison.

"These are the two lads I traveled with," she motioned, while looking at the Captain. He, together with the other officers at the table, nodded to them.

"Welcome aboard, boys" the Captain smiled.

The Chief Officer came in and sat on the left hand of the Captain, on the same side of the table as the apprentices. He was a tall, gangly man; his uniform loose on his thin frame. He looked rather like the film star, Gary Cooper. A serious, almost sullen looking man until he smiled; then his whole countenance changed to a very pleasant one. Next to him was the Second Mate, another film star look-alike, but this time it was Robert Taylor. He was medium height and good looking, with dark hair and a five-o'clock shadow, and strong, dark haired hands. Beside the Second Mate was Doug's empty chair, then John, and finally Edward. Edward started checking around the room; Gregory Peck had to be there somewhere.

On the other side next to Mrs. Landy was the Radio Officer, a bespectacled, curly haired individual in his early twenties. He was sitting with his right arm draped over the back of his chair, the wrist of which was held tightly by his left hand. He looked at the newcomers and just nodded. Then there was the Third Mate (whom Edward would be on watch with at 2000hrs), and two empty chairs. One of these was the Chief Steward's; a large, overweight individual who, as it turned out, rarely sat there, electing to eat in the pantry instead. All the people at this table had cabins in the amidships accommodation.

The table on the starboard side had all the Engineers, including three Engineer Apprentices. They all sat by rank, much the same as the Deck Officers, with the Chief Engineer at the head. The Chief, as the senior engineer was referred to, was a large man that always seemed out of breath. His uniform jacket was unbuttoned showing his protruding belly. His hair was cut short, the top of which was level, like a brush. He looked a stern individual, but Edward would find that he was a very pleasant man. The Engineers' cabins were in the after accommodations on the first deck, below the boat deck, and above the crew accommodations and the Engine Room.

Both The Chief and The Captain had four gold stripes on their sleeves. Chief Officer (First Mate) and Second Engineer had three, Second Mate and Third Engineer two and the Third Mate and Fourth Engineer had one. All the stripes had a diamond shape in the centre. The apprentices had the small single vertical gold stripe with a small brass button on its upper end, on both upper lapels.

This was all very new to Edward and he loved it, even though he was very well aware that he was the only one in the room that had not been to sea yet. At last, his first ship and the beginning of his first trip. His heart was pounding and he was a little nervous; a strange mixture of feelings. His hands shook slightly as he ate.

There were no real formalities other than politeness at the tables and all spoke in soft voices except The Chief, who had a loud boisterous voice, probably due to years spent in noisy engine rooms. The steward, dressed in his high collared white jacket with its single vertical row of brass buttons, black trousers with a sharp crease, and black polished shoes, served all meals. These were brought from a serving kitchen (the pantry) across the hallway from the dining room. From the galley, which was situated at the rear end of the after accommodation overlooking the poop deck, food was delivered to the pantry and placed in heated cabinets. Everyone was in uniform, apart from Mrs. Landry of course. It may have been a working ship, but there was one thing that would always be in place at Shell in all the years that followed, and that was ceremony. Even at sea, except when working on deck, for the Deck Apprentices; and in the case of the Engineers, when in the engine room, uniforms were always mandatory.

John and Edward finished their dinner, drank the strong percolated coffee they were given, and with Edward following John's lead, excused themselves and went back to their cabin. Their suitcases were on the deck where they had left them and had to be stowed away. At the end of their hallway, with doors to both the hallway and the deck, was the small deck office. Doug was standing outside on the deck, and John asked him where they should stow their suitcases. He went into the office and opened a locker on the bulkhead that had three rows of keys inside, hanging from large brass hooks.

"Follow me," he said as he chose a key. Edward and John followed him down to the main deck, where he turned into a storage and utility space in the center castle, under the amidships accommodation. They stepped over the storm sill, also known as shin knockers, for obvious reasons, and into this space. They made their way over to the port side, stepping over pipelines and ducking under other pipes strung along the deckhead; overhead in the Royal Navy; ceiling to the landlubber. Edward banged his head more than once, much to the amusement of the other two. He was already finding out that being tall could, in some cases, be a distinct disadvantage on an old ship.

When they'd stowed their suitcases along with everyone else's, John looked at Edward, and said enthusiastically, "Come on, let's do a quick tour!"

It was 1800 hrs. Edward followed John out onto the after main deck, and then up a series of stairs to the flying bridge deck, then to the boat deck, and finally up to the Bridge deck. They were on the wing of the bridge; John walked over to the large wooden door that led to the wheelhouse and with some effort, slid it open. They walked in. The center piece was the large wooden ship's wheel, behind a large compass binnacle with its varnished wooden cylindrical body, and a large brass cover that looked rather like a deep sea diver's helmet. Alongside this was a read-out display of the gyro compass, easily visible for a sailor who would be constantly steering whilst at sea, "no automatic steering" observed John as he tapped the steering wheel. Hanging down from the deck head was a metal cylindrical tube with an angled mirror in its curved open end just above eye level for anyone at the helm. Edward peered into this seeing the reflection of the magnetic compass card in the binnacle on the deck above. The row of windows gave a panoramic view of the ship forward, and of the surrounding docks. On the rear bulkhead was a door leading to the Chartroom, the two of them entered. On top of the glass-covered chart table was a folded chart of the docks, and to one side, the charts of various scale required to leave these waterways, out into the Mediterranean Sea. A large window above the chart table looked out into the wheelhouse and the forward windows. At the end of the chart table, near the door, was the Chronometer, a very accurate time piece used for navigation, in a cabinet with a glass top. At the rear of the chartroom was a narrow bench seat with drawers underneath, and alongside that, a door, behind which were narrow stairs that led down to a landing outside the Captain's cabin. This, in turn, had stairs down to the corridor outside the dining room. Entry to this stairway for general use was taboo; Captain's domain only. A fore and aft bulkhead separated the chartroom from the Wireless Room, or Radio Room; the station of the Radio Officer, or as he was commonly known, Sparky! On the back starboard bulkhead was a door behind which was a small room that contained the gyro compass.

Back out in the wheelhouse, John looked around, then walked out onto the wing of the bridge and looked up to the short flag mast and yardarm on the deck above. This was the Monkey Island. Edward had followed him and looked up enquiringly.

"Something wrong, John?"

"She has no radar."

"Is that bad?" enquired Edward.

"Well, it will be different. Come on." With that, John proceeded to climb a fixed vertical polished wood ladder, up to the Monkey Island. The deck there was wood, having at the forward end a raised wooden platform with varnished wooden sides; in the centre of this stood another compass binnacle. A tube with an angled mirror, rather like a periscope, protruded down from the deck head in the wheelhouse below them in front and above the ship's wheel, gave a read-out of this magnetic compass.

In the centre of this deck rose a short mast with a large yardarm. At an upwards angle on the back of the mast was an Ensign yard, from which the Red Ensign, the Merchant Navy flag, could be flown when at sea. A flag was flying on the starboard yardarm, a red burgee. This was the explosives flag. It was the letter B in the international code of flags and meant, 'I have explosives onboard.' This was a required flag in all ports when carrying oil cargoes.

The ship had two large masts; one on the fore deck, the foremast, and one on the main deck, the mainmast. Between the tops of these two masts hung the triatic stay and from this, above their heads, the main aerial came down to the radio room below their feet. The forward mast had a yardarm high above the deck and on the starboard side of this yardarm flew the tri-colored French flag, the courtesy flag. The national flag of whichever country was being visited was flown from this yard arm as a courtesy. On the top of the main mast, one hundred feet high, flew the Shell house flag. The Red Ensign, it turned out, flew at the stern on the short ensign staff.

They left the bridge, after sliding closed the wheelhouse door, and made their way to their cabin. It was getting close to time for Edward to be on deck. At the cabin he changed into his work gear and felt like a right twerp. The creases were on the sides of the thick denim trousers, and they were stiff and uncomfortable.

"Should have washed this stuff before I packed it," he said to John. The denim jacket wasn't much better; it also felt like it was starched. A light blue shirt and sturdy work shoes completed his look.

"Good God, talk about a first tripper!"

"You'll be just fine," laughed John.

12

At 1845hrs Edward was outside the ship's office, to meet with Doug at 1900. His Dad's training was in effect here; *Never be late.* He felt uncomfortable and out of place in his new work gear.

"This stuff is horrible," he said to Doug as he motioned to himself and the stiff denims.

"Don't worry Ed, you'll soon break it in," replied Doug with a chuckle. "Come on."

Edward followed him to the outside door of the office. Doug pointed to a chalkboard hanging on the railing opposite the office door that indicated all of the ship's cargo holds; nine rows of three. Some of the squares had feet and inches written in them, which were the Ullages. The ullage is the distance from the deck to the surface of the oil in the tank. Other squares had the letter F for Full, with the letters MT in others; MT meaning Empty. This reminded Edward of the origin of the Esso name; S.O., Standard Oil.

On the main deck below them the First Mate; whose watch was the 4 – 8, was talking to a medium height, strongly built man.

"That's the Pumpman," informed Doug, "he's responsible for the pump room and the smooth running of the pumps. There are two pumps in that pump room" he said, pointing in front of them to the skylights where Edward had heard the pumps running when they first came onboard. "There is another pump room on the fore deck with two more pumps."

Just astern of where they stood were the ship's manifolds. These are ship-to-shore connections to the ship's pipeline system, four feet above the deck, through which the oil cargoes were loaded and discharged. Four pipes in all with vertical valves on each, with large valve wheels on top; these were accessible by a small catwalk behind them, on top of the pipes. This system was duplicated on the port side of the ship. Attached to the manifolds were two ten inch rubber hoses, which snaked ashore and were in turn attached to manifold valves on the shore. The hoses were kept clear of the deck and rails by a wire from the ship's derrick. They pulsed and vibrated with the oil that was being pumped through them. Stepping back into the office, Doug pointed out a large framed plan of the ship's pipeline system that ran along the bottom of the cargo tanks. It indicated the valves for each tank, together with crossover and master valves. It looked complicated, but turned out to be quite easy to learn. Doug briefly explained it to Edward.

"You will have to know this like the back of your hand Ed, but it's not as bad as it first looks." Edward said nothing, just nodded while looking intently at the schematic.

"These," continued Doug, pointing to two more framed plans, "are the two pump room layouts." Again Edward just nodded, feeling a little overwhelmed.

"Come on Ed, it's time to take the 7 o'clock ullages," he handed Edward a folded piece of paper and a pencil, "you can write them down."

Edward followed him down onto the main deck, where he picked up a quart size can with a wire handle. It had wire gauze covering the top, on which sat an oily wooden disc attached to the end of a cloth tape measure enclosed in a round leather case. This was the ullage tape.

"This is the number eight starboard tank," Doug informed him after they had walked down the deck aft.

The wooden disc was dropped into this tank via an ullage plug, and allowed to run out until the wooden disc hit the surface of the oil. The tape was then bobbed up and down and the ullage measured at the top edge of the plug. Doug handed the tape to Edward.

"Bounce it up and down, you'll feel it hitting the oil," Edward did so and nodded to Doug as he handed back the tape. Doug read out the tape measurement, the ullage, and Edward wrote it down. The tape was then reeled in as fast as he could go, being careful not to touch the edge of the ullage plug, so as to keep the tape as clean as possible as it returned to its brown leather case. The oil covered wooden disc was placed on the gauze on top of the tape can, where the oil could drip from it without making a mess. Then they moved over to the number eight center tank, and then to the eight port tank, repeating their measurement drill in these and all the nine tanks that were presently being pumped ashore. They went back up to the office, where the First Mate stood watching them while Doug put all these latest measurements on the chalkboard; it was now 1910hrs.

Edward was shown around the deck to familiarize him with all the tanks and their corresponding valves, with ullages being taken every half hour. Valves were everywhere on deck; the individual tank valve wheels were painted red, crossovers were green, and master valves painted white. Edward had a reasonable understanding of what was happening on deck and what his duties were. At 1945 Doug took Edward to the fo'c'sle and the poop deck (the aftermost part of the ship) to check the mooring lines. During the unloading process the ship rises out of the water, so they had to ensure that the lines had not become too tight. They did slacken the head lines a little, and everything was fine. Final ullages for Doug's watch were taken, and then with a clean rag and a handful of cotton waste, Doug proceeded to clean the ullage tape.

"This is always the last job of the watch," he said to Edward. "Always make sure the tape is clean for the next guy coming on which in this case is you," he said, smiling as he handed Edward the rag and cotton waste.

"Come on. Let's go see the Third Mate."

At 2000hrs (8pm) the watch had changed and the Third Mate was on duty. Edward would be with him on deck for the next four hours, until midnight. The First Mate went over the numbers on the chalkboard with the Third Mate, afterwards leaving the deck for his cabin, although he remained on call for the entire unloading process. Doug introduced Edward to the Third Mate, to whom he gave a brief run down on what had been covered with Edward. Doug turned to Edward and gave him a friendly slap on his upper arm.

"You'll be fine Ed, I'll see you later," and vanished towards his cabin.

Edward shook hands with the Third Mate, who didn't look much older than himself. He was of medium height, fine reddish brown hair combed straight back, pale freckled face and an infectious smile. He was in fact twenty-one years old. Edward liked him immediately. They stood side by side, leaning on the hand rail, looking over the deck aft, and exchanged pleasantries.

"Well Paige," the officers rarely addressed apprentices by their first name, "let's walk around the deck and check out what's happening, and get ourselves organized."

The next four hours were quite busy, and involved the emptying of the oil tanks presently being discharged, and opening up others that were still full. There wasn't too much empty space on the main deck; each tank had a circular steel hatchway, dogged down tight around its rim. The hatchway was raised about ten inches off the deck and surrounded by a single safety rail about three feet high. In the centre of each of the tank lids was a circular plug about eight inches across known as the sighting port. One hatchway for each tank meant that there were twenty-seven on the Combia. Six inch pipes ran across the deck; these were gas lines for each tank that went to, and along the flying bridge, to the masts and up for about half the mast's height. They were for the release of gas pressure from the tanks, and each had its own pressure-vacuum valve at the deck level where the pipe opened to the tank. Together with the one foot high ullage plug for each tank the deck was a veritable obstacle course.

Emptying the tanks involved the pumpman, who was known as Pumps, slowing down the pumps for 'stripping' the last of the oil from the various tanks, occasionally cracking open a full tank in order to keep the pumps primed. The empty tanks were closed up and the chalkboard updated with the letters MT. When full tanks were opened, the pumps were run at full speed.

The rest of the watch for Edward was just taking ullages. Between times, he took the opportunity to study the pipeline systems on the schematics, then walked round the deck matching the depicted valves with their actual location. As it had become dark, the Third Mate had shown Edward where the deck floodlight switches were, and these had all been switched on. On the top of the small mast on the monkey island, a red light had been switched on to represent the red burgee, the explosives flag, that was left flying anyway.

At 2345hrs, 15 minutes before watch change, Edward woke up the Second Mate and John; made coffee in the small pantry across from the dining room, and set off once more to take ullages and clean the ullage tape. At midnight the new watch was brought up to date and Edward stayed out on deck talking to John and having a cup of cocoa, before saying his 'Good nights,' to go and get showered and turn in.

13

The next he knew it was 0715hrs and he was being woken up by Doug. Edward had slept like a baby, not even hearing John come in around 0400 when his watch had finished. John was fast asleep in the other bunk, and Edward tried not to disturb him as he got up and washed, put on his uniform, and went round to the dining room for breakfast. This turned out to be his favorite meal; cornflakes, egg, bacon, fried tomato, toast and marmalade, finished off with a steaming hot cup of coffee. He returned to his cabin, changed into his newly oil-streaked working gear, and went out on deck to relieve Doug. He felt good. The watch was much the same as his previous one, except that, just after ten, when he had finished the round of ullages and was still on the main deck, the Chief Officer had called his name.

"Paige!"

Edward turned to see the Chief Officer up on the flying bridge, "Yes Sir?"

"Nip up there and free the house flag," The Chief Officer pointed up to the top of the mainmast.

Edward looked skyward at the flag that had impaled itself on the lightning rod; a short spike sticking vertically from the mast truck; a disc shaped piece of metal on the top of the mast. The flag was attached to a six foot long bamboo pole that held it clear of the top of the mast. Efforts to bring it down by the lanyards had failed, it was just hanging there.

"Yes Sir!" replied Edward and scrambled up to the flying bridge and then to the mast where he climbed onto the hand rail of the flying bridge and then onto the fixed ladder that ran up the port side of the mast. He had loved climbing trees as a kid, so saw no problems with this… little did he know.

He scrambled his way up holding onto the sides of the ladder rather than the rungs, and eventually reached the top of the section where the thick wire shrouds stretched out to the edges of the deck below. It was here that Edward saw that this was, in fact, a telescopic mast and he was at the point where the top half of the mast could originally be lowered into the bottom half; but this ability was long past as the canvas cover protecting the joint and wedges had for years been painted over. For some reason he thought of the old Royal Navy saying, *If it moves, salute it; if it doesn't move, paint it.* The challenge here was; to allow the top of the mast to be lowered, the top portion of the ladder had to be collapsible. It was a wire frame with round metal rungs; a rope ladder. Undaunted, Edward reached up to this section and pulled on it to test its security, and then continued his way upwards. Arriving at the top he wrapped one arm around one of the stays; another wire support that stretched down to the deck below, next to the shrouds; reached up, and freed the impaled flag. Then he made a big mistake... he looked down. He did this to supposedly call down to the Chief Officer to ask if he was to just free the flag or bring it down. He didn't speak a word, he froze. A lump came up in his throat, was that his heart in his mouth? The deck below looked so far down, and so narrow, he thought that if he fell off he would actually miss the ship and go into the water, or hit the jetty. He took a few deep breaths and, holding on for dear life, made his way down, one rung at a time. The scariest part of all this was that he didn't really know what was going on; he'd never felt this way before. He may have scrambled up, but he sure wasn't going to scramble down. On reaching the bottom, at the flying bridge, his legs were so wobbly that he sat down at the top of the steps leading down to the main deck.

"You alright?" asked the First Mate.

Edward looked round and up to the Mate, "Shit, that's a long way up, Sir!"

The Mate laughed, tapping him on the shoulder as he walked away, "Good job, Paige."

Maybe he was just seeing what I was made of, thought Edward. *Well now he knows; it's jelly. No, I mean spring steel... that's me.*

Smiling to himself he jumped up, still feeling a little wobbly, and went down to the main deck to get on with the duties of his watch, after which he went up to the ship's office. As he put the latest ullages on the board, the Third Mate was standing with his elbows on the top rail, one foot up on the bottom rail.

"Did you enjoy yourself, up there?" he asked.

"Great view," was his response, smiling to himself as he had not even noticed what the view was like!

"Go for a 'smoko', I think you just earned it."

Edward went into the accommodation, after kicking off his shoes at the doorway. He made himself a cup of tea and stood chatting to Ray, the amidships steward, for his allotted ten minute break. There was no smoking allowed in the amidships accommodation whilst alongside. There was, however, an officer's smoke room cum lounge, in the forward end of the after accommodation that he could have gone to, but didn't bother. The ship was getting quite high out of the water now, especially the bows, where the watch deckhands had slackened the mooring lines. Discharge of the cargo would be complete during the afternoon watch, and then there was the matter of taking on ballast. Departure from Port-de-Bouc was set for 2000hrs; this expected time of departure, ETD, was posted on a small chalk board at the top of the gangway. This departure time would be the start of his next watch. Edward was very excited about the prospect of being on the bridge when they left.

14

After he had been relieved by John, Edward got showered, put on his uniform and went to lunch. Doug was just finishing his, and turned to greet him.

"Want to go ashore for a couple of hours after lunch Ed, do some last minute shopping?"

"That would be great," was his immediate response.

"Put your civvies on."

At 1330hrs the two of them were making their way down the gangway to shore, and a brisk walk brought them to a small square in the centre of the little town. Edward was happy to just tag along as Doug bought toothpaste and brush, working socks and t-shirts, and a souvenir ashtray.

"Let's go get a drink," suggested Doug. The two of them settled at a table just inside the door of a small café. The weather was clear and sunny but with a cool breeze. They each had a glass of beer; the fact that Edward was not yet seventeen did not come into question. They sat and chatted about where they were from, family, the usual things.

"I heard The Mate had you to the top of the main mast today?"

Edward was a little surprised. "Yes," he said, looking at Doug questioningly.

"You should not have been sent up there; first-trippers are supposed to go no more than ten feet off any deck. The Mate's a good man but I don't know what he was thinking. Don't worry I doubt that it'll happen again."

"I'm not worried," was Edward's solemn response, and the subject was never broached again.

They left the café and wandered around, dodging round a few of the local people who were scurrying about their business on the narrow pavements edging the small streets. They ended up back at the square, where there was a red brick toilet building on one side.

"I have to be back for my watch soon, but I need a piss" said Doug.

The urinal was a cement wall draining off at the base to one corner, and across from the wall were three cubicles. As they stood side by side facing the wall, a scuffle at the entrance made Edward turn his head. A woman walked behind them and went into one of the stalls.

"What the hell was that?" whispered Edward in surprise.

"Welcome to France. They don't seem to be as hung-up about segregation as we Brits are," Doug laughed.

They made their way back to the ship, laughing about the incident.

"What the hell was that!" mocked Doug, and teased Edward about the look of shock on his face. The three Deck Apprentices, it would seem, were going to get along just fine.

Back at the ship, the large discharge hoses had been disconnected, and blank flanges had been bolted over the valve openings, ready for sea. Unloading was complete and the pumps were now being used to pump in ballast ready for departure. Back in his cabin, Edward changed into his uniform and sat reading a book while waiting for dinner time. The Chisholm Trail was a Western by Zane Grey. It was a thick book and would keep Edward busy for quite some time. Doug had changed and was now on watch. John, who had been in the shower on the other side of the amidships accommodation, came in with a towel around his waist.

"How was the trip ashore, Ed?"

As John got dressed Edward told him of the incident in the lavatory and they both laughed. Edward looked at John,

"You remind me of the story of a woman who had told her husband that she didn't like visiting their daughter's house because their son-in-law often came into the room wearing just a towel."

"What's wrong with that?" her husband asked.

"It's round his neck!" retorted his wife.

Still joking around, they finally made their way to the dining room.

After dinner, Edward accompanied John aft to the officer's lounge. As they walked in they were greeted by a wall of thick pipe and cigarette smoke, something that not much thought was given to at that time. It reminded Edward of a 'North Sea Fog'. No portholes were open, as pumping ballast into the cargo tanks was ejecting volatile gases into the air outside, around the accommodation. A rather ineffectual fan was oscillating in one corner. The Chief Engineer sat in an arm chair in one corner puffing on a pipe, surrounded by various ranks of Engineers, all chatting amiably.

The Chief pointed his pipe at Edward and smilingly asked,

"You the young fella I saw up the mast today?"

"Yes, it was Chief," he said, while thinking, *Holy shit, I'm famous.*

"You got my vote, son. It sure looked scary on that top half. Was it?"

"Only when I got to the top and looked down Chief," Edward replied with a smile.

The Chief gave a hearty laugh,

"It's a strange thing son that the closer we get to God the more insecure we feel." He was still laughing as John and Edward went over to the other side of the lounge and slumped down into chairs below the forward facing port holes, and lit cigarettes.

A question from a landlubber… If the windows on this side are called portholes, are the ones on the other side called starboard holes? Edward smiled at his silly mood, he was feeling good.

On the after bulkhead across from them was a dart board, with half a dozen plastic-flight darts stuck in it.

"Do you play darts, John?"

John laughed, "Not very well Ed, how about you?"

"I used to play a lot at a youth club back home, I really like it"

"Well, I'm sure there will be lots of guys to take you on".

As they sat and chatted with others around them, Edward learnt that they would be going from here to Tripoli, in Lebanon, to load crude oil for Shellhaven in the UK. The cargo they had just discharged had also been from Tripoli, so they were doing a return trip.

Half an hour before his watch was to start, Edward, still in uniform, was on the deck outside his cabin leaning on the rail looking over the shore. The view was dominated by the oil storage tanks of the refinery.

Doug came round the corner, having completed his round of the main and fore decks. He'd put all the ullage plug caps on, effectively sealing up the deck ready for sea.

"Come on Edward let's go up to the bridge." It was here that Edward was informed, who would be stationed where, when leaving port.

Doug, in working gear, would be up on the fo'c'sle with the First Mate. John, also in working gear, would be aft, on the poop deck with the Second Mate. With Shell, when an apprentice was 'on station', leaving or arriving in port, it was a working station, which meant that they helped the sailors with handling the mooring lines. It was a learning process and Edward would be on the bridge with the Third Mate because it was his watch. The Third Mate was always on the bridge for arrivals and departures. Had it not been Edward's watch, he would have been on the poop deck with the Second Mate. Also on the bridge would be the Captain, a Harbor Pilot, and, of course, a helmsman. Edward's station was at the rear of the wheelhouse on the starboard side, next to a pigeon holed locker of all the international code flags. It was here, Doug explained, that the 'Movement Book' was kept. The movement book was a small log book used to record all activities when leaving or arriving in port, and it was the responsibility of the apprentice on watch to enter all pertinent information into this book. Doug leafed through the pages of entries that had been recorded on the ship's arrival, to give Edward an idea of what he should be recording.

He was also advised to stay in this area of the wheelhouse, and "Stay out of the way."

"One golden rule with the movement book Ed, is that you can't put too much information in it, ok?"

"Yes, ok."

"You will need your cap. They're always worn when a pilot is onboard. Go get it and then standby up here. I would have a piss while you're down there," he smiled. "Go when you can, not when you have to." It was advice that Edward would always remember.

"I'll bring the pilot up when he comes onboard, and I will inform the Captain. Shouldn't be long now, I'll put the Pilot Flag up even though it's getting dark."

The Pilot Flag is the international code flag H; a vertically divided red and white flag that simply means, 'I have a Pilot onboard'.

The Third Mate came onto the bridge and looked at Edward, "All set?" he asked.

"All set."

The Pilot came into the wheelhouse from the starboard wing. Edward looked at the time on the brass clock above the wheelhouse windows, directly in front of where he was standing, and made his first entry into the movement book. The Captain bustled in from the chartroom, having come up the inside stairs from his cabin below, and greetings were exchanged between him and the pilot.

15

The Captain went to the engine room telephone, "Are we all set down there? Good! Stand-by Engines, Third Mate." The Third Mate pulled the lever of the telegraph down and back round, making it ring loudly, and stopped it on Stand-by Engines. The inner pointer did the same thing, which was the response from the Engine Room. Another entry made in the movement book; and so it would continue. The helmsman came in and stood behind the wheel, waiting. A tug came alongside on the port bow and a tow rope was lowered down to them. The tug's deck hands fed the eye through a fairlead, a space, often with rollers, at the vessels side for a rope to pass through without causing undue stress to the rope, and dropped it over a bollard on their fore deck. The tug backed off, and slack was fed out to them until one of the tug hands held his arms crossed above his head, and the rope was 'made fast' on the port side bollard; the tug took up the slack. The vessel was 'singled up'; one rope forward and one rope aft. The Third Mate operated the telegraph, and the telephone, to the Second Mate on the stern. The Captain spoke to The Mate on the fo'c'sle on another phone, or sometimes just called out to him from the wing of the bridge. The Captain was there to oversee everything and to ensure the safety of his ship. The Pilot gave his steering orders directly to the helmsman, and the engine movements directly to the Third Mate. The Captain observed intently and said nothing, as long as he agreed.

Occasionally, the Third Mate would prompt Edward to make certain entries in the movement book. All ropes were let go and the ship was pulled away from the wharf, bow first. Engines were put slow ahead, and the ship swung round in the harbor to a south westerly direction, towards the entrance. The tug was let go, and the Skipper gave one short blast on the whistle in farewell. Clearing the entrance, they continued on to the fairway buoy where a Pilot Boat was waiting to pick up the Pilot. The Pilot shook hands with the Captain.

"Have a good trip, Captain." He left the bridge closely followed by Edward, who, as a politeness to the Pilot, escorted him to the ship's rail. A watch sailor was standing by the pilot ladder, which was a rope ladder with flat wooden rungs, and long stabilizer bars resting against the ship's side to keep it from twisting. Even though the engines were stopped and the ship was oriented to protect the Pilot Boat from the wind, descending one of these ladders to a boat bouncing up and down on the swell was not for the faint of heart. The Pilot stepped onto the small boat and it pulled away from the ship's side. The Third Mate was watching from the starboard wing.

"Pilot clear, sir!" he called, and walked back into the wheelhouse.

"Half Ahead," said the Captain to the Third Mate. Edward helped the deckhand pull the pilot ladder inboard then scrambled back up to the bridge.

Edward made his entries into the Movement Book of all the recent activities. The order, as are all orders, was repeated, and the Third Mate rang the telegraph. The Captain gave the helmsman the course to steer, which was a south easterly course that would take the ship off the southwesterly coast of Sardinia. Port de Bouc, Edward observed, was not a complicated place to leave, as once clear of the harbor the vessel was in the Mediterranean. The weather was good, with fresh southwesterly breezes. The order for Full Ahead was given by the Captain, who was usually referred to in conversation as 'The Old Man' which was not a derogatory title at all, more an affectionate one. He watched and listened intently as the sailors up for'd ran all the mooring lines down a hatchway into the fo'c'sle head. The ship's Carpenter, 'Chippy', heaved down on the windlass brakes for the anchor cable, and forward of the windlass, large claw stopper chains were being tightened over the anchor cables to secure them in place. The ship was ready for sea. In the meantime the Third Mate, because there was no radar, took a few bearings from the compass binnacle on the port bridge wing. He then plotted the ship's accurate position on the navigation chart in the chart room, which was right on the plotted course line. The courses for the trip were plotted by the Second Mate before departure. The Captain looked at the chart and returned to the wheelhouse.

"A beautiful evening Third Mate. Ring Full Away."

"Aye Aye, Sir."

This was done by swinging the telegraph lever two or three times and coming to rest back on Full Ahead. This was the signal to the engine room that no more engine movements were expected and they could settle the engines to their full ahead speed. All storm doors were closed up forward, and all lights put out, plunging the forward part of the ship into darkness. This was done in order to be able to see past the bow, to the sea ahead.

"Get the standby man to show this young fella," said the Captain nodding in Edward's direction, "how to stream the log, Third Mate."

"Yes Sir."

"She's all yours Third Mate, you know where I am if you need me," were the departing words of the Captain as he left the bridge.

Edward met the standby man on the port side of the poop deck.

"Hi! I'm Edward," he said while shaking hands with a pleasant but tough looking sailor.

"George," was the short, smiling reply.

The braided log line was coiled up on the deck next to the rail, near the short boom with the brass log clock already secured to its end. Edward watched and listened as George 'streamed the log'; the term simply meaning deploying the log over the side. First flaking-the-line up and down the side alleyway to ensure there were no kinks or knots in the line. Edward saw that the line had a bronze rotor on one end and a governor wheel on the other. The rotor spins on the end of a long line while being towed behind the ship. At the ships end, the line is fastened to a clock that records the ships speed according to the spinning rotor. The clock is secured on the end of a short boom that is at the ships side to keep the spinning rotor out of the ships wake.

"It's best to flake the line along the deck so you don't 'av any kinks in it," George instructed.

Having completed this he clipped the governor end onto the clock; leaning over the rail to do so, and then started to pay out the line in a loop over the ship's side until all he had left in his hands was the rotor. Stepping to the ship's rail, George heaved the rotor over the side, seaward of the line. The ship's forward motion took up the slack in the line, and the rotor settled below the surface. The turning rotor set the governor wheel spinning, and the log was streamed. The electric cord from the clock was plugged in, just under the deckhead above them, and screwed down, watertight. Now the ship's speed, according to the log, would be seen on a read-out on the bridge.

"That's it," said George. "Never put the rotor out first. It's harder on the hands, and it starts spinning right away. Then when you let go the line, the governor will spin like crazy because of the twist in the line, and you will have to reset the clock, after it settles down"

"Thanks a lot, George." They shook hands once more before Edward returned to the bridge.

Edward's heart was pounding… he was on his way. His first voyage and he was on watch; excellent! The Full Away was the last entry in the Movement Book for Edward, and the Third Mate's first entry in the Ship's Log Book, which was kept on the chart table; where one left off, the other continued.

"Keep a watch for ships from the wing, Paige, and let me know when you see anything," instructed the Third Mate.

"Yes, Third Mate." Edward walked out onto the wing, leaned on the dodger, and scanned the horizon. He saw the navigation lights of several ships and duly reported them. The Third Mate explained how to report the direction of the various ships in points. Each quarter, from right ahead to the beam was eight points; four points being 45 degrees from the bow and so on.

"Also, keep a watch abaft the beam for any ships that may be overtaking us," (abaft being towards the stern), were the departing words from the Third Mate as he walked back into the wheelhouse.

Each watch was made up of five personnel; the officer-of-the-watch, an apprentice, and three sailors. The sailors split up the duties of being on the wheel, on the fo'c'sle on lookout, and on standby. At 2200hrs, the helmsman was relieved; no auto pilot on this ship, and Edward was sent down to the midships kitchen to make coffee for himself and the Third Mate. He stayed away from his cabin as John would be fast asleep. He took the two steaming mugs of coffee back up to the bridge, gave one to the Third Mate, and took up his station again on the bridge wing. The lookout forward reported a ship on the port bow with two loud rings of the ship's bell. This large brass bell with the ship's name on it was situated on the after part of the fo'c'sle head. Three rings of the bell would be given for a vessel that was right ahead, and one ring if on the starboard side. The Third Mate was busy with the ship traffic, and with taking bearings of various lights in order to plot the ship's position on the navigation chart. At the ring of the bell, he gave the reported ship a careful look through his beer bottle shaped binoculars.

It was a quiet but exciting watch for Edward; the Third Mate just leaving him to his thoughts on this, his first trip, and his first watch at sea. At one point his thoughts turned to his Mum and Dad, *If you could only see me now…* He smiled proudly to himself as he looked at the star studded heavens above.

Before the watch ended there were no shore lights to be seen; only the glow of the lights of Marseilles on the horizon on the port quarter. The Third Mate called Edward into the chartroom to show him a large chart of the Mediterranean, and the various courses that would take them to Tripoli. This was so exciting that Edward's heart was pounding again. The trip would take them round the southwest corner of Sardinia, some 260 miles and over 24 hours away. From there, a southeasterly course would take them along the southwestern coast of Sicily. It was this coast that made Edward look closer. He pointed excitedly to the town of Gela at the centre of a long curving bay.

"This is where General Patton and his troops landed in 1943, on his push to Palermo." Edward's finger moved to the northwest and pointed to Sicily's capitol.

"Really…" retorted the Third Mate, taken aback by this burst of enthusiasm, "and you know this how?"

"My father has a ton of books about the war, mostly pictorial, and I enjoyed reading them," was Edwards reply. "That was the start of the Allied push through Sicily and then Italy, against the Germans and the Italians. General Montgomery, at the same time, landed round the corner here, at the Gulf of Noto, for his push to Messina." Edward moved his hand away from the chart, a little embarrassed by his outburst. He looked at the Third Mate,

"Sorry".

"That's OK," said the Third Mate, shaking his head slightly in surprise at this knowledge. He then continued his showing of the trip. From Sicily, a more easterly course would take them along the southern coast of Crete, then east to the southern coast of Cyprus, and then the short hop across to the far eastern end of the Mediterranean to Tripoli. It was some 2,000 miles in total and would take them about eight days. It was on this trip that Edward would be introduced to the grueling process of tank cleaning.

16

The three apprentices would break off watches starting at midnight, so John would not be relieving Edward. Instead, the two of them would be on deck at 0600. They would work until 12 noon, and then Doug would relieve them and work until 1800hrs (6pm), so they would be working six on and six off. It was done this way for the first day so that Edward could be taught the tank cleaning process, after which they would do their normal watches. Cleaning would take three to four days. Of the twenty-seven cargo tanks, except for four wing tanks and a centre tank that now held the ballast, all had held cargo so they needed to be cleaned. Cleaning was done with 'Butterworth' machines. This is a bronze, bottle shaped machine about eighteen inches long, with a double nozzle on one side. Hot sea water is pumped through this machine via a high pressure hose which causes the nozzles to spin at high speed and high pressure. The machine itself also turns on the end of the hose. The machine is lowered into the tank through a fourteen inch flange opening in the deck, and is supported on a saddle that fits over the opening. Because all this spinning causes static electricity, a large grounding wire attached to the machine is bolted down to the deck next to the hose saddle. The machine is first lowered ten feet into the tank and left for thirty minutes to do its work on the top part of the tank. It's then lowered to twenty feet for another thirty minutes. On the Combia, this was sufficient to clean the entire tank. In the larger center tanks two machines were used. All the time that this is going on, the oily water has to be stripped (pumped) out of the tank into a slop tank; usually the nine center tank. This tank is situated just forward of the after accommodation and separated from the Engine Room by a four foot wide tank that went right across the ship called a cofferdam. This is a very desirable feature as any leakage of oil from these last cargo

70

tanks would go into this cofferdam and not the Engine Room. This same feature, a cofferdam, was also situated between the forward cargo tanks and the fore hold.

Butterworth machines were run on the fore and aft deck simultaneously. The water from the slop tank was occasionally run out to sea, up to the oil on its surface. All slop oil was left in the tank and in this case, when they got to Tripoli, the new cargo would be loaded on top of it, as it would be the same type of oil. If the oil to be loaded was of a different kind, the slop would be pumped ashore, where facilities allowed. One thing about Shell even in the fifties, was that they tried to set standards to avoid polluting the oceans; this did not, unfortunately, stop some ships personnel from pumping oil into the oceans - nature of the beast. With any change in ballast or dropping the water out of the slop tanks, there always remained a risk of some oily discharge, but as long as care was taken it would be minimal. Crude oils being the biggest problem.

Tank cleaning was a busy, non-stop process that, after six hours, left the apprentices exhausted. Supervision for all cleaning and any additional ballasting was done by the Chief Officer. Pumps were operated and maintained by the pumpman. The grunt work of moving the tank cleaning equipment, 'swinging' the tank valves, ullages and soundings of the slop tank was done by the apprentices.

The day after departure, the duty free store was opened and Edward was able to get a carton of 200 Senior Service cigarettes. He was also allowed six cans of beer for the week; in this case they were the Dutch beer, Amstel. He was also given a beer can opener, this punctured a diamond shaped hole in the top of the can for drinking through, drinking made easier by punching a smaller hole on the opposite side of the top. He also received a bottle opener, more commonly referred to as a 'top end spanner'.

17

Tripoli was a sea terminal; that is, the vessel did not go alongside a wharf, but would be tied up to mooring buoys offshore. Required mooring lines for the bow were brought up onto the fo'c'sle, but the stern lines had not been stowed, and were still on the poop deck. On arrival, a Pilot was picked up to expertly maneuvre the vessel into place. Edward had hoisted the Lebanese 'courtesy' flag on the starboard yardarm on the foremast, intrigued by its symbol, the pine tree. Something he associated with the cold climates of the north rather than a middle eastern Mediterranean country. The ship was to be moored to two large, flat topped cylindrical buoys fore and aft, with a small marker buoy lying amidships. The starboard anchor had been dropped, and the ship was backed and pushed into position by a tug, as the anchor cable was slackened off. Wire 'spring' cables were put out, and the vessel was secured in position. Tug and Pilot departed, and a small boat containing shore personnel came alongside to the amidships marker buoy. This buoy had a flexible pipeline attached to it by a cable. The ship's derrick was swung over the side, and the hook lowered down to the buoy. The shore personnel attached the hook to the cable, and the weight was taken-up. The cable was then detached from the buoy, and the pipeline was hauled up above the deck level. The shore personnel came onboard and swung the pipeline into place, and it was securely bolted onto the ship's manifold, at the large gate valve indicated by the Chief Officer. A wire from the ships derrick supported the hose and kept it clear of the ships rail, to ensure no 'rubbing' took place.

In the meantime, the ship's ballast was pumped out, after which all tanks were sounded and inspected under the supervision of shore representatives, who cleared the ship for loading. Her cargo of Persian

Gulf Crude was from storage tanks ashore that had been filled via a pipeline from the Persian Gulf.

The process of loading cargo was much more hectic than discharging it. Again, this was the Chief Officer's responsibility. The cargo of oil is loaded, as well as unloaded, in such a manner as to ensure that no undue stress is put on the ship's structure. This became a lot more involved as new ships got larger and longer. Great care had to be taken as the tanks became full, and the watch sailors were out on deck to help with this process, standing by to open and close valves. Ullages had to be taken with the cloth tape and noted on the chalkboard outside the ship's office. Ullages were a little more difficult, as air and gas was now being pushed out of the ullage plugs. The wooden float on the tape had to be pushed into the ullage plug, and then a hand put over the top of the plug in order to make the float drop into the tank. The oil was topped-up in the tanks with the aid of an ullage stick, which looked like a seven foot black wooden sword. This was lowered into the tank via the ullage plug, and the oil level constantly checked for the desired ullage; in this case 2ft 6ins. As it neared this mark, the tank valve was eased closed, and an empty tank eased open to take off the pressure. When at the mark, the valve was closed down tightly, and others opened more until the set of tanks being loaded were complete, and the next set of tanks were all fully open. Edward had been previously instructed on the correct procedure with cargo valves; when a valve is fully opened, it is then eased back a little to ensure free movement of the valve wheel. This allows an easy check that the valve is open, and also allows quick movement when it has to be closed. Jamming a valve open can cause problems, and could lead to it being mistaken for a closed valve. There were small indicators on the valves; a pointer that ran up and down on a thread on the valve stem, but many of these had broken off over the years. A closed valve was closed as tight as it would go.

The process of topping-up was repeated until the ship was fully loaded, the last tank being completed by the shore personnel closing the valve on their terminal. With the ship fully loaded, draught was noted fore, aft, and amidships, and the vessel was checked for list. Complete tonnage of cargo was calculated with all final ullages, along with the temperature and specific gravity of the oil. This was checked along with shore personnel to make sure that all parties agreed on the amount of cargo loaded; bearing in mind the amount of oil in the slop tank, that had been loaded on top of. The total process had taken twenty hours. All battening down lugs on the tank lids were checked for tightness, any loose gear was stowed away, and all ullage plugs were screwed down tight with large bronze spanners. These spanners, or wrenches, are made of bronze because bronze does not cause sparks if dropped or struck against a hard surface, as steel will; a good idea when working around volatile cargoes and their gases.

They were ready to go.

18

With the Pilot onboard, the vessel was singled up, and the windlass put into gear to start heaving in the starboard anchor. Lines were let go, and they were clear of the terminal. It was Saturday, 1300hrs. This time, Edward was on the poop deck with the Second Mate, who had him stand by the telephone to the bridge, and observe what was going on. Departure was a simple process, and after the Pilot disembarked, they were on their way west in no time at all. Once under way, all mooring lines were stowed away, and the ship's decks were hosed down by the daytime crew. She was all ship-shape and ready for the voyage ahead. Loaded, the ship had a freeboard (distance of the main deck above the sea) of around six feet, so it didn't take much of a wave to ship water onto the main deck. Storm doors on the forward ends of the accommodations were closed tight, even though the weather was great, as there would not be too much activity on deck for the weekend. The three apprentices were to keep their normal watches for the trip to the UK. During the day they worked on deck, and at night on the bridge; something Edward was really looking forward to.

Edward's time was his own until 2000hrs. He spent a while on the deck outside his cabin, looking north over the Mediterranean Sea. The westerly breeze was made stronger by the fact that the ship was heading west. His heart was filled with joy as he watched the sea go by the ship, which was barely rolling as it ploughed its way west at a steady ten knots. The rhythmic thump of the diesel engine was plainly heard through the open skylights of the engine room, aft. *This is definitely the life,* he thought, *sure better than working down the fish docks. All that work at Trinity House was definitely worth it.* With those thoughts on his mind he made his way to his cabin, where smoking was now allowed. He hooked the cabin door back and pulled the curtain across the doorway. The porthole was open and a cool breeze drifted through. He sat reading, propped up against his bunk, and fell into a peaceful sleep. He woke up refreshed, a little after 1600hrs, as John came into the cabin. John was just coming off watch, having been working on deck. Doug had relieved him, and was now on watch on the bridge. After dinner, John and Edward made their way aft to the lounge, which was unoccupied, and clear of smoke. They played a few games of darts, 301, which Edward barely won, and generally relaxed and smoked a few cigarettes. At 1900 John left to go to bed and at 2000hrs Edward was on the Bridge relieving Doug.

19

The westerly course they were on would again take them off the southern tip of Cyprus, Cape Gata, about 170 miles from Tripoli. So on this watch there would be no landfall, as by midnight they would still be some 60 miles from the cape. From there it would be to the southern coast of Crete, and south of the island of Gavdos, approximately 500 miles away. Edward had not realized how big the Mediterranean was; the distance from Tripoli to The Straight of Gibraltar is approximately 2300 miles; more than the distance across the Atlantic Ocean from Land's End to Newfoundland!

This, then, was to be a very quiet watch with light breezes from the southwest, a beautiful clear starry sky, and just the occasional vessel seen. The lookout was on the fo'c'sle, and George was the man on the wheel, who also kept watch and reported any ships that he saw.

The Third Mate took Edward into the chartroom and showed him the star chart that was under the glass of the chart table.

"Let's teach you some of the principal stars, Paige," was his invitation. Edward followed eagerly.

"We'll look at the North Star, here, and how to find it, and then this circle of stars to the east." He pointed to the chart, indicating with a sweep of his index finger a large circle with, as he pointed out, Orion's belt at its centre.

"The three stars of Orion's belt point down to the brightest star in the heavens, Sirius. That's the bright star you see astern of us in the East, also known as the Dog Star. Then in a clockwise direction we go to Procyon, then to The Twins, Pollux and Castor; just remember Cast Iron Bollocks for these two." Edward laughed as he eagerly followed the instruction.

"Then we go round to Capella," the Third Mate continued, "then to Aldebaran, down to Rigel, then back across Orion's Belt to Betelgeuse, and that completes the circle. You going to remember all this, Paige?" he asked jokingly.

"I will," was Edward's excited response.

"Come on let's go outside," added the Third Mate.

On the starboard bridge wing the Third Mate, after a careful scan of the horizon for any shipping, pointed off to the starboard beam and with his finger, outlined The Big Dipper, which is also known as The Plough or Ursa Major. This, to Edward, looked more like a saucepan standing on its handle.

"The two stars at the top of The Big Dipper point to the North Star, there." Edward looked intently as the Third Mate pointed to the star.

"It's not very bright but it sure is beautiful to a navigator; its true north bearing only varies by about one degree," remarked the Third Mate.

Hanging down by its handle from the North Star was The Little Dipper, Ursa Minor.

"The long curved handle of The Big Dipper points to a wonderful bright star called Arcturus, but that is below the horizon," he said off-handedly.

"Let's look to the East," he continued, and Edward followed him through the wheelhouse onto the port bridge wing. Pointing astern, high off the port quarter he continued his instruction. "As I showed you on the chart, there are the three stars of Orion's Belt, pointing to the brightest star in the heavens, Sirius, his finger dropped down towards an incredibly bright star above the horizon.

"Wow! With its direction that could be the Star of Bethlehem," remarked Edward.

"Yes it could," was all the Third Mate responded. Continuing with the circle he pointed to all the stars he had named in the chartroom, ending with Betelgeuse.

"What do you think, Paige, you going to remember these?"

"Yes, definitely," replied Edward, "Orion and Rigel look more like a Scottie Dog," observed Edward. "Is that why they call Sirius the Dog Star?"

"Probably" was the Third Mates laughing reply.

"Can I go to the chartroom to write all these down?" he asked.

"Absolutely" was the simple response.

On a sheet of paper Edward drew himself a chart of these stars vowing that he would have them all memorized before his next night watch. Back on the wing of the bridge, he practiced all the names, referring to his notes when he got stuck.

The Third mate came out onto the wing, "Just as a conclusion for tonight, Paige; the star to the west there," he pointed off the starboard bow, "in what looks like the letter D on its back, the star at the top is Deneb, and is at the top of The Northern Cross." He traced the cross in the sky, turned, and went back into the wheelhouse. Edward was one happy apprentice right then and could not think of anything that he would rather be doing at that moment in time.

The watch went by fast, and Edward was relieved by John at midnight. The two of them stood talking on the bridge wing for half an hour, while they sipped their hot drinks; coffee for John, cocoa for Edward. Inside the wheelhouse, the Second and Third Mates were talking quietly as the new helmsman stood yawning behind the wheel. This was the start of the 12 to 4 watch, also known as the graveyard watch, because it was as quiet as a graveyard. All but watch keepers were sleeping during these hours. The best watch to be on was widely considered to be the 4 to 8, even though you had to be up at 0345hrs every morning.

Edward remembered something Doug had said. *The working class can kiss my ass I'm on the Chief Officers watch at last!* He smiled at the memory. It was a beautiful watch to be on as it gave you sunrise and sunset, dusk and dawn, and it was at these times that the Chief Officer 'took stars'. Usually four to six stars were observed with the sextant, and the ship's position was then plotted on the chart. 'Sights' of the sun were taken by both the Third and Second Mates at approximately 0900hrs each morning when not in sight of land and, of course, when the weather and cloud cover permitted. Both also took noon sights, and again the ship's position was plotted on the chart. This was the Second Mate's responsibility, who was generally accepted to be *the* Navigating Officer.

Edward learnt that the Second Mate's job was a busy one. He generally got to bed at 0430 hrs, and was up having breakfast by 0830, then on the bridge by 0900 to take sights with the Third Mate. Apart from being responsible for plotting all the ship's courses on all the different scale charts, he was also responsible for keeping all the world charts up to date. The chartroom table had large slide-out shelves, these contained 26 large canvas folders of all the world charts; hundreds of them in all. The Admiralty issues weekly 'Notices to Mariners', with navigational updates listed; corrections, changes, and additions, etc. These updates were made by the Second Mate using an ink dipped pen with a very fine nib, almost like a needle. These would later be replaced by a specially made fountain pen. So, after sights at 0900 he would stay on the bridge to do these chart corrections. If that was not enough, he was also responsible for the maintenance of the Gyro compass. This was housed in a special room off the chartroom. On this ship it was the Mark XIV, with a rotor that weighed some 64lbs. It was this that gave true north, rather than magnetic, and had one read-out for the helmsman and another one on the forward bulkhead of the wheelhouse for the Officer-of-the-Watch. It was a reliable machine but with one big fault; a power failure to the gyro would take it off-line, and if not caught right away it could take hours for it to settle down again. For this reason, when the Engineers changed over generators it was usually done on the Second Mates watch, so that he could stand by the power switch. If it tripped he could restart it right away without any loss of function. The Gyro was much appreciated by the helmsman, as steering by the magnetic compass was, as George put it, 'a right pain in the ass.'

20

Edward relieved Doug at 0800 at which time he learned that after discharging their cargo, they were to go to drydock in Barry, South Wales.

"Orders have been changed to Land's End for Orders," he was informed by Doug, "but we shall probably still go to Shellhaven on the Thames."

"What's Lands End for Orders mean?" Edward asked.

"It's really just a point of reference to give us a place to head to; Land's End. Then before getting to the English Channel we will be informed of our actual destination," Doug explained.

"This morning you will be on deck working with the Bosun (Boatswain); he's in the centrecastle. See you later, I'm going for breakfast. I could eat a horse," laughed Doug, and was gone.

The Bosun, usually referred to as Bose, was a large, burly man covered in thick black/graying hair; a large pot belly protruding over his pants belt. Edward would find that this was a great friendly man, a gentle giant, but not a man to be messed with. He was typical of 'walk softly and carry a big stick'. He was in charge of all the deck crew, who had great respect for him, and received orders of the day from the First Mate. They would get on very well together, and he became yet another father figure to Edward. Other deck Petty Officers were The Storekeeper; a middle aged Polish man by the name of Jesinski, who was always referred to as Stores; and the ship's Carpenter, referred to as Chippy, who was a young man from Fowey, in Cornwall, England. These three men protected Edward in many ways and kept him out of harm's way. They would be the catalyst by which Edward would begin his learning of ships and seamanship, as well as ship maintenance; tasks that he would undertake with great enthusiasm.

The wind had freshened and was coming from the southwest, and because the ship was loaded, and lower in the water, spray would occasionally come over the bow. It didn't look much, but if it caught you, you'd be soaked through. The occasional wave would also be shipped on the after deck, and would run aft and hit the after accommodation.

"Be sure to use the flying bridge young fella, when going fore or aft. Stay off the main deck in the exposed areas, and remember the golden rule; one hand for yourself at all times, and one hand for the ship," advised the Bosun.

With that, he left Edward with Stores, in his shop in the centrecastle. He was going to be doing some rope work. *Right up my alley,* thought Edward.

"Because we are going to drydock," explained Stores, "we are going to get rid of all the old ropes and lines, and replace them with new ones from the storeroom. Those will, in turn, be replaced with new stock when we get to drydock.

"On the port side of the Poop deck there are some heaving lines. Go and get them, we'll start on those."

Edward made his way aft along the flying bridge, and at the after accommodation turned to port to go round to the Poop deck. Mistake! Just as he approached the corner of the accommodation to turn aft, the ship rolled, and with the wind and sea coming from the Southwest, shipped a lazy rolling wave over the bulwark just aft of the midships accommodation on the port side, about four feet high. The wave ran along the deck, spreading itself out and hissing as it hit the tank lids and pipelines. Edward stopped and held on tight and braced himself. The water hit the bulkhead and bulwark below him with a crash; sprayed upwards and hit him full-on, soaking him through to the skin. He stood there for a few seconds, mouth wide open, hair plastered to his head, dripping with cold salty water.

"Shit!" was all he could manage.

The water receded and he looked round, embarrassed, to see if anyone was watching. He made his way aft, feet squelching in his shoes, and burst out laughing.

"Guess I should have gone round the starboard side," he laughed out loud.

He found the three heaving lines at the corner of the galley, where the cook saw him. "Been for a swim?" he asked smiling.

"Yeah the water was lovely," he replied and they both burst out laughing.

With a more somber note the cook added, "Be careful out there son, and keep a weather-eye out. And one hand for yourself and one for the ship." The latter comment he would learn was, when carrying something you did so with one hand, the other was for grabbing onto the ship should balance be lost.

Edward made his way back midships, round the starboard side this time, with the heaving lines draped over his left shoulder, his right hand gliding along the top of the railings, ready to grab hold. He reached midships without further incident and walked into the storeroom, where Stores looked him up and down and burst out laughing.

"What the fuck happened to you?"

"I went round the wrong side aft, at the wrong time."

"Well I guess you won't be doing that again in a hurry. Go and get changed, and then we'll get started on these." He pointed to the heaving lines that Edward had dropped in a pile on the deck.

"Bring your wet things down here we'll hang them on the pipes to dry," Stores instructed, still chuckling to himself and shaking his head.

Edward changed into dry clothes, putting on his sea-boot stockings and sea boots; Wellingtons – named after the British General, The Duke of Wellington, and also referred to as Wellies.

They spent the rest of the morning making up various lines and ropes, doing back splices and eye splices. Stores was impressed how quickly and easily Edward did these. One thing Edward could not do though was a Turk's Head knot. He watched in fascination as Stores did them, and attached these large round knots to the end of the heaving lines. These were the smaller gauge lines, attached to the large mooring lines, to be thrown ashore hence the large Turk's Head knot that added weight to the throwing end of the line. The shore personnel used the heaving lines to heave the mooring lines ashore, dropping the eye splice over a mooring bollard. It was a fun morning, even though Edward's fingers were awfully sore with all the prying open of the ropes strands in order to splice, they had talked and joked most of the time.

"So what brought you to sea, Edward?" asked Stores.

"My Father; he was a deep sea fisherman for 20 years, as was his Father, and his Father before him." was Edwards reply.

"Salt in the blood, eh?" Stores nodded.

"I guess so." laughed Edward.

21

The weather remained good for the remainder of the trip west across the Mediterranean. It took some nine and a half days to reach the Strait of Gibraltar, the roughest part of the trip being the stretch from Crete to Malta. They again went north of Malta, and Edward was on his evening watch. Studying the chart, Edward looked at the area they had just crossed, in this, the widest part of The Medi, (its usual reference). His finger went down to Tripoli (so that's where it is), and his thoughts went to a book he had read about the exploits of a group of British soldiers, the Long Range Desert Group. The LRDG who had played a key role in taking Tripoli back from the Germans, and was the pre-cursor of the British Special Air Service; the SAS. They'd come in from across the desert, as other forces had approached from the sea; all part of Montgomery's offensive in North Africa.

The following day they passed Cape Bon, near Tunis, to run down the Algerian coast heading for Gibraltar; still some 950 miles and four days away. Edward was thrilled to be running along this coast! It was the Barbary Coast of old. Pirates! Many of the pirates along this coast were French, and were more commonly referred to as Corsairs. They became such a menace to shipping, and disrupted merchant trade so badly, that the Royal navy sent out a fleet of war ships to deal with them; and deal with them they did.

The weather got better, and at 1000hrs the following day The Old Man had a lifeboat drill; not a surprise as everyone had been told. All the crew, except the key watch personnel in the Engine Room and on the Bridge, went to their pre-assigned boat stations in their bulky, uncomfortable lifejackets. The boat covers were taken off and the boats lowered so that their gunnels were level with the boat deck. Painters (head lines) stretched out forward to the main deck, attended to by an AB (Able Bodied seaman). There were four lifeboats; two at the midships accommodation, and two aft. Two lifeboats would hold all of the crew. This is necessary because if the ship was listed, it made the two lifeboats on the high side virtually useless. Rules regarding having enough lifeboats on one side of the vessel to hold all the ship's personnel came about as a result of the Titanic disaster. The drills were in some cases a pain in the butt, but an absolute essential, as everyone had their roles to play and the practice did away with any confusion.

The life boats and their stores and upkeep were the Third Mate's responsibility, so, as the ship was going to drydock, they were to be inspected. This was done in the afternoon and Edward was to help. It was an opportune time to do this as the lifeboat covers, having been removed for the drill, had been left off. Of the four lifeboats, one was a motor boat, and the Fourth Engineer; the engineering counterpart of the Third mate, was inspecting and testing its engine.

All lines and ropes were checked, including the lifelines that hung vertically down from a wire strung between the davits; these had figure-of-eight knots at intervals down their lengths to aid decent down into the boat when lowered. The loops of rope strung around the boat that aided getting into the boat from the sea were also inspected. The ropes were untwisted to inspect the inside part; if still new-looking it was good, if not, and the strands broke when twisted they were replaced. All boats had a mast and single canvas sail that lay along the thwarts. The mast was lifted into place and the sail hoisted and tested. The fresh water tanks were emptied rinsed out and refilled, and the tins of glucose candies (for energy) were replaced. The old ones were mostly eaten by the apprentices; they were good, but the wrappers were a devil to get off after spending months in the small locker in the boat.

Each boat also had a sea anchor, and this was taken out and the line strung along the boat deck. The Third Mate explained its use to Edward.

The anchor itself is a four foot long, cone shaped canvas bag, open at both ends, rather like a wind sock at an airfield. It's never intended to go anywhere near the bottom of a body of water. Rather, it's put out to control the drift of a boat. On the end of the anchor rope is a three legged harness that fastens to the larger rim of the anchor. One of these legs is fastened by a wooden peg that could be 'tripped' in order to haul the anchor back in. A fathom (six feet) up the line, was fastened a canvas bag about ten inches square which, in rough weather, was filled with vegetable oil. The idea was to string this sea anchor out from the lifeboat's bow, and the drag created keeps the bow to the wind, sea and weather. The oil in the small canvas bag seeps through the canvas, putting down an oil slick that calms the sea in which the boat was sitting. If the sea anchor was lost, a bailing bucket tied to a line apparently worked very well also.

"Hope we never have to put this to the test," was Edward's comment.

"You got that right! was the Third mates solemn reply.

The lifeboats were made of aluminum, and riveted to the inside bottom-centre of the boat was a bilge pump, with a hose attached that was long enough to reach over the gunwale, (the top edge of the boat). A long handle was moved back and forth to pump water out of the bottom of the boat; it sure beat a bailer. On the casing of the pump was a lever that, when moved to its secondary position, could pump water from the sea.

"In case of a fire in the boat," explained the Third Mate.

"You've got to be kidding," was Edward's response.

The Third Mate just laughed. "Pull the lever over, Paige, let's see if it works."

Edward pulled on the lever, but it was stuck. "It won't move, Third Mate. It probably hasn't been tested in years by the looks of it."

"Come on Paige put your back into it. Give it a good yank."

Edward braced himself, and heaved on the lever with all his might. He fell backwards over the thwart, landing at the Third Mate's feet. The Third Mate looked down at him and then at the pump, still held by its handle in Edward's hand.

"Holy fuck Paige, I didn't mean for you wreck the boat!" the Third Mate said sternly, looking at the large hole in the bottom of the boat where the pump was supposed to be.

"Remind me not to tell you to 'put your back into it' again," he said, looking at Edward lying in the bottom of the boat still holding the pump; then burst out laughing .

"Come on, get up and go and ask the Fourth Engineer if he can fix this," pointing to the hole and still laughing. "Good job we're going to drydock; you'd better make sure there's an extra bailer in this boat," he concluded sarcastically.

The rest of the lifeboat inspections went well; being sure not to touch another bilge pump, the levers of which were all set for pumping water from the boat into the sea.

They finished their inspections at 1600hrs, in time to get cleaned-up and have dinner. The Fourth Engineer, in the meantime, had bolted a temporary patch over the hole in the boat, making it watertight with a greased gasket. On his Engine Room watch that night, he freed up the seized pump, and attached it to a new piece of plating. The following afternoon he replaced the temporary patch; it looked as good as new. Edward would be teased many times with regard to this incident; for example, when closing valves tightly he would get the comment, 'Don't break it'.

22

It was Christmas Day when Edward got his first look at The Rock of Gibraltar. It was magnificent, even though it was a lot further away than he would have liked. He enquired about the eastern side as he stared at it through binoculars. It was smooth and turned out to be a man-made concrete fresh water catcher. Another first was to come for Edward as they traversed the Strait and entered the Atlantic Ocean; he'd heard and read many tales about this unforgiving ocean and, of course, he'd seen films at the picture houses (cinemas) back in Grimsby. He especially remembered stories about the large shipping convoys during the war; fighting this stormy ocean, as well as having the hunting packs of U-Boats to contend with. His father had fished off the Newfoundland Banks and Iceland, so knew all too well what this ocean could do. He had also fished off Murmansk in the Barents Sea, which could have terrible weather; his father had referred to the latter as a White Sea trip or fishing the White Sea, due to the constant foamy spray and spume from the white-caps and breakers. They never actually went into the White Sea itself

Ray, the midships steward, had decorated the dining room for Christmas dinner, and the Captain had put wine on the tables for everyone. It was a fabulous meal. They had turkey, which was another first for Edward. They started with a vegetable soup, then small pastry appetizers with some fancy French name, followed by the turkey, along with stuffing, vegetables, and thick gravy; finally followed by Christmas pudding. Edward's thoughts went briefly to home, where he used to help his Mum mix the Christmas pudding and he got to 'lick the bowl' afterwards. They always had a goose at Christmas, and ended up with a large basin of goose dripping, which was fabulous spread on bread with pepper and salt. *Hope they're enjoying themselves as much as I am*, he thought.

There were Christmas crackers on the table, and they all pulled them, laughing and enjoying the moment. They all looked rather silly wearing the paper hats from inside the crackers, but no one cared. It was Christmas. Mrs. Landry was really enjoying herself. It turned out that the reason she was onboard was to spend Christmas with her husband, the Captain, whom she normally saw very little of. The price they all paid for being sailors, or being married to one, as they were often-as-not away for a year at a time.

After the meal they all congregated in the officers smoke room aft and had drinks and a sing-song of Christmas carols. Edward had a beer; he did not drink the bitter tasting wine at dinner; never having seen it before never mind drink it. He recited his father's favorite Christmas time ditties much to the delight of everyone;

"Up spoke the brave old warrior
His face as bold as brass
I don't want your Christmas pudding
You can stick it .... on the wall."
...

His father had never completed the obvious rhyme and Edward had never heard him swear. When Edward used the occasional profanity he always felt a little self-conscious and wondered what his father would have to say if he had heard him.

....
"The boy stood on the burning deck
His feet were full of blisters
His father stood at yonder pub,
With beer running down his whiskers."
....
"It was Christmas day in the workhouse
The snow was raining fast
A bare footed man with clogs on
Came slowly running past"

And of course:

"It was Christmas day in the workhouse
The happiest day of the year
Our hearts were full of gladness
Our bellies full of beer."

At home, in the front room (or best room as some called it), a room that was only used on 'special occasions', they had a gramophone in one corner that had to be wound up by a handle on its side. There was also a compartment that was full of '78' records. Edward used to love to play these, and one of his favorites was George Formby's rendition of Jingle Bells, that was called 'Sitting on the Ice in the Ice Rink'.

Edward's six years in the church choir had not made him timid about singing and away he went, singing the words as he best remembered and understood them from the scratchy 78 record. The first verse was the usual words and tune of Jingle Bells, and then continued with Formby's rendition.

"Jingle bells, jingle bells, jingle all the way,
Oh what fun it is to ride in a one horse open sleigh,
Jingle bells, jingle bells, jingle all the way,
Oh what fun it is to ride in a one horse open sleigh.

Last night I went out walking with a pretty little Miss
She said I like you very much and give me one big kiss.
She was a perfect little blond; and not so very old
She let me hold her in my arms; but by gum she was cold.

Cos she'd been sitting on the ice in the ice rink
Sitting on the ice with her skates on
It's the finest fun I've ever had
Sitting on the ice it will never grow bad

There's lots of nice young ladies,
and how I like to tease 'em
If they don't give way I say OK,
I sit 'em on the ice and freeze 'em.

Jingle Bells, jingle bells, jingle all the way..." and so on.

There were great cheers and laughter and they made Edward sing it again. The song is a bit sexist but it was George Formby and that was him of the time. Just like his better known "When I'm cleaning windows" (or rather 'winda's) and "Leaning on a lamppost ... at the corner of the street waiting for a certain little lady to pass by..." all in good fun; apart from his recordings, the old 78's, Formby toured the theatre on stage, made films (movies) and he also had a comic strip, busy man. They all had a great time and 2000hrs came round too quickly, when Edward and the Third Mate left to go on watch.

The North Atlantic can be a nasty place to be in the winter, and here they were. Its reputation is such that all ships under the Lloyd's Registry have a Plimsoll line on the ship's side, at midships, which has set loading marks. One of these, giving the highest freeboard, was WNA; Winter North Atlantic. The WNA mark has to be at or above water level when crossing the North Atlantic in the winter. This system was named after Samuel Plimsoll, a nineteenth century leader of shipping reform.

When loading in a port where the water the vessel is floating in is of a lower density than that of sea water, this line can be submerged by the fresh water allowance of tons per inch. When the vessel enters salt water it will come up out of the water by that amount, to put the desired load line at the sea surface.

....

A strange thing happened on this trip; for some reason the ship ran out of butter, so beef dripping, which Edward was all too familiar with and did not mind, was put on the tables, and the only meat that was left was beef! Edward thought nothing of it, he liked beef anyway, but there were some not too kind comments made about it all.

Once clear of the Strait of Gibraltar, the Combia had made a north-westerly course, heading for Cape St. Vincent, across the Gulf of Cadiz. The wind had freshened, and now came from the west. Light spray was pretty much constant over the bow, which occasionally dipped lazily into a trough, sending solid water cascading over the fo'c'sle, and crashing over the windlass. The anchor chains were stretched forward to the haws pipes, as if bracing for the onslaught.

It took the better part of a day to cross this gulf, and Edward was on watch when they reached Cape St. Vincent. The weather had eased, with just light breezes, and the ship rolled and pitched with calm repetitiveness.

Edward stood leaning on the dodger watching the flashing light of the cape's light house. The sky was beautiful and Edward was soon gazing up at the stars. The Third Mate came and stood alongside him.

"Well Paige, do you remember the stars?" he asked, nodding at the sky. Edward, pointing upwards, named all the stars he had been shown.

"Good lad," was the Third Mates response as he turned and walked back into the wheelhouse.

As Edward again looked at the light of Cape St Vincent, his thoughts went to an article he had read about Nelson and his victory against the Spanish, out of Cadiz, in the battle off this cape at the end of the 18th century. The young Nelson had actually led a boarding party onto a Spanish galleon, which eventually surrendered, and the Spanish fleet was routed.

23

It was 2300hrs on 26th December when they altered course to the north, for their run up the Portuguese coast to Finisterre. The weather was quite calm. The Old Man was on the bridge for this occasion, as he often was for course alterations. George, the helmsman, was just steadying her on the new course when there was an almighty thunderous crash from aft, and the ship faltered from her new course lurching to Starboard. The helmsman swung the wheel and steadied her back. Edward turned to look astern as The Old Man and the Third Mate rushed out of the wheelhouse. Three pairs of eyes watched as water cascaded off the starboard side of the after accommodation from the boat deck. It came down like a waterfall, pouring onto the main deck and over the side, from the boatdeck back into the sea.

The Third Mate ran back into the wheelhouse and switched on the after deck flood lights, then ran back out again calling, "Keep her steady on course," to the helmsman.

They stared unbelieving at what they saw. Although the sea was relatively calm, the 'Rogue Wave' that had hit them had really left its mark.

"Make a note in the log book, Third Mate, I'll detail a report later" ordered the Captain.

The First Mate appeared on the bridge wing still putting on his overcoat. "I'll go and check it out Captain," and he disappeared. He returned twenty minutes later with his report.

The bulkheads on the starboard front corner, from the main deck to the boat deck were buckled inwards. The boat deck bulwark, which is probably the thinnest steel plate on the ship, was flattened to the deck, with the wooden taffrail broken and twisted, a section of which pointed skyward. The lifeboat on that side was twisted sideways and off the davit but held firmly by the two securing wires around its hull. The Engine Room skylights were open on the starboard side, which was actually the lee side, and some water had gone into the Engine Room, but no damage was done except to 'scare the living shit' out of the watch below. Six, one inch thick glass portholes were broken, but thankfully no one was injured. An AB, whose cabin was on the forward end at the main deck level, had been lying on his bunk reading, when the one inch thick piece of glass from his porthole crashed into his cabin and smashed on the bulkhead above his head. He was very lucky that he had not been standing up!

"Scared the fuck out of me." was his only comment.

One other port-glass was smashed, in a shower room on the main deck level, the other four, in cabins going aft, were badly cracked. These were later taped and the steel plates that all portholes on these war time ships had on the inside of the ports, were dogged down tight. The ship continued on its way, deemed seaworthy for the rest of the trip; otherwise it would have had to make port, especially at this time of year, which would have been Lisbon.

At 0800hrs the next morning, Edward was assigned to the Bosun to help square away the mess aft. Daylight really showed the damage that had been done by the unseen wave. Another reminder that they all plied the oceans by the grace of Mother Sea, and that she would never be tamed. If she was in a bad mood - watch out! Chippy had already cut off the broken taffrail, a large piece of oak, which he'd stowed away, and was now working on replacing the two smashed port glasses with spares from his shop. Edward helped the daytime sailors right the lifeboat back into its davit, and the Engine Room skylight covers were inspected and found undamaged. There was very little else that could be done, except to rope off the damaged bulwarks.

The weather was good, with stiff winds coming from the west, right onto the port beam. The sun was shining brightly, and it was a beautiful day; like nothing had happened, almost like the Gods were smiling at the damaged ship. Pleased with their little reminder of their powers.

They were on the main north-south shipping route for vessels going to and from the UK, to the Mediterranean, the western African countries, South Africa, and the Cape of Good Hope. It was this north-south route that had given rise to the expression 'Posh', on the Castle

Company liners to South Africa. Affluent passengers, in order to get away from the hot afternoon sun, booked their cabins on the port side of the ship going out, south, and on the starboard side when coming home, north; Port side Out and Starboard side Home. These initials were on their tickets. They were said to be traveling POSH.

24

As the ship got further north towards Finisterre, the wind freshened and moved round to the northwest. The sea began to get angry, with waves breaking, and spray and spume lines started forming on the surface, spreading downwind as if singling the ship out and pointing at them. By the time they got to Finisterre for the start of their northeasterly run across the Bay of Biscay, they were in a full-blown gale, force 8 to 9. The Combia began to pitch and roll heavily, shipping heavy seas across the deck as she dipped into the troughs.

The Old Man ordered a reduction in speed, and made a more northerly course to get the sea off the beam and more onto the bow. It certainly helped, but the ship still rolled and pitched heavily, making it difficult to move around without holding on for dear life. The ship would dip into the oncoming seas, shipping solid water over the bows. She'd stagger under the weight, then shudder as she rose, shaking off the water from her decks, only to be pounded once more. At times it looked like a great waterfall.

Because of the weather, the apprentices kept all their watches on the bridge, much to the delight of Edward. He was now allowed to stand inside the wheelhouse, on the port side near the tightly closed door so that he was out of the way. His arms and elbows were on the window sills legs spread wide, and just watching in awe. He loved it! Some of the rolls almost put Edward's knee on the deck as he braced with left leg on a port roll and bent the right knee towards the upcoming deck. Standing closer to the centre line of the ship made it easier to handle the rolling, than standing on the wing, but he loved standing on the wing. It was like riding in a lift or some crazy ride at the fairground, and a little scary, as you looked up at a wall of water coming toward you; then as the ship rolled back, looking up at the sky. He was told to stay in the wheelhouse. The helmsman had a real tough job fighting the helm to keep on course, and relief's on the wheel were every hour; the men were worn out by then.

Their position during this crossing was obtained by radio beacons on shore using the DF (direction finder), which Sparky operated. Beacons were from the north coast of Spain, Bordeaux, Brest, and Jersey. They were averaging just four knots; at that rate it was going to take four days to get across the bay!

Meals were fun! The dining tables had ledges around the edges that, when lifted into place, made the table like a shallow box. The white table cloths were dampened with water so that the dishes would not slide. Even so, you had to hold onto your plate and eat with one hand. The heroes of the day were the cooks, who somehow still produced meals. The stoves in the galley had rails around them with clamps that held the pans in place, it was a miserable place to be, on the poop deck, as the crazy movement of the ship in the gale was probably at its worst there, but still they prevailed; heroes.

On one morning watch, the Captain came up onto the bridge and looked at Edward, who had his arms on the window sill watching forward.

"How are you doing, son?"

"I'm doing fine thanks, Captain."

"What do you think of this weather?"

"It's great Sir." was his reply.

The Captain shook his head and turned and left the bridge. It turned out that Mrs. Landry had confined herself to their cabin, as she was rather ill due to the weather.

Edward reported a ship over on the starboard bow. He and the Third Mate stood watching it as it ploughed its way south, disappearing from their view as it dipped into a trough. Because of their more northerly course, most of the shipping was over to Starboard for those coming from the English Channel. They did have to alter course to starboard for one vessel though.

"Probably coming from the Irish sea," the Third Mate muttered.

There was a good reason why the apprentices were keeping watches on the bridge, along with the watch officers and sailors it was another pair of eyes. Smaller vessels were difficult to see in the large rolling seas. Their alteration of course to starboard had caused large waves to break over the foredeck, the water crashing across the deck hitting the entrance to the pumprooms bulkhead, sending spray smashing into the wheelhouse windows. The same happened on the main deck, sending water crashing into the after accommodation. Thankfully, this eased as the ship was brought back onto her adjusted course.

The Bay of Biscay had a reputation of being angry, or as the Third Mate put it, 'pissed off.' This is because of the continental shelf running round the coastline of the bay, with a depth of about 100 fathoms, this dropped off into the bay to over 1000 fathoms. The seas, especially from the northwest, hit this shelf and cause the havoc that they were in.

Being loaded, of course, made it worse because of the smaller freeboard. The reserve buoyancy came mainly from the Engine Room, which if breached, Edward was informed, would cause a loaded tanker to sink. Other reserve buoyancy was from the fore peak tanks and the forehold, any empty cargo tanks, and the cofferdams. One thing that had to be avoided, the Third Mate explained, was partially filled cargo tanks, as the free surface was large enough to increase the ship's rolling, causing the center of gravity, G, to move around. The oil cargo was topped up almost to the decks so that the large fore and aft deck I-beams broke up the oil surface to avoid this free-surface effect.

They finally made it across Biscay, altering their course gradually more to the east, which allowed them to make landfall on Ile d'Ouessant. It had taken four days – twice as long as normal for this ship. It was midnight on New Year's Day; a day that had gone by with no fanfare; just another day in the workhouse. The Captain was on the bridge when the Second Mate relieved the Third, and John relieved Edward. They had just gone onto their new northeasterly course, which would take them to their next landfall at Alderney, the northern-most island of the Channel Islands, some 160 miles and eighteen hours away. The weather had eased its onslaught on the battered Combia and was now coming from abaft the port beam. It was as if the ship gave its final defiant shake of the water off her decks, and all her crew gave a big sigh of relief.

"The 'old girl' did well" was The Captains remark as he happily asked the Engine Room for full speed ahead, and the new watch was left to their quieter graveyard watch vigil.

Before leaving the bridge Edward had a look at the chart and observed that from Alderney it was a straight run across the widest part of the Channel, where just 11 years earlier the massive allied invasion of Europe at Normandy had occurred. Then it was onto Beachy Head, Dungeness and round to Dover.

Edward made himself a mug of hot chocolate and sat reading in his cabin for the next hour; sleep would be a lot more comfortable tonight. The ship was still rolling and pitching but not as violently as it had been over the past four days. His bunk was relatively narrow, with a high side board. He had been sleeping in the fetal position, with his back against the side board, and his knees jammed up against the bulkhead to keep himself from rolling around. John had laughingly told him one morning that when he'd come in after his watch at 0400, that he, Edward, had been rolling backwards and forwards from side to side, hitting the bunk-board and then the bulkhead, and was fast asleep!

"If only you could have seen yourself, it was hard to believe you were asleep!" John had laughed.

25

J ust after lunch one and a half days later, they were passing Dover.
Edward, bundled up against the cold, stood leaning on the port rail
amidships, watching this wonderful, emotional, and motivating
view of the white cliffs. He felt like he had been away for a long time, as
so much had happened, but it was less than a month ago that he, John,
and Mrs. Landry had crossed this very strait on their way to Calais; the
start of his incredible adventure. As they headed north to the Thames,
he stayed on deck until the cliffs could no longer be seen. This was to be
his life; at that moment he would not have changed it for anything.

That evening, on Edward's watch, they tied up at Shellhaven. The
most exciting parts of the trip up the Thames for Edward, had been
passing Southend-on-Sea, and seeing the large pier that he had heard
about but never seen before, and the large number of sailing fishing
vessels that could be seen fishing in the estuary.

The unloading procedure started with connecting two large rubber
hoses - more of a rubber pipeline really - to the manifolds and, along
with a shore representative, Edward had gone round all the tanks to
take ullages in order to verify the exact amount of cargo that they were
to pump ashore. He had also sounded the empty tanks to ensure that
their had been no leakage into these. They were starboard-to the dock,
which would always be the case on the north bank of the Thames in
order to keep the bows of the ship pointing upriver to cope with the
strong ebb tide, which was much stronger than the flood. The tidal
movement here was quite large, and a constant watch had to be kept on
the mooring lines. Here it was done by the watch sailors. Experience was
needed for this job, and on occasion Edward would tag along in order to
learn. When the ropes got really tight, it was a dangerous job and great
care had to be taken, even for the experienced. The ropes were put in a

figure-of-eight pattern around the bollard, usually five turns, or layers. Edward watched carefully as the sailors started on the first mooring line. The top two turns of rope were easy to take off. The three bottom ones were the tightest and the circumference was reduced by the tension that was on them; in this case by the rise of the ship in the tide. As the ship unloaded her cargo the rise of the ship due to this would also contribute, and magnify the problem. The now top turn was pulled by one of the sailors, where the rope crossed in the centre, and then quickly let go. The rope snapped around the bollard as it slackened off making Edward jump with the violence of it. It was a nasty job to do and one that had to be done with great awareness. Hands could easily be caught in the slackening turns, and for this reason it was rare that you saw a sailor wearing gloves – too easy to get trapped in the rope. This procedure was repeated with the other mooring lines, Edward watching intently as he stood well back out of the way.

When John relieved Edward at midnight unloading was underway and there was the industrious sound of the reciprocating cargo pumps, thumping away far below in the pumprooms.

The following afternoon Edward went ashore to do some shopping, having got an advance from his pay. Before arrival in each port advance requests, or 'subs', as they were commonly referred to , were collected from all the crew, and the total was radioed to Company representatives ashore who delivered it upon arrival. This was, of course, done in local currency. The advance is signed for by each crew member upon receipt, and the Captain 'kept the books' for this activity. When a crew member left a ship and 'signed off The Articles', he was paid-off from these books.

Chippy and Sparky were also making their way ashore. They were both in their mid twenties, Chippy being from Fowey, in Cornwall, while Sparky was from Bristol. The three of them struck up a conversation as they walked down the jetty together and made their way to the refinery gate. From this, a friendship developed that would last for the remainder of their stay together on the Combia. Although Edward learned that Chippy's first name was Brian, and Sparky's was Trevor, the names Chippy and Sparky prevailed for each of them. Both were single. They stayed together, electing to eat ashore, and later had a beer at the pub near the gates; well, Edward had a pint of shandy, which is half beer and half lemonade (Sprite or 7-Up) or ginger beer. They all returned to the ship in time for Edward's watch. There were to be many future trips ashore for the trio, and they became affectionately known by other ship's personnel as The Three Musketeers.

Discharge of cargo and ballasting was completed by the next evening, and they departed for their trip round to Barry in South Wales. Company inspectors had come onboard to inspect the damage caused by the rogue wave, in order to make their recommendations for the necessary repairs. They had also inspected the log entries of the incident as this repair was, apparently, an insurance claim.

The trip back round the English Channel was a busy one, working round the clock cleaning and de-scaling tanks and gas-freeing the vessel for drydock. De-scaling is the manual removal of broken sheets of rust that fall from the steel bulkheads of the tanks. This is hauled out by the bucket load and ditched over the side. The accumulation of this 'scale' can be quite sizable and can interfere with the flow of oil in the bottom of the tanks when draining, or stripping, them; it also holds oil and gases, hence its removal. The gas-freeing is done by lowering a long canvas tube into the tank tops. The top of these tubes had two wings that opened out, rather like the hood of a cobra. This faced the wind, blowing clean air in, and pushing the gas out; just a large, portable ventilator really.

Notable landmarks that Edward enjoyed along the way were Beachy Head, The Isle of Wight, Start Point, Lizard Point, and Land's End. Then on to Barry Island, just about as far south as you can be in Wales. Another place Edward had never been.

26

Once alongside in Barry at a tank cleaning berth, a flexible hose was attached, ship to shore, at the loading/discharge manifold. Contents of the slop tank from the tank cleaning, was then pumped ashore. This last remaining tank was then cleaned, stripping the residue directly to shore. The tank then had to be gas-freed, and once done and tested safe, hordes of drydock workers came onboard to start on the list of repairs and inspections.

Welding gear, generators, pipes, wires, gas cylinders, blow torches, and other paraphernalia that was required for the next three to four weeks of work was dropped on deck by the shore-side cranes, making the deck more of an obstacle course than usual. A few days was spent tied up alongside, before finally moving into a nearby drydock.

The vessel was centered in the dock and secured; the gangway was put ashore, and a large cargo net draped underneath it for security of personnel when the drydock was, indeed, dry. Work continued on deck as the water was pumped out of the dock, until the ship settled onto the keel blocks. Once the dock supervisors were satisfied that the vessel was positioned correctly and safely, the bilge supports, (long large logs of wood) were put into place. Then similar looking supports, or props, were installed from shore to ship, down both sides, securing the Combia firmly into place. The sides of the dock were 'stepped' rather than being straight down making the positioning of these side props much easier. Here she was to stay for a couple of weeks.

When the dock was empty, the Chief Officer, being responsible for overseeing all work done on the ship and checking off satisfactory completion on the repair list, walked around and under the ship with the Captain inspecting the hull. One surprising find was that the forward third of the port bilge keel was missing; ripped away from the angle bar to which it had been attached. It had held true to its design where, in the case of accident, such as touching bottom, if severe enough to rip the bilge keel off, it would do so by coming away from its angle bar and not damaging the hull. Later, a log book entry was found from earlier in the year, when the ship had been 'out east' (the term used for trading around Singapore and Indonesia). It had been noted that the ship had in fact touched bottom when approaching the discharge port of Jakarta, in Java. In Dutch Colonial days this port was known as Batavia. This event was noted, for insurance, as the reason for the missing piece of steel. The loss of this portion of the bilge keel would also account for some of the violent rolling they had experienced when crossing the Bay of Biscay, as it does play an important part in the stability of a ship.

Over the next few weeks many repairs were carried out, and the 'rogue wave' damage repaired. The four lifeboats were replaced, as inspection found the hulls of all four to be structurally unsound; especially the one that Edward had pulled the bilge pump out of! Edward and John moved the Glucose tablets, sea anchor ropes, and other gear out of the old boats and into the new. This activity, by the apprentices, was fine by the dock foreman. Care had to be taken in what work was done by ship personnel to ensure that work wasn't taken away from dock workers; their Union protecting their interests.

Watches had been discontinued for the drydock period, so the three apprentices were working days from 0800 to 1700, with the weekends off. Once in the drydock most of the crew had been paid off. Some would return after just a few weeks at home, the majority of them being single. As some would jokingly say, they were 'married to the sea.'

Trips ashore, and long nights in bed catching up on sleep, were great extra benefits for being in dry dock, and the three apprentices enjoyed both. On Saturday evenings there was a dance at the local dance hall, and the three of them went together to enjoy the company of the local girls, and the madness of rock'n roll. One memorable evening was when the drummer of the group played the number one hit drum solo, Skin Deep. An amazing solo that stopped everyone dancing; they just stood and watched the drummer, cheering and shouting for more when it ended. The three of them always returned to the ship together at one o'clock in the morning, jostling and pushing each other and having a grand old time, finally collapsing exhausted into their bunks.

Although monetary funds were very limited, shopping was another important pastime; building up on essentials for their continued adventures at sea. One extremely useful item that Edward found was a travel iron, to iron his shirts and press his pants. It was small, and the red handle unscrewed and folded down flat, making it easier to pack in a suitcase. It was also the right voltage for the ship; 110 as opposed to the 220 ashore. He would also need this for the tropics; how he longed for the chance to wear his white tropical gear! He also bought starch, washing powder, toothpaste and brushes, shoe polish, shoe whitener for his tropical shoes, chocolate, and candies, especially scotch mints, of course! Years later Shell would actually put a shop onboard with all these supplies, because many places tankers went, you couldn't buy these things, and if you were in port for just one day, on a Sunday in the UK, no shops were open.

One big update to the ship was the addition of Radar. This was being installed on the starboard side of the wheelhouse. Edward had occasion to go up to the wheelhouse, and watched in awe as the shore-side radar tech sat cross-legged on the deck, sorting through a pile of wires that erupted up through a hole in the deck. To Edward, it looked like a colorful pile of spaghetti, alongside which stood the radar unit itself.

"How on earth do you sort that lot out?" he asked.

"With great difficulty sometimes," the technician replied, smiling up at his young inquisitor.

Edward stood and watched for a while and then returned to the deck below, thinking how great it was going to be to have radar to help navigate by. He remembered that John had noted its absence when they had joined the ship some two months earlier. *One hell of an exciting two months,* Edward reflected.

That evening John had gone ashore, and Edward was sitting in his cabin, reflecting over the past couple of months and the events that had brought him this far. He was very content, and put his thoughts to paper in a rare moment of poetry.

My First Trip to Sea
Fifteen years old and time to leave school
Worked down the fish docks, what a fool
Moving kits of fish heavier than me
This is no life, I'm going to sea.

To Trinity House Navigation School in Hull
The next twelve months sure wasn't dull
As if Navigation and Ship Construction wasn't enough
Had to learn geometry, and algebra, trig and stuff.

The year has gone and it's time at last
To Shell Tankers I go, oh what a blast
A train to London and Shell's Ibex House
Sit in the waiting room, quiet as a mouse.

Gave my tickets and travel plans a quick glance
Stay in London overnight and then it's off to France
A train down to Dover and across on the ferry
To Calais we go feeling quite merry.

On a train through Paris, Lyon and on to Marseilles
What am I doing here, can anyone say?
Such an adventure, have I done the right thing
Too late now, is that my ears that have that ring?

Combia was the ship, oh what a mess
Unloading crude oil in Port de Bouc no less
A tanker with oily decks, pipes and wires galore
The deck was an obstacle course for sure.

Looking like a first tripper with all this new gear
All the creases and folds that I had to wear
Four hours on deck and I looked like the others
Two other Apprentices, these are my brothers.

Taking ullages and soundings of the tanks being pumped
To the shore it goes like its being dumped
Getting the knack of bouncing the float on the oil
Keep the tape measure clean, all this strife and toil.

At the end of the watch get everything clean
For the next apprentice on deck, where has he been?
It's off to the showers to get off the dirt
All spruced up in a nice clean shirt.

Discharge of cargo is complete and off we sail
Thoughts of home and the newly posted mail
To the eastern Medi to Tripoli we go
There is no hurry, we are awfully slow.

Loaded with Cargo we head back west
Shell Haven in England is our next quest
We run out of butter, so bread and dripping we had
The only meat was beef, but that's not so bad.

Gibraltar to the north and then through the Strait
First time in the Atlantic this was really great
Up to Cape St Vincent in a good breeze
Alter course to the north in heavier seas.

A large unseen rogue wave starboard aft was shipped
Bent steel, broken glass and taffrail stripped
The life boat in the davit moved and all askew
What the rogue looked like nobody knew.

The Biscay crossing was at just four knots
Upheaval of stomachs of which there were lots
Spume lines on the ocean and stinging spray
Sea so rough the ship could hardly make way.

The waves hit the decks constant and fast
A thought came to mind, would the ship last
The rolling heavy in these rough seas
On the bridge some brought you right to your knees.

Waves crashing hard over the deck
Well at least the decks clean so what the heck
Everything battened down tight as a drum
Why did I suddenly think of my Mum?

Finally into the English Channel we get
Smoother courses northeasterly are now set
England from the sea, may this feeling never be over
I'm right back again to the white cliffs of Dover.

Into the Thames and to Shell Haven to unload
Steam and flame of the refinery a sight to behold
Now back to work get hoses hooked up once more
Get the pumps going and pump the cargo ashore

New stores onboard with butter helping the cause
A luxury dinner of roast pork and apple sauce
A fresh glass of milk fresh bread and tea
Let's get this cargo ashore and get back to sea

On the move again, apprentices cleaning the tanks
Good weather in The Channel for that we gave thanks
Get her ready for drydock, to Wales and Barrie we run
Well this is still my first trip and it sure is fun.

Edward Paige.

He laughed at the result, rather simplistic but very pleased with the outcome of his thoughts. He showed his handy work to John upon his return who thought it "Rather Good". He decided he would send it home to his Mum in his next letter.

27

Edward loved to go down to the bottom of the drydock and walk around and under the ship; it was only a small ship, as ships go, but looked gigantic when underneath it. The 'stockless' anchors had been lowered down to the dock bottom and the cable flaked out for inspection. The 'stock' of an anchor is that long bar near the top that is set ninety degrees from the flukes (the flukes being the two pointed pieces that stick into the sea bed). The stock is long and designed to turn the anchor so that the flukes do in-fact dig in to the sea bed. These modern anchors did not have this 'stock'. A tripping bar is designed on the flukes that ensure they dig-in. The anchor cable, Edward noted, was divided into shackles every 15 fathoms (90 feet). There were eight of these shackles on the port side anchor and nine on the starboard side. These shackles had been opened up, cleaned and inspected, and were now painted white, along with the links on either side, corresponding to their number. The first shackle from the anchor had one link on either side painted, the second two on either side and so on. This was done so that when the ship dropped anchor, Chippy could slow, then stop the cable at one of these points to verify the number of shackles, and hence the length of cable put out, which was generally two and a half to three times the depth of water.

The cable was made up of the familiar studded links. Studded links are like regular chain links, except there's a crossbar, or stud, across the middle of the link, from one side to the other. The reason for this is to prevent kinking of the chain in the chain locker. The last thing needed was a kink in the chain hitting the bottom of the spurling pipe, (a vertical pipe through which the cable left the locker and ran up to the deck via the windlass), as the impact would probably break the cable. Imagine the loose end of a cable whipping out over the windlass and hitting the deck before plunging down the hawse pipe into the sea! The studs also contributed to the overall strength of the chain; a great secondary benefit.

Edward watched for a while as the cables were being stowed back onboard, and then wandered aft to look at the ships stern. Walking along the port side he noted the new section of bilge keel that was now in place. At the stern he stopped and watched the finishing touches being done to the bronze propeller, which had been cleaned and buffed, and looked like new. They actually carried a spare propeller on the after main deck, but that one was made of steel.

Around the arch of the hull where the propeller was located, new zinc anodes had been welded into place. It was explained to Edward that at sea, when a ship's propeller is turning, it creates a static charge between itself and the steel hull, and actually corrodes the steel. In this case, the charge is attracted to the anode, and over time corrodes this away instead of the hull, leaving just the steel bracket to which it was attached.

The stern draft marks had been re-painted, as had the forward and midships ones, and all were looking very spruce. Each number was six inches tall, with six inches between, so if, for instance, the water surface was on the bottom of the number 20, it indicated a twenty foot draft. On the top of the number 20, indicated twenty feet six inches. Edward climbed the concrete stairs back onto the dockside, made his way up the gangway and back onboard, and gave his update to the Third Mate, as to the progress below.

They were now into their fourth week in drydock and work was nearly completed by the dock workers. Shore equipment was slowly being removed from the decks. The section of hull above the waterline had a new coat of black PF4, and the Plimsoll marks on both sides amidships were re-painted. The last to be painted was the underwater section of the hull, which was done with red-oxide antifouling paint. Curiously, the dock is then flooded before the paint dries. Over the next year the paint actually washes off, thus stopping the accumulation of barnacles and the like. At least that was the theory. On completion, the ship looked fabulous in its new coat of paint.

This reminded Edward of the response from the Third Mate when he had asked, "Why is a ship always referred to as *She?*"

The answer:

Because she is all 'decked' out.
She has a waist and stays.
It takes a lot of paint to keep her looking good.
It's not the initial expense that breaks you, it's the upkeep.
It takes a good man to handle her right.
She hides her bottom, shows her uppers.
And when going into port always heads for the buoys.

He smiled to himself knowing that this definition would not amuse some women…

The dock flooded, they moved out and back alongside the wharf. Over the next few days deck work would be finalized, and the completely overhauled engine would be tested. Edward was getting excited about the prospects of getting back under way, although he had enjoyed his stay in Barry. He was here for a life at sea, not being tied up alongside; although one big plus was that he had learnt a great deal about the ship. He had found the Welsh people very pleasant and agreeable, and a part of him was sad to be leaving.

As soon as they were securely tied up alongside, the Chief Officer prepared to start running sea water into designated cargo tanks as ballast, to ready the vessel for sea. He first ensured that there was no one in the tanks concerned, and instructed the pumpman to open the sea valves in the forward pumproom. Once the ship's bows had come down and she was more level and deeper in the water, the sea valves in the after pumproom were also opened, to speed up the process. Steam power was still provided by the shore, but now that the ship was where she belonged – back in the water - her own boilers could be fired-up. Once running the ballast into the tanks by gravity alone was no longer effective, the cargo pumps were started and completed the job. The apprentices were put in charge of this.

They had completed ballasting and John and Edward were in the ship's office. They were tidying up the place and trying to get warm, when the First Mate appeared at the door.

"Get yourselves up to the Captain's cabin and take Mrs. Landry's luggage ashore. There's a taxi waiting there."

The two suitcases were not too heavy, and after putting them in the taxi Edward helped Mrs. Landry down the gangway while John stood at the bottom. Before getting into the taxi she gave each of them a hug and a peck on the cheek.

"You two boys look after yourselves." she turned, looked up to the boatdeck amidships, and waved to the Captain, who stood leaning on the rail. The taxi whisked her away. They were sorry to see such a cheerful lady leave, and would miss their 'Mother figure'.

Work was complete, crew signed on; some new, some returning back from the previous trip, and last minute shopping ashore done. Provisions, fresh water, and bunkers (fuel oil) had been loaded, and the paint locker on the port side of the fo'c'sle had been jammed full of paint supplies for the next twelve months. The ship and her crew were bracing themselves for the voyage ahead.

28

I t was 1000hrs, 10th February 1956 and they were getting ready to leave. Edward was on the bridge feeling good to be back on watch again. The new radar mast on the monkey island looked good; its parabolic reflector turning steadily on top. The radar screen was a mass of reflections from the docks and surrounding area. Tugs were alongside; the singled-up lines were let go, and they were on their way out into the Bristol Channel. Under the instructions of the Compass Adjuster and the Pilot, they steamed in circles for the next few hours while the magnetic compasses were adjusted and a new deviation chart was drawn up. The Second Mate had had the gyro compass running for the past two days and he was busy checking it out.

Lying alongside on the same heading for the past month had changed the magnetism of the ship, which was itself a large magnetic bar, and this had to be compensated for by adjusting the positions of permanent magnets within the various compass binnacles. Edward stayed out of the way on the bridge wing reporting the various shipping, while the Third Mate was busy keeping the position of the ship on the navigation chart. He was using shore navigational aids as well as the radar, and they seemed to confirm the accuracy of each other.

"New fandangled thing." as the Old Man referred to it.

After compass adjusting was complete, a couple of runs up and down the coast at full speed were made to test the ship's newly serviced diesel engine, under the careful watch of the shore and ship's engineers.

The ship's orders were to go to Thames Haven, next to Shell Haven on the River Thames. There, they were to load waxy distillate for Ellesmere Port on the River Mersey (actually it was in the Manchester ship canal). The senior shore engineer was also to travel to Thames

Haven, to ensure proper running of the ship's engine, as part of the dock yard service, and for insurance purposes.

They were on their way! The Pilot and Compass Adjuster were dropped off at the Pilot Cutter, and they were Full Away, steaming westerly down the Bristol Channel, fighting a stiff Atlantic breeze. It was cold as the daylight faded, and the dark of the night enveloped the ship. Her new radar eye scanned ahead, to help keep them safe from any danger. The newly painted hull sliced through the cold, choppy sea, bows dipping lazily in the long Atlantic swell. Their trip round to the Thames River would take a little over two days.

Edward was again on watch with the Third Mate, and got to check-out the radar. The Third Mate showed Edward the screen and the echoes from Wales' south coast, and they compared it with the chart. They took a couple of bearings from the radar, that were relative bearings, on the starboard side. To this, the ship's heading had to be applied; in this case it was added, in order to get the true bearing for applying to the chart. Distances from the shore were also taken and applied to plot the ship's position. The radar was certainly a good addition to the Bridge. Although this new 'fandangled' thing would develop over the years, at the time it was really quite primitive, with limited range. It was operated 'head-up'; that is, the cursor (a movable line running from the center to the edge of the screen) would always be on zero degrees, so all bearings taken were relative. The cursor could be put on the ship's course, and then bearings were as they were read. The Old Man, however, could not get his head around steering, for example, 180 degrees and hence going 'backwards' on the radar. So head-up it was.

The run southwesterly along the Cornish coast was quite uncomfortable, as there was no protection at all from land, and the northwesterly that was blowing had the ship rolling heavily. More ballast was pumped in to make her more stable. The wind was about a 5 on the Beaufort scale; this is a scale that indicates the force of the wind by numbers from 0 to 17, 0 being calm, 5 a fresh breeze, 10 a whole gale, 11 a storm and 12 to 17 being a hurricane. The original nineteenth century scale was 0 to 12. Although there was just a fresh breeze the swell running in was high and long, causing the heavy rolling. You certainly had to have one hand for yourself when moving around.

This had always been a notorious coast to be too close-to, as under present weather conditions you had a lee-shore, especially undesirable for sailing vessels. A lee-shore meant that the coast was down-wind, there was, therefore, the danger of being driven up on the rocks. During the Second World War, there had been many mines laid down along this coast, and they had taken their toll on shipping; as had the German U-boats that had patrolled this area. Nasty times!

The next morning Edward was working with Stores and Chippy, unpacking crates of supplies and stowing them away. Chippy carefully broke down the crates and neatly bundled the wood and stowed it away in his shop. Edward was helping him with this, and stowing a bundle under the work bench, where it came up against large cables that ran round the ship. They ran along the decks in the scupper-ways, right around the outer edge of the ship, through the accommodations, making a complete circle. As Edward was stowing another bundle of wood, the ship rolled heavily and he banged his head on the bottom of the bench. He just grunted, rubbed his head, and pushed the wood into place, much to the amusement of Chippy.

"These are awfully big electric cables Chippy," remarked Edward.

Chippy laughed. "Actually they're coils, and it's the 'degaussing' gear. An electric current is run through 'em, from the Engine Room, and it's supposed to neutralize the magnetic effect of the ship, and not attract magnetic mines."

"Really," replied Edward. "Does it work; the demagnetizing I mean?"

"Don't know, it's supposed to. Hard to say I guess," was Chippy's solemn reply.

"How would you know," responded Edward, "unless… oh never mind," he waved over his shoulder, as he sat down on the deck still rubbing his head, and the subject was dropped.

Noon hour the following day saw them rounding Land's End, then it was on to Lizard Point, and into the English Channel. They were now protected by the landmass of Cornwall, the wind was abaft the port beam, and life onboard was a lot easier for all. Now that the ship was relatively still, Edward found himself unable, initially, to walk down the flying bridge without bumping the rails to either side of him, his body trying to deal with a roll that was no longer there, but it soon acclimatized. Sailors on shore were known to have 'the western sea roll', walking with feet apart.

Next morning, Edward was on watch on the bridge while going through the Strait of Dover. He was standing on the port wing; the shore side. The Third Mate came out onto the wing and took the bearing of a ship some two points on the port bow, and 6 miles away.

"Keep a watch on the bearing of that ship, Paige, and let me know what its doing."

Edward stood behind the compass and looked through and over the prism at the approaching ship. After watching it for about one minute he reported that it was still on the bearing that the Third Mate had left it.

Four more minutes passed, an eternity. The approaching ship was closer and the bearing had not changed at all. The Third Mate and Captain, whom the Third Mate had called onto the bridge, came out onto the wing.

"Any change, Paige?" the Captain asked.

"No Sir! Still bearing 025 degrees."

The Combia was traveling at 12 knots so in the past 5 minutes had traveled just one mile. The approaching cargo ship, doing about the same speed, was now just four and a half miles away, and still end-on to them; heading straight for them. The Captain sounded six rapid blasts on the ship's whistle; a warning to the other ship, that was the giving way vessel that she was standing into danger: The Rules of the Road state that when two power driven vessels are crossing in such a manner as to cause risk of collision <u>the vessel that has the other on her own starboard bow shall give way to the other.</u> This means that the vessel approaching the Combia was the giving-way vessel and should take such action as to avoid risk of collision. This would normally be done by simply altering her course to starboard and pass astern of the Combia. The Combia, in this case, is referred to as the Stand-on vessel.

There was still no action from the approaching ship, and they were getting closer. Both the Captain and the Third Mate had binoculars on the approaching ship.

"Do you see anyone on the bridge, Third Mate?"

"No Sir," was all he replied.

Now only a mile apart, which at sea is awfully close, the Captain continued to sound the six rapid blasts on the whistle; still no response from the approaching cargo ship. It was obvious that there was going to be a collision.

Edward was now standing at the after end of the port bridge wing, out of the way.

"Call the Engine Room, Third Mate, and tell them to hang on."

He then gave the order to the helmsman, "Hard to Starboard."

This moved the Combia away from the approaching vessel, and if she also altered course to her Starboard, which she should have done in the first place, allow a wider space as she passed astern. The approaching vessel altered her course to **port**! Disaster! *What was this idiot doing?!*

Edward, still stood near the back rail of the bridge wing, instinctively reached to one side and behind him, and grabbed the taffrail. The cargo vessel followed the Combia round and struck her squarely on the port bow Edward, holding his breath, stood watching, transfixed to the spot. He expected the vessel, for some reason, to hit them and then bounce off after just pushing them away; little did he know. The plated bow of the cargo ship tore into the Combia's side near the after end of the fo'c'sle, stopping at the large mooring bollard, which kept it from ripping further into the bow. The Combia seemed to stall, staggering and listing over slightly to starboard. The noise of ripping steel was incredible and sparks flew everywhere. It was a good job the Combia had not just discharged a cargo, which would have left the tanks full of volatile gases!

The sea around the stern of the cargo ship looked like it was boiling; her engines were going astern. This pulled her bow away from the Combia, but also brought her stern towards them. The two bows pulled away from each other with more screeching and tearing of steel plates. The motion of the ships now brought them side-by-side, the Combia going forward, the cargo ship going backwards along the Combia's port side, about 20 feet away. Edward looked up at the starboard wing of the other ship into the eyes of a shirt sleeved individual, which seemed odd since it was February in the English Channel! He was leaning on the rail looking between the two ships. He looked up, returning Edward's stare, then turned and walked away without saying a word; but it wasn't over yet. The stern of the cargo ship came round, missing the

Combia's stern, but the two ships came together again. The starboard side of the midships area of the cargo ship, hit the Combia's port quarter accommodation. The crashing impact stalled the motion of the ships even further; the Combia being pushed over to port, briefly rocking from side to side, and then they drifted apart.

The silence was deafening. Edward noted the gaping hole in the other ship's round-plated bow right back to her hawse pipes, her starboard anchor was twisted from its stowed position. All damage was well above her water line; she, like the Combia, was in ballast. Had they both, or even just one of them been loaded, the extra weight would have caused much more damage.

The Combia was steadied on course and the Third Mate was checking other shipping in the area. Edward was told to make a note of the time, even though he'd seen the Old Man look at his watch, and the name and place of registry of the offending ship.

Sparky, standing outside the wireless room door, was called over by the Captain.

"Sparky, contact that vessel's Captain. Tell him he has struck my ship and that I hold him responsible for all damage done to it. Paige, give Sparky the bastard's name and port of registry." This was the first sign of emotion from the Captain, who, Edward noticed, had remained so calm.

"Third Mate, plot our position on the chart and make an entry in the log book. I will detail it later."

Edward gave Sparky a slip of paper that contained a simple message:

'1103 12th February 1956, Argentine vessel Argon'

Edward had not been able to see the port of registry, which is always painted below a ship's name on the stern, but he had noted, as had others, the pale blue and white of the Argentine flag, flying on her jack staff. Sparky returned to his wireless room not saying a word. He appeared not long after and told the Captain that the Argon had acknowledged receipt of his message. She was registered in Buenos Aires.

"I'll write you a message Sparky, to send to Head Office."

Chippy appeared on the starboard wing and the Captain, seeing him, beckoned him over. "Thanks for coming up Chippy. Sound the fore peak, fore hold, and the forward cofferdam. See if we are taking in water."

Chippy about turned, gave a quick nod to Edward, and ran back down the stairway. The Chief Officer had also appeared on the bridge, and informed the Captain that he was on his way to check the damage, and see if there were any injuries.

"Thanks. Let me know as soon as possible," the Captain nodded.

On his way, The Mate was joined by the Bosun and they set off together. The Captain, meanwhile, walked over to the Engine Room telephone and called below.

"Is everyone alright down there?" he listened for a few seconds. "Just a little mishap up here," a typical English understatement, "it's all over now. Give me Half Ahead please." Then he walked over to the ship's telegraph and rang his order down to the Engine Room. The loud clanging ring was repeated as the Engine Room replied. The Third Mate made a note of this in the log book. The engineers were very quick to respond considering they had not been on standby, and the ship slowed down. This was all done while they were getting back to their proper heading.

The whole incident, from the Captain signaling the warning rapid blasts on the ship's whistle, had taken less than twenty minutes!

The reality of what had just happened began to settle in and the Captain, looking down at the deck at his feet, was rubbing his hands through his hair, his mouth clamped tightly closed. He looked sadly across to Edward.

"Go down below son, and ask the steward to bring some coffee up here."

Edward scurried the two decks down, and found Ray standing at the port rail looking aft. Edward also noted, what looked like every crew member was now wandering around the deck, some explaining to puzzled others what had just happened. He passed on his message to Ray and returned to the port wing of the bridge.

Looking aft, Edward saw the Argon some 2 miles astern, showing her starboard side beam-on. As he watched, she turned away from them. He picked up the binoculars and saw the port of registry on her stern, confirming Buenos Aires.

Looking forward Edward saw that the Second Mate was surveying the damage. The Argon had gone right through the newly stocked paint locker; thankfully no one was inside. It was completely destroyed, and mixed paint (making a beige colour) was running down the scuppers and out over the side. The temperature outside was hovering near freezing and the paint was already congealing in thick globs.

So much for the new paint job, Edward thought wryly.

Thankfully, no one had been injured by the collision. Just a few frayed nerves, especially from those in the port side accommodation aft. Edward couldn't imagine what that had to have been like; being in one of those cabins when the Argon crashed into your outside bulkhead! There were more broken portholes. Scary stuff! The ship was sound, as far as no breach of the hull below the waterline was apparent. They went to full speed and continued on their way towards the Thames.

At noon hour Edward was relieved by John. They had a brief conversation as to what had happened, and then he went down to his cabin and sat smoking a cigarette, thinking of his eventful morning, and then went to lunch. He sat eating slowly, listening to the speculations of the day. The general consensus being that The Old Man had done everything by the book, and that fault lay with the Argentine ship.

Some three hours later they were off North Foreland, about to head westerly to the Thames when orders came through from head office. They were to go to Rotterdam for repairs, so their course was altered to a northeasterly one, heading for the Hook of Holland and the River Maas, some ten hours away.

29

The following morning they arrived at the Maas, and when Edward went on watch at 0800hrs they were already tied up alongside in Vlaadingen, on the north bank about five miles downriver from Rotterdam. Edward was surprised that he had not been called out for the mooring, but it had been decided to let him sleep. It was expected that they would be there for two to three weeks. Edward learnt from Doug that they were breaking watches, and were now on day-work. Edward and John would join Doug after lunch, at 1300hrs, working until 1700, then they would be free until 0800 the next day. A shore night watchman would be on duty overnight.

In the meantime, Edward was assigned to help Stores salvage what they could from the devastated paint locker. It was a messy, sticky and cold job, and Stores had put some old canvas and rags down on the deck for them to stand on. Edward got his first close-up look at the damage. Some of the paint drums were wrapped up by the steel hull where it had curled back, and wind and snow was blowing through the gaping hole, making him shiver.

They salvaged about twenty percent of the paint, much to their surprise, and stored it out of the way inside the starboard side of the fo'c'sle. Some of the drums, which were all five gallons of leaded paint, were only dented and were stored separately to one side. They also cleared the area around the damage just to get stuff out of the way. It was heavy work, and Edward's arms and shoulders ached with all the pulling and lifting. The badly damaged cans and the mess were left to shore personnel to dispose of as they deemed fit. Shore people in hard hats were milling around doing their survey of the damage and deciding how they were going to deal with it.

Damage aft, although extensive, was limited to buckled plates, frames, and railings, and two broken porthole glasses, and, of course, the new paint job was ruined! The port side crew accommodation here was mainly for Firemen and Oilers, who were moved to spare cabins or spaces, or doubled-up with others.

Edward found that the Dutch workers were friendly, pleasant people, and they all spoke fluent English. They were also industrious, and got about doing their work without complaint, and had a good sense of humor. Edward had never seen so many leather coats being worn at once, and they were all bundled up against the horrible cold. The breeze blowing off the ice-covered river was bitter, and light snow was swirling around the ship.

A large canvas awning was rigged around the collision damage on the bow to give workers some shelter from the bitter weather. After careful assessment, the damaged areas were marked and numbered, and the workers set about cutting away the mangled steel with acetylene torches; sparks flying everywhere. Rows of the rivets that secured the Combia's steel plating were removed; the large rounded heads being burnt off, and the rivets punched out with spikes and hammers. It was a hive of activity.

Of the damage aft, two large hull plates had to be removed and replaced, along with their corresponding frames. Other plates, with lesser damage, could be heated and hammered back into shape. The whole area here was also covered by large canvas sheets. It was as if they were doing their work in secret, hiding from prying eyes! But, of course, it was to give the workers some protection from the bitter cold.

Shore leave here was a lot of fun, and although the weather was cold, the people certainly were not. Well, most of them! One evening the three apprentices went ashore to see a movie. They walked outside the dock area and got a bus into Schiedam, as they walked to the bus stop in front of a row of houses Edward noticed mirrors on the walls alongside the windows, rather like a rearview mirror on a lorry, all the houses had them,

"Why do they have mirrors on the walls'" he asked. It was Doug who replied

"So they can watch all the passers by."

"That's a bit nosey, isn't it?" The response from John and Doug was their laughter. As they approached the bus stop Edward looked up at one of the mirrors and saw a woman's face. He waved cheekily, to which there was no response.

The bus they finally boarded took them to Koemarkt, a square in what they took to be the centre of Schiedam. Leading off the square was an arcade with shops and a cinema. The arcade ran through to the street behind the square, and the three of them walked through to the far end where the cinema was located on their left. The shops on either side of the arcade were closed as it was after 1800hrs.

Unlike England, you couldn't walk into the cinema in the middle of a film here in Holland, patrons had to wait until the feature was over, then go in for the start of the next showing. As it was not long to wait, and there was no smoking allowed inside, again unlike England, they decided to wait outside the entrance and have a cigarette. There were quite a few people milling around, mostly going through the arcade, so they stood in the doorway of a closed shop across from the cinema just to get out of the way. Two uniformed policemen approached them. They were dressed in long shiny leather coats, calf length leather boots, leather gloves, and high peaked caps. Leather belts around their waists supported a covered leather gun holster. Edward took particular notice, since the police in the UK were not armed. Looking at them, he thought how smart they were but, *Holy God, they look like the Gestapo,* he thought. They stopped, side by side, facing the three young Englishmen.

"Move out of the doorway," one of them commanded in English. *Wow, were they that obvious?* Thought Edward.

"We're just waiting for the film to start," replied John pointing across the arcade to the cinema.

"Move out of the doorway," the same one repeated, this time more slowly.

"We will be going in to see the film soon," this time it was Doug.

"Move!" was the angry response, and he put his right hand on top of the gun holster.

The three of them, as if joined together, scampered out of the doorway, aware of the eyes of the passers-by looking at them. The two policemen went on their way, hands clasped behind them, walking in step.

"Fuck, I wonder what pissed them off," whispered Doug. "Didn't *we* liberate this country?"

"I think we did," replied John. "I guess we should have moved on the first order!"

"Looked like the fucking Gestapo," Edward said softly. While thinking, *it was the Canadians that had liberated Holland.*

The three of them looked at each other and burst out laughing, then worriedly looked behind them, but the two 'Gestapo' had gone.

"That was fucking scary," concluded Doug. The others just nodded.

They paid their guilders and sat watching the film, which was in English with Dutch subtitles. Edward's guess was that not too many of the locals watching needed them.

After about half an hour Doug leaned over and whispered, "How about we leave this shit and go get a beer?"

They got up and left! They were at the end of a row near the back so their exit was quick and silent. Edward was all too pleased to move as his knees had been jammed up against the seat in front of him, and they had all been fidgety. It would appear that their encounter with the two cops had disturbed them, because as they stepped out of the cinema they furtively looked up and down the arcade. No coppers to be seen, so they made their way to the square. Strange to call it 'the square', since it was circular, and was the terminus for buses and trams. One of these trams, the number 4, went into Rotterdam to the Central Station. They opted to walk around Schiedam, found a small watering hole, and sat and had a few beers, and smoked a few cigarettes. They chatted to the barman; a tall, rotund, jovial man, who laughed and joked with them while ceaselessly washing and drying glasses. It was a busy little spot and they relaxed and enjoyed each others company, and the hubbub of voices around them. By 2230 they had had enough, in more ways than one, and left the bar to make their way to the bus that would take them back to Vlaadingen and home; their ship. By midnight the three of them were crashed in their bunks, and slept the sleep of the innocent until 0700, when routine once more prevailed.

Work was proceeding well on the repairs, and it looked like they would be ready to leave in about two weeks. It was the weekend, Saturday to be exact, and it was Edward's seventeenth birthday. At lunch Ray had got a small cake with Happy Birthday written on it, and everyone sang 'Happy Birthday', much to Edward's embarrassment, but it made him feel very happy.

30

Chippy and Sparky were going ashore after lunch to do some shopping in Rotterdam, and asked the three apprentices if they wanted to go along. Only Edward accepted - the three musketeers together again. They got a taxi into Schiedam, as Sparky and Chippy couldn't be bothered with the bus, and took the number 4 tram from Koemarkt into Rotterdam. Edward enjoyed the tram ride, reminded of the trams that ran in his home town down Corporation Road from the bridge, just round the corner from the Palace Theatre.

Edward really liked Rotterdam, and its shops and people. He had a great time; Sparky and Chippy being terrific company. In one shop he found a German-made drawing set. A leather-bound velvet lined case, with all the different drawing instruments; dividers and compasses with various attachments - some for ink, and all snugly enclosed in their special recesses. He bought it as a birthday present to himself. It turned out to be a great buy as it would see him through all the exams that he would be taking in the future; correspondence courses over the next four years, yearly exams for Shell, and then the biggies – Second Mates, First Mates, and finally, Masters Certificates. The latter would be about ten years in the future, due to required sea-time in order to sit the exam.

Their shopping and wandering around was conducted at a brisk walk because of the cold. They found a nice little restaurant near the railway station where they stopped and had a wonderful meal of steak, mushrooms, and chips, followed by apple pie and small cups of strong black coffee. Edward was having the time of his life, and the meal was his birthday treat.

"Do you fancy a night on the town, you two?" inquired Sparky.

"Sure!" Chippy and Edward replied in unison, which made them all laugh.

"What did you have in mind?" asked Chippy.

"I know a little bar with lots of female company where we can have some fun."

"Lead on McDuff," was Chippy's response, with a big smile.

They left the restaurant, hailed a taxi and bundled into the back seat. Although the driver was bundled up against the cold, the inside of the taxi was like an oven. It reminded Edward of the night watchman onboard ship in the small ship's office. He too would be bundled up against the cold and have the office heat cranked on full. *Must be a Dutch thing,* he thought.

"The Seven Seas bar," Sparky told the driver. He nodded and pulled quickly away from the curb, pressing the three of them against the back of the seat. *Time is money for taxi drivers,* Edward guessed.

The bar wasn't very big, but was busy, noisy, and very smoky; Edward loved it. They found a table in a corner and hung their coats on a peg on the wall. They sat down and ordered beer from a cute waitress, who was at the table almost before they were. Chippy and Edward lit cigarettes, and Sparky lit his pipe; all contributing further to the already well-polluted air. The waitress returned, banged the small glasses down on beer mats, and left.

"Doesn't she need paying for the beers?" asked Edward.

"No, we run up a tab and pay before we leave," he was informed.

"Oh," was all Edward could manage. At home you paid as you got served.

"Cheers!" They touched glasses and drank heartily. It was strange, but even though Edward had only just reached his seventeenth birthday, he had never been questioned about his age in a bar. It made him feel good, and grown-up.

Before they had finished their first beer they were joined by three young women, who had previously been sat at the bar.

"You boys want company?" one asked as they pulled up chairs and sat down between each of them.

"Sure," replied Chippy rather unnecessarily, "what would you like to drink?"

They ordered their fancy expensive drinks and started making small talk. They were actually good company and made a pleasant change with their conversation, as opposed to the usual guy-talk. They were, Edward guessed, all in their early twenties. Two tall slim blondes sat with Chippy and Sparky, and a shorter, heavier set, auburn haired girl sidled up to Edward. The three of them were Dutch, but spoke better English than most English people do. They were very pleasant, but a little 'hard looking'. Their main job seemed to be to sell drinks and run up the bar tab, but Sparky kept this to a reasonable level, no doubt by experience. Chippy told them it was Edward's eighteenth birthday; after all they were in a bar so they upped it by a year!

They spent a couple of hours laughing and joking, during which the girls' other occupation became more evident. To Edward's surprise, his two shipmates made it clear that they would not be going home with their two girls; much to their chagrin, but they continued to try very hard. Auburn hair, she said her name was Heidi, cozied up to Edward.

"Are you a virgin Edward?"

"No," he lied trying to be indignant.

"Are you going to stay a virgin?" she asked, unconvinced by his reply.

Sparky and Chippy just sat back and watched, enjoying the moment of their friend's unease.

"If your friends go with them two, I'll do you for nothing," she whispered in his ear, "birthday present!"

Edward just shook his head and she moved away, rubbing her hand down his leg and squeezing his knee. He was actually a little scared, but would admit that to no one. He would think of this offer for a long time to come in his male dominated world at sea, and berate himself for being a *chicken shit*; Sparky and Chippy, or no Sparky and Chippy.

Shortly afterwards they paid the bill, to which Edward was not allowed to contribute. They stepped outside to the taxi waiting at the curb that the bartender had summoned for them. The wind was blowing and it was absolutely freezing outside. Certainly the coldest Edward had ever experienced. They jumped into the taxi, slamming the door to keep out the cold.

"Vlaadingen ship docks," Chippy requested, and they were off. No public transport tonight.

"Too fucking cold!" as Chippy put it.

"I'm surprised you two didn't go off with them girls, they were quite cute," Edward observed, still confused about his own emotions.

"Didn't fancy mine very much" replied Sparky

"Not your type?' asked Chippy

"Hell no!" he replied, "They take you home, take your money, fuck your brains out, and then throw you out to get on with your life, exactly my type!" They laughed drunkenly, jostling and joking all the way back to the ship. Edward was teased about 'his girl', and how he should have 'gone for it'.

The taxi dropped them off at the foot of the ship's gangway and they clambered up, heads bent against the wind and bitter cold. After quick goodnights, Sparky and Edward made their way amidships and Chippy aft, to his cabin.

John was still up reading a book as Edward entered the cabin. He recounted the day's events to John, as he got ready for bed. He said goodnight and climbed into his bunk.

"One hell of a birthday!" he concluded. He was asleep in no time.

31

Work was complete and the Combia looked as good as new. Well, that was stretching it a little, but at least she was whole again. In a bay just off the river they tied up amidships to a buoy, and tugs pushed the ship in circles around it, to once again adjust compasses.

They were to go across the river from where they had been tied up for the past three weeks, to load at Pernis, the large Rotterdam refinery. The cargo would be 100 octane gasoline, known as red gas; and Avtur - Aviation Turbine Fuel; a cargo for the Swedish Air Force that was to be delivered to Norrkoping. This was an ideal time to load the Avtur, as the cleanliness of the tanks; free from contaminants, was critical. Even so, when they were alongside, scale samples from the tanks to be loaded with Avtur were taken ashore to be tested in their lab. Special attention was paid to those tanks that ballast had remained in during the repairs.

Loading would take two days. It was a long, drawn out process. First, approximately six to twelve inches of Avtur was loaded into each of the appropriate tanks, through a dedicated line. Samples were then taken for testing ashore. One of these tanks was then pumped ashore to dedicate a pump and line for its discharge, and then the process repeated for this tank until the shore reps were satisfied. The pipeline system on these tanker ships allowed a two valve separation between different products; a safety precaution to ensure that different products, or different grades of cargo, were kept separate from each other. If a high octane gasoline and a low octane gasoline are carried at the same time, the high octane is discharged first and then the low. This is so the product left in the pipeline system is high octane, which is then pumped ashore with the low octane, rather than the other way round.

They were finally on the move again. A Pilot took them down river to the Hook of Holland and, after dropping him off at the Pilot Cutter, they made their way north in a choppy sea. A stiff northerly breeze caused constant spray over the fo'c'sle, and short seas to break over the decks of the loaded, low riding ship.

At the East Frisian Islands, the breeze had dropped off and changed to a southeasterly direction. Here they picked up a German Pilot, who was to navigate them, in a buoyed channel, through a left-over German mine field. The mines had been laid off this part of the German coast during the Second World War to protect the approach to Bremerhaven, Wilhelmshaven, and the entrance to the River Elbe, and hence the port of Hamburg.

That night, visibility became especially poor due to fog, which was the result of cold air coming off the land, over a relatively warm sea. They were very thankful of their new radar as their way was clearly marked, thanks to the radar reflectors on the top of the buoys in the channel. There were squared-off areas marked on the chart where the mines had been cleared. These areas allowed ships to get out of the channel and anchor. The Captain, looking at the fog now enveloping the bow, looked over to the Pilot.

"We can anchor for the night if you wish, Pilot"

"No, it is fine Captain, we have the radar so we can proceed," he said in a deep guttural voice.

"We have Avtur and one hundred octane gasoline onboard, Pilot," the Captain responded.

"We will go and anchor Captain!" the Pilot replied without a second's hesitation. He walked over to the radar and gave his orders to take them to the next anchorage area.

"Third Mate, call the Chief Officer and get the standby to inform Chippy we are going to anchor."

"Sir!" was the Third Mates reply as he walked over to the phone on the after bulkhead.

The apprentices were keeping watches, and Edward was presently on duty. As he stood inside the wheelhouse on the starboard side, between the radar and the starboard door, he was looking out the forward window at the fog swirling around the fo'c'sle head as they slowly steamed forward. When he had come on watch Doug had shown him on the chart in use where they were, and the courses they would be making. On a smaller scale chart he'd slid his finger almost due west across the North Sea, pointing to Grimsby.

"There's your home town, about three hundred miles away."

"Wow, right on!" was all he could manage. It was 9th March, Edward's youngest sister's birthday. He hadn't forgotten, and had sent a card to her while shopping in Rotterdam.

Really strange, he thought, *to be so close to home on this date.* His sister, Eva, would turn out to be his constant link with home, Edward receiving letters from her in almost every port he visited.

He looked down at the flying bridge and watched as the First Mate, Chippy, and the watch standby sailor, made their way forward to get the anchor ready for dropping. He was pleased that he had been allowed to stand inside the wheelhouse as it was bitterly cold outside, and he also got to look at the radar screen - fascinating!

His thoughts, however, still went to the Pilot; the first German he had seen. The war had only ended ten years previously. The films he had seen, books he had read, and stories he had heard, and his own memories of being huddled in the air raid shelter listening to his home town being bombed, all contributed to his mixed emotions about this nationality. Probably unfair, but he didn't like the Pilot. He wondered how the Captain felt, as Edward knew that the Captain had been a Second Mate on tankers that had been part of the North Atlantic convoys during the war, having to deal with the wolf packs of U-boats. Here now was a German on board his ship, giving orders!

Maybe it's a non-issue, thought Edward. *They do say that time is the healer of all wounds. Anyway, one thing is for sure, you have to move on and try to let go.*

Thirty minutes later they were in the anchorage area and the starboard anchor was dropped; the cable rumbled and crashed over the windlass and through the hawse pipe into the cold depths below. She came-to her anchor and settled down for a peaceful night. The watch sailor hoisted the anchor light onto the forward stay, above the fo'c'sle. The Pilot was shown to the small Pilot's cabin behind the wheelhouse, and the Captain also retired to his cabin. It was in this peaceful state, with the radar screen lit by all its returned echoes, that midnight came around. The Second Mate relieved the Third Mate, and John relieved

Edward. The two apprentices chatted in the corner drinking hot coffee before Edward departed thirty minutes later to his waiting, and welcome bunk.

....

He was awakened by Doug for his morning watch at 0715 to find that they were, once again, under way. After eating his favorite meal, breakfast, he eagerly went to the Bridge, just glad that they were at sea. He'd had enough of being tied up alongside.

They were approaching the River Elbe, with the island of Heligoland to the north. The weather was calm and sunny, but still very cold, and the river was busy with lots of sea traffic. The watch went quickly, and by noon, when John and the Second Mate came onto the bridge, they were approaching Brunsbuttelkoog, the entrance to the Kiel Canal.

"Come on Paige, let's go get lunch," said the Third Mate "we'll be needed again shortly for going into the locks."

They ate their lunch quickly the Third Mate relating to Edward the hazards of anchoring here: The ebb current in the Elbe is very strong; ships were known to have broken their anchor cables while anchoring here. Once anchored it is usually fine but during the act of anchoring great care had to be taken when 'bringing the ship up to the anchor' that is, holder her in position in the river, the ships engine had to be used to ease the strain on the cable until this could be done.

Fortunately they did not have to anchor on this occasion. After lunch the Third Mate went back up to the bridge, Edward got changed and went aft to the poop deck, along with the Second Mate, the First Mate going forward to the Fo'c'sle.

Tugs were tied up alongside to aide them into the locks, and especially to hold them in position against the tide. There were two sets of locks, and as they were entering one lock, a Russian ship was leaving in the other lock beside them. Their poop decks became level as they slowly passed and the sailors on the Combia stood ogling a tall buxom blonde woman on the Russian ship.

"Probably the cook." a sailor standing near Edward remarked.

One of the sailors on the Russian ship, seeing what was going on, crept up behind the woman and good naturedly wrapped a heaving line round her shoulders, and made as if to throw the other end to the ogling sailors. The Combia sailors were cheering and indicating for the line to be thrown to them. The sailors on both ships were all laughing, including the blonde woman, and all waved as the two ships went their separate ways. The blonde lady pushed the Russian sailor away with a friendly laugh as they walked away from the rail.

The trip through the canal took a little over fourteen hours, so it was the following morning that they cleared Kiel. When Edward relieved Doug on the Bridge at 0800, Doug explained that they were off the southern tip of Zealand at Gedser. The weather was cold, minus 10F, but clear with a light breeze. The sea was a grey/blue, with no white caps, it looked awfully cold making Edward give a little shiver. Two ships, heading for the canal, were passing off their port side. As Edward scanned the sea ahead, the stern of a ship going the same way could be seen, pulling away from them. Other vessels were at varying distances and courses. This was a busy place.

Edward asked the Third Mate if it was ok to look at the chart, and upon his enthusiastic scrutiny noted that at the northern tip of Zealand, some eighty miles distant, was the capital, Copenhagen, home of the famous bronze mermaid that sat in the harbor.

While looking at the chart, Edward compared where they were in relation to the UK. The furthest north he had ever been was the city of York, which was about the same latitude as the entrance to the River Elbe. So now, entering the Baltic Sea was the furthest north he had been. Looking at the latitude of Norrkoping, Edward saw that it was just a few miles south of the latitude of John o'Groats in Scotland, which is about as far north as you can go on the mainland of the UK. *That's getting up there,* he thought. Edward had read many accounts of the travels of explorers to the North and South Poles and was intrigued by the hardship and romance of these journeys. So for him at this time to be traveling north towards the Arctic Circle was very exciting. Even if, it was to just say, he had been here.

Their northeasterly course would take them north of the Danish Island of Bornholm, then northerly along the east coast of the Swedish island of Oland and up to Norrkoping. This, he was told, would take them a total of two days.

The whole thing was exhilarating for Edward as it was so different to anywhere he had been, and certainly lots to write home about.

32

The entrance into Norrkoping was absolutely beautiful. There was ice at the shore line, but the water in the centre was clear, and like a mirror. Ducks were still there on the water and as the ship approached they tried to take flight, skimming along the surface leaving a wake trail behind them.

"Look at them," the Swedish pilot laughed, "they're so fat they can't fly." Edward watched them with amusement.

Discharging the cargo was a slow affair and they were alongside for two days. The only 'shore thing' that Edward did here was to go ashore and walk among the trees that surrounded them. He loved the woods and his stroll was very peaceful and, much to his delight, he saw his first red squirrel. The whole experience was a pleasant getaway from installations, docks, towns and, for that matter, the ship.

After discharge was complete they ballasted. The water here was clean and clear, and that, along with the nature of the cargo they had discharged, meant there would be very little tank cleaning to be done; mostly gas-freeing. Their next port was Thames Haven, on the river Thames, where they would be loading a cargo of waxy distillate for Ellesmere Port in the Manchester Ship Canal; so it was back to the UK!

They made their way south once more, to the Kiel Canal. Their passage through the canal was slow, the weather cold and foggy. The fog was awful as it froze on the ship's upper superstructure; the masts and stays became encased in ice. Fortunately, by the time they got to the south end of the canal the fog thinned and the temperature had risen slightly. The Triatic Stay, between the tops of the two masts, became the biggest hazard as the thick ice that had accumulated on it started to drop off in large pieces, crashing down onto the flying bridge below.

The safest passage fore and aft was along the main deck away from the flying bridge, the Bosun having tied-off each end to ensure it was not used until all the ice had fallen. Stations fore and aft, for going through the locks at Brunsbuttelkoog were made easier by scattering sand on the slippery decks but fortunately there was no heavy build-up on them. Once into the River Elbe heading west, the ice slowly disappeared from the ship.

This, Edward thought, must be the fog that his father had told him about; 'Black Frost'. It was a real danger to small fishing vessels; some boats fishing off Iceland had become so encased in ice that they became top-heavy and capsized, many with the loss of all the poor souls onboard. To read accounts of these events, especially by those that did survive, was enough to make the stoutest of souls cry.

33

During the crossing of the North Sea to the Thames, the apprentices were kept busy with tank cleaning. This time it was a relatively easy affair that was really just a quick flush. The tanks containing ballast, under the supervision of the First Mate, were overflowed through the open tank lid by pumping sea water into them. This flushed out any surface residue which went straight over the side. No pollution, Edward was told, as the gasoline and Avtur they had carried would just evaporate off the sea's surface. It wasn't until awareness of such things became more prevalent that it was realized that the pollutants were still somewhere in the environment; but there again it was when gas freeing was done and very little could be done about that, and the natural evaporation of the cargos – nature of the beast.

During the crossing there were a couple of strange incidents when fog was again encountered. The ship became a haven for birds; hundreds of starlings took refuge on the rails and stays, particularly the triatic stay. They appeared to be shivering as they huddled against the cold. Some didn't make it; either from the cold or from hitting the ship's masts or rigging. Two mornings in a row, dead birds were picked up off the deck and unceremoniously thrown over the side into the cold North Sea; it made Edward sad. Dozens of the starlings took refuge inside the skylights of the Engine Room, basking in the warmth that emanated from below. Some of these did not survive either, and much to the distress of the Engineers, fell to the engine and plating below.

The starlings were joined by Homing Pigeons, all with rings round their legs. Taking refuge from the bitter weather, these birds preferred the railings around the accommodations. One of Edward's uncles back in Grimsby had kept homing pigeons, and often shipped them off by train in large wicker baskets. They'd be released at their destination, usually in the south of England, and the distances and times of their return home were noted. With a smile, Edward remembered throwing seed at them on the rooftops to entice them back into the coop. Did this flock get lost in the fog? Had they lost their bearings? How did they navigate back to that small coop where they were looked after with such care and affection? Edward wondered if their owners would ever see them again… he sure hoped so.

On the approach to the River Thames, and in sight of land, all the surviving birds took flight and disappeared. Maybe they weren't lost at all, just bumming a ride. Maybe their home was on the other side of the North Sea!

At Thames Haven they discharged all the ballast and the Engineers checked the heating coils in the cargo tanks. These coils are steam pipes approximately two and a half inches in diameter attached by brackets to the bottom of the tanks. They are raised just a few inches above, and cover the entire bottom of the tanks. Steam is put through these pipes from the Engine Room. The Engineers were checking that there were no leaks. Apart from not wanting steam being released into the cargo, which would become water; the Engineers also wanted to ensure that the steam made it back to the Engine Room. There, it would go through a condenser to return it back to its liquid state; then pumped back into the boilers. You couldn't waste the condensed water that was required for the boilers, and the Engineers were very vigilant about that.

The reason for all this inspection was that the Waxy Distillate that they were going to be loading had to be kept above sixty degrees Fahrenheit. If it got below this it would be difficult to pump ashore; if it got well below sixty degrees it would be impossible. Waxy Distillate was one of the products left after crude oil was refined, and was used in the manufacture of soap, candles and petroleum-wax seals. The Third Mate had explained the process to Edward.

This cargo would prove to be a very tiresome one for the apprentices, as temperatures of all the cargo had to be taken every eight hours, and recorded in a dedicated log book. They each had their turn at this; Edward at 1000hrs, Doug at 1800hrs and John, bless his soul, at 0200hrs.

On the three day trip to Ellesmere Port this routine was strictly observed. Any downward trends of temperature in a particular tank would mean increasing the steam flow to that tank by means of steam valves located on the side of the flying bridge. Adjustments also had to be made if the temperature got too high. Temperatures were taken by means of a copper cased thermometer that had a reservoir at the thermometer bulb. It was lowered by a line and held in the cargo, then hauled out and the temperature read. It was a messy job, and a hazardous one being down on the main deck, shipping water in rough seas. If the cargo cooled off in any particular tank, the thermometer had to be weighted in order for it to get below the surface.

One morning watch, Edward was to take temperatures. They were crossing Cardigan Bay (Wales) in St George's Channel and the wind was strong from the north, coming down from the Irish Sea, to which they were heading. He was standing on the port wing of the Bridge with the Third Mate, watching the seas breaking over the main deck fore and aft.

"Let's see if we can make this easier for you, Paige," the Third Mate said. He then instructed the helmsman to 'bring her up into the wind' watching as the shipping seas diminished.

"Hold her on that course. Ok Paige, get the standby man to give you a hand, and keep a weather eye out."

Edward started on the fore deck; they were about half way down the deck near the forward pumproom when a lazy three foot wave came onboard and swept towards them.

"Watch out!" the standby man cried, and they both grabbed the railing around the tank lid where they were standing. The sailor jumped onto the tank lid and then jumped upwards as the water swept beneath him, landing back on the tank lid as the water passed. Edward was not so fortunate. Holding onto the rail, he had put his left foot over the ullage plug to stop the water going in, but was too late to get his right foot up, and the sea rushing by them swirled above his knee, filling his rubber boot.

"Shit that's cold!" he gasped, "and my Mum told me not to get my feet wet!" The two looked at each other and burst out laughing.

Before they had finished taking all the temperatures they had cause to dodge a few more waves. On the main deck aft, while walking to the next tank, a 'four-footer' came over the bulwark behind the midships accommodation, making them run for the shelter of the flying bridge, where they hung on for dear life. Edward managed to get his other boot filled with water. He was somewhat gratified though, when he found that both of his companion's boots had been filled. Wet and cold, they finally finished, and Edward went up to the bridge.

"All finished Third Mate."

The Mate nodded his thanks. "Get yourself cleaned up and changed," he said.

As the ship was brought back onto her original course, a large wave cascaded over the port bow. *Glad I wasn't down there for that one,* Edward thought as he made his way below, giving the temperature log book to the First Mate for his review.

Sitting on the storm step at the entrance to the midships accommodation, which faced aft, Edward kicked off his boots, then peeled off his sea boot stockings and wrung the water out of them. He pulled off his jeans and walked down the alleyway to his cabin to change, shivering from the outside cold. John was sat reading, and looked up as he entered.

"Having fun yet?" he asked and laughed at the comical picture Edward presented. As he entered the cabin, he was still wearing his storm coat, but with no pants, and bare feet.

"Fuck off," Edward retorted good naturedly as they laughed together.

After having a hot shower, Edward changed into his Battle Dress Uniform. This waist length jacket with shoulder epaulets was more comfortable than the more traditional doe skin 'Blues' uniform, and the three apprentices had come to prefer wearing them. They were not as warm though, so a sweater was also needed. He sat and had a cigarette with John, then put his oilskin (storm jacket) on, and made his way aft to the steering flat to pump fresh water into the midships holding tank. He would never be forgiven if the Third Mate came off watch and decided to get showered, and there was no water left, especially when Edward was the one that had used it.

The weather worsened as they got into the Irish Sea. Heavy seas swept across the decks from the port side, and poured back into the sea on the starboard side. Fortunately this only lasted until they rounded Anglesey, northwest Wales. They then made an easterly course towards the River Mersey, which put the weather on their port quarter, making life a lot more pleasant for all.

Having picked up a Mersey Pilot, they made their way to the locks at the entrance to The Manchester Ship Canal. This was also known, according to some of the sailors, as The Manchester Shit Canal.

As one of them eloquently put it, "Twenty six miles up to Manchester; twenty six miles up the arshole of the world".

Stop sugar coating it and tell us how you really feel! Edward thought.

One thing was for sure; it certainly did not have a good reputation for cleanliness. It was said that if a person fell into the canal at the Manchester end and swallowed the water, their chances of survival were pretty slim. Thankfully, over the years this would change for the better.

34

Ellesmere Port was just a few miles up and was a square, locked dock, alongside the canal. Its saving grace was a little pub just outside the gates, walking distance from the ship. It was a wonderful, cozy little spot with a fireplace, and was frequented by all. The proprietor, a large rotund man with a red face and short-cropped grey hair, would match drink for drink with you, as long as you were buying, and always drank gin.

"If you ever want to go on a binge young fella," he said to Edward sitting at the bar, "always drink gin. It won't give you a hangover like that stuff." He indicated a scotch that one of the sailors was drinking.

"I'll remember that," Edward said politely.

Posted on the exit door of the pub was a wonderful sign that Edward loved;

The proprietors of this establishment will not be held responsible for any injuries caused to patrons when rushing for the door after Time has been called.

'Time' was called at 2300hrs, and a bell was rung at the bar. Edward thought the sign was particularly funny because when this happened, as in all bars – no one moved!

They were to spend the next two months making this same run from Thames Haven to Ellesmere Port, and the monotonous routine got very tiring. On the way back to Thames Haven, tank cleaning was a grueling affair that took the apprentices the whole return trip to complete. It had to be done, even though the same grade of cargo was being loaded, to avoid the build-up of the wax. The slop tank was no problem though, and the new cargo was loaded on top. The water used for cleaning was very hot, and pumped at high pressure from the

Engine room, making the hoses and machines hard to handle. There were, though, some not-so-routine moments.

The heating coils in one of the centre tanks failed, and the cargo became too thick to pump ashore. Heating units had to be brought in from the shore and lowered into the tank, in order to get the viscosity of the wax to a stage where it could be pumped. The coils were repaired before departure, a blocked pipe being the culprit.

....

Bicycles appeared on board; Sparky, Chippy and Doug had one each, as did some of the crew. One day, on a beautiful weekend, Edward borrowed Doug's bike, and the Three Musketeers cycled to the seaside town of Hoylake. The northern bank of the River Mersey is the county of Lancashire while the south bank is Cheshire the west side of which borders on Wales. Hoylake is on the tip of the peninsula that has the Mersey on one side and the estuary of the River Dee on the other. In Hoylake they found a nice little pub and had a beer; actually, Edward had his first ginger beer shandy, and cycled back again, a round trip of some 30 miles!

"For a beer?" asked a shipmate. "Are you crazy?"

One morning in Ellesmere Port, while discharging cargo, a uniformed police constable came onboard, striding towards them, midships.

"Hi! How are you doing? How can we help you?" asked the Third Mate politely. Police coming onboard was rarely a good sign.

"That?" asked the police constable, pointing skyward towards the top of the main mast. They all looked up. Suspended from the top of the mast, hoisted up by the flag halyard, was a bicycle.

"Haven't got a clue Constable," was The Third Mates response. He looked over at Edward who, tight lipped, just shrugged his shoulders.

"Hang on a minute." The Third Mate nipped up to the wheelhouse, bringing down with him a pair of binoculars, which he used to focus on the bike in question.

"What do you think?" he asked, handing them to Edward.

"It's Sparky's bike!" laughed Edward.

"I thought so."

"Sparky's?" asked the policeman.

"The Radio Officer." answered Edward.

"You mean it's your bicycle?" asked the policeman.

"Yes."

"That's fine then, thought one of your sailors had 'borrowed' it from shore, happens all the time. Have a nice day." He strolled across the deck and back ashore.

"Paige, get one of the watch sailors to help you get it down - *after* you tell Sparky where it is," instructed the Third Mate.

Edward went up to Sparky's cabin, enjoying the moment. They lowered the bike down and Sparky, good natured as always, wheeled it amidships to stow it back in the centre castle. They never did find who had put it up there, but it didn't matter; just a practical joke by one of the crew.

One memorable moment for Edward was on an evening watch when, information provided by the Third Mate, one of Aristotle Onassis' ships, the 'Olympic Flame', the fleet being referred to as The Olympic Boats, came into the same dock as they were in and tied up on the opposite side to them to discharge her cargo. She was a new ship, owned by the Greek shipping magnate, and the hull and superstructure were painted white, and the deck green. The ship was absolutely immaculate, with onboard flood lights lighting up the whole ship. She made the Combia awfully drab looking, but *what the hell, this is home*, thought Edward.

On another occasion, Edward had to go ashore to see a dentist. A filling had fallen out, and he needed to have it replaced. It was all arranged by Shell's agents, and a car was sent to the ship to pick him up. The ride from Ellesmere Port turned out to be quite an adventure; through the city of Birkenhead, then through the Mersey Tunnel, under the river, to Liverpool, and then to a Dentist's school, of all places. There had to be thirty chairs in the room he was taken to, and then some student tried his hand at fixing the tooth. Thankfully, this was done under the supervision of an instructor. It turned out OK, but Edward reminded himself not to get a tooth ache at this end of the trip again!

April brought the spring weather. It was beautiful, with leaves and gorgeous blossoms coming out on the trees. The weather was calm, with cool breezes and sunny days. The Third Mate walked out on deck one morning, while loading in Thames Haven. He stretched his arms high while looking along the shore and recited a verse that Edward had heard many times;

Ah! The spring is sprung, the grass is riz
I wonder where the boydees is
The boydees are upon the wing
But that's obsoyd, the wing is on the boyd.

He sounded like Jimmy Durante, much to the amusement of those around him.

35

Their monotonous coastal assignment was complete. They had discharged their final cargo of waxy distillate, and had orders to go to Curacao, in the Dutch Antilles. What a lift of spirits this was for all onboard; Edward especially, who had long dreamed of crossing the mighty North Atlantic Ocean. His dream was about to come true. Better still, they were going to the West Indies.

"Awesome!" was all he could say.

It was the middle of May and they were again enjoying good weather. Edward hoped that the change from the constant toil of the coast would also stop all the 'First Tripper' nonsense that had been going on for the past two months. Sailors and officers alike appeared to delight in playing practical jokes on a first tripper. On reflection, Edward realized that these were time-tested wind-ups; not to be taken personally, but that didn't make them any easier to bear at the time. He'd been sent to look for Chippy in the chain locker - the place that housed the anchor cable, a very awkward place to get to below the fore part of the fo'c'sle, and a place that Chippy would never be. Another time he was sent to the engine room to ask for 'a long weight'. This one had particularly embarrassed Edward; he had stood for half an hour in the noisy engine room, covered in sweat.

"So do you think that's long enough? The engineer officer on watch had enquired.

"What?" Edward said, puzzled.

"The long wait you asked for."

Then it clicked. He had asked for a 'long weight', and had received 'a long wait'. He returned to the deck feeling humiliated, much to the amusement of the Third mate who had sent him down there.

Another had been when he was sent to get a 'sky hook' from the storekeeper. He had been suspicious of this one but, just in case, had timidly asked the storekeeper if there was such a thing.

His shoe laces had been tied together when his work shoes were left on the deck outside the accommodation door.

The worst though, had been when his work shoes had fallen apart, and he was temporarily working in his dress shoes; a highly polished pair of brown brogues that he wore when going ashore. He'd left these outside the door whilst on a coffee break, and when he returned found the toe caps and heel caps painted white. He had been livid, and actually went aft, looking for the guilty sailor. Fortunately the Bosun had stopped him inside the sailor's aft accommodation, and calmed him down. He then accompanied Edward back amidships, a large, thick, black-haired arm across his back. He later thanked Bose for this, as on reflection he could have got himself into a whole lot of trouble.

As John had put it, "Are you mad? Did you have a death wish?"

For the Combia, the trip across the Atlantic would take about three weeks. They would pass through the islands of the Azores, about eight days away, which was the preferred passage for most ship's Captains going to the Caribbean. A Great Circle route would have taken them well north of the Azores and was the shortest distance, but the trip through the Azores was preferred because the weather was usually better; which doesn't necessarily mean that the weather was good. Bad weather, or more accurately, worse weather, being the risk on the great circle route. It was reasoned that the better weather more than compensated for the longer route.

From the Azores, their chosen entry into the Caribbean was through the Guadeloupe Passage in the Leeward Islands of the Lesser Antilles, and then down to Curacao. This was a trip that still made Edward's heart race; finally an ocean voyage of some consequence, and to the Caribbean, no less. A favorite haunt of pirates in the days of sail!

The apprentices, once clear of the River Mersey, took up their usual routine of tank cleaning, for which they would remain on their respective watches. Less than a day out saw them rounding Carnsore Point, the southeast tip of Ireland, and a southwesterly course was set for their next landfall at the Azores. A long, westerly Atlantic swell was running, making the ship roll steadily in her ballasted state, although the sea was relatively calm; the sea and waves being a separate weather entity to the swell.

Upon completion of tank cleaning three days later, the apprentices were taken off their watches and put onto day work. They worked from 0800 to 1700, which was wonderful; full night sleeps, and the three apprentices got to work and socialize together.

The majority of days for the apprentices were spent alongside the crew soogying (washing down) the outside bulkheads and deckheads. After rinsing with fresh water they were painted; first a primer and then a coat of high gloss leaded paint. All painting was done with a three inch pure bristle brush. The soap they used for all scrubbing down, as well as dhobiing (laundering) their work gear, was Teepol. It was a slimy soap concoction made by Shell that came in 5 gallon tubs. It could actually be purchased by those onboard Shell ships, and Shell would send a tub of the stuff to your home. It was a good buy and inexpensive, and Edward had one sent home to his Mum, who thought it 'absolutely wonderful'.

It was a much needed clean up, and the ship was starting to look good. If the areas being done were badly chipped or rusted they were completely stripped of paint using chipping hammers. This was a noisy, tiresome job, where clumsy protective goggles had to be worn. Once clean of old paint, the area was wire brushed and then primed with 'red lead'. This red lead was mixed from powder by the storekeeper in a cut down 40 gallon drum. It apparently worked best, according to Stores, if the mixture was urinated in! Apparently the acidity and make up of the urine made a much smoother mixture than paint thinner alone! After the red lead was applied and dry, two coats of primer were added, followed by the high gloss finishing coat that gave good protection to the steel.

One thing for sure was that maintenance onboard a ship was a constant battle against rust, the enemy, of course, being the salt water. The biggest problem was the main decks. They were coated in a horrible substance known as PF4, which was a black tar-like residue derived from the refining of crude. Whoever thought that this substance would protect the decks from rust had probably never been to sea. Maybe it was the same person that had recommended the 'required clothing list'. Large areas of the PF4 would separate from the deck, and the sea water would get underneath it. The deck would then just rust away to its heart's content, unseen. Once you started to remove the PF4, the damage that was being done became apparent. It did not appear to stick very well to the ship's steel, but it sure stuck well to skin and clothing! When the deck was made free of rust and scale, it was re-coated to start the process all over again. By the end of a day doing this work, the apprentices ached in places they didn't know they had places. Shell would later realize the folly of using the PF4, and ships were sand blasted to remove the stuff, and real paint was used.

The apprentices, however, were to get a daily break from all this, as at 1500hrs each weekday, after cleaning up and getting into uniform, they all reported to the Captain for 'lessons'. This was a great two hours learning each day. It took place in the Pilot's cabin, aft of the wheelhouse. The Captain had a board with a wooden model of a river, with moveable shoals and buoys. The buoys were various shapes; conical, can, round, stick, and tower, with colours black, red, green, or a combination of colours. There were also other types of navigational aids. After the board was set-up, the apprentices were asked to navigate a model ship up and down the river, explaining their route as they went. It was a great teaching/learning tool.

The main focus was on the Rules of the Road, which they had to learn word-for-word. This represented some thirty pages of text in the seamanship books that each of them had. Having said that however, the Captain did not want parrots; He expected the apprentices to have a complete understanding of these rules. Learning something word for word is useless if you have no idea what it means. In reciting the rules to the Captain, the apprentices would often be stopped mid-stream to explain what was meant. When the Captain was satisfied that they understood the rule, they'd be told to continue. If you were able to continue where you left off with the memorization, then you had a good understanding of the rule. 'Parrots' would have to start over at the beginning! It was tough going but the Captain was incredibly fair, and all the apprentices had the highest regard for him, and worked hard to get things right. He was a great teacher, and had their best interests at heart. In all the years that followed Edward would never know another Captain that did this. The knowledge gained from these lessons with Captain Landry would play a large part in enabling Edward to obtain his first required certificate, the Second Mate's Certificate, which had to be taken after apprenticeship was completed; if you wanted to continue going to sea and become a Navigating Officer, that is.

Every Sunday morning at 0900hrs, the apprentices reported to the Bridge for another study activity. They took morning sights of the sun; the Third and Second Mates having already done likewise. This 'sighting' entails taking the altitude of the sun using a sextant, and recording the exact time that the altitude is obtained, to the nearest half second, using the ship's chronometer. A fellow apprentice would stand by the chronometer and, upon 'time' being called by the sight taker, would record the time. (There was no bell involved in this calling of time; unlike the pub!) The idea was that, by means of the sextant, the lower limb of the sun's image is brought down to the horizon using a slight rocking motion of the sextant, and at the moment that the sun's lower limb sweeps along the horizon, the altitude and time are recorded. From this information, and using spherical trigonometry, plus Nories Tables and six figure logarithms, a position line is obtained. This is a line that, because it runs at right angles across the bearing of the sun, you are known to be somewhere along its length at the time of the sighting, but you don't know where.

At noon another sighting is taken of the sun at its zenith; then, by means of a simple calculation the ship's latitude is obtained, this is another position line. The earlier position line obtained at 0900 is then transferred, that is, running this position line down the ship's course for three hours at the ship's speed. Where the transferred position line crosses the latitude obtained, is the ship's position at noon. It is from this noon position that any course adjustment that may be required is made.

It was a fun time, and a friendly rivalry ensued to see which of the apprentices got the nearest position to the Third and Second Mates', who were naturally always assumed to be correct. At dusk and dawn 'star sights' are also taken; usually by the First Mate, on his watch. Sights of four to six stars are usual and as a result four to six position lines are obtained. These position lines are then plotted on a special plotting chart, and where these position lines intersect is the ship's position at the time the star sights were taken.

As the vessel proceeded westward, the clocks onboard had to be adjusted on a regular basis, as fifteen degrees of longitude change represents one hour, according to the world's time zones. This was done in order to keep the noon hour on the ship's clocks as close as possible to the sun's zenith, noon, as well as to be on local time when arriving at the destination port. The chronometer, however, is never changed. It stays on Greenwich Time; the time used in all calculations and by which the navigation tables are calculated. All times for positions and watches are always kept at local time.

The chronometer was checked daily for accuracy, using a Greenwich Time signal that Sparky obtained. The Combia's chronometer gained half a second every two to three days, and this accumulated error was applied to the time taken at sights. In order to maintain consistency, the chronometer was wound by the same person, the Second Mate, at the same time every day. It took about seven quarter turns to fully wind it. It sounds unlikely, but when a mechanical timepiece is wound at different times of the day, or by different people who don't usually tend to do things the same way, accuracy is affected.

The Combia had just one chronometer which, like all ship's chronometers, was set in gimbals in a glass-topped cabinet. It stood at the side of the chart table; well protected from harm. In the future, newer ships had two chronometers, for safety's sake.

36

Seven days out they made their landfall on the Azores, a group of isolated islands in the North Atlantic. Edward tried to imagine what these massive mountains looked like under the water, the islands being just the peaks, sticking out of the ocean. The Portuguese referred to them simply as, The Islands. It was from these that the Portuguese discovered the fishing grounds of the Newfoundland Banks, long before the mainland of North America was 'discovered' by Columbus.

The Islands were beautiful, and while passing through them, much to Edward's delight, he saw his first whales, Right Whales. He watched in awe as they blew, *thar she blows*, arching their backs out of the water then disappearing from view only to appear again blowing their fine spray of mist, their give-a-way, for those terrible hunters, man. Whaling, unfortunately, was still a large commercial enterprise in the world. The locals here hunted them from open boats much in the same manner as the sailing ship days. When Edward asked about their name, he was told that because this whale was slower than their cousins, and easier to harpoon, they were the 'right whales' to hunt. Consequently, their numbers were being decimated. After feeling such joy at seeing the whales, Edward found this information to be rather sad. Although his family's history was fishing, reaping the harvest of the sea, and he saw nothing wrong with that, hunting these massive incredible mammals seemed wrong somhow!

Each morning at 0730hrs, Doug, because he was the senior apprentice, reported to the First Mate on the bridge in order to get their orders for the day. At breakfast, he shared this activity information with John and Edward. One particular day they were to clean out the main fresh water tank, which was located aft of the Engine Room, actually the Boiler Room, and below the steering flat. During the morning 4

-8, the Engineers had transferred the water from this tank to the fore peak tank, and removed the large inspection hatch of the tank to be cleaned.

They had breakfast and got changed, then the three apprentices made there way aft to look at their job of the day. The tank was a dark, hot, hell hole, to put it kindly, and a typical apprentice's job. The three of them stripped down to shorts and wellies, and entered the tank through the small oval shaped opening. They climbed down a vertical iron ladder armed with long handled scrapers to see what they were up against. Sealed portable flood lights, which were actually safe in explosive environments, were suspended from above to light their way. The tank was cube shaped, each dimension measuring about thirty feet. The inside surfaces were disgusting.

"Hard to believe we've been drinking the water from this," Doug expressed dejectedly. "Let's get to it".

They started with a high pressure hose, blasting the dirt, scale, and rust from the deckhead and bulkheads while carefully avoiding the lights, and used a portable ladder in order to scrape the top half of the tank. The hose above them was attended to by a watch sailor who also kept an eye out for their safety. After half an hour of blasting they yelled for the water to be turned off and climbed out of the tank. They looked like drowned rats as they lay on the steel deck gasping for air. They rested while the engineers on watch emptied the tank, pumping the filthy water into the sea.

John sat up. "Now I know what a Butterworth machine feels like," he said, referring to the machines they used to clean the cargo tanks. The others just snorted and smiled.

In the open air, they quickly became chilled, and the watchman brought them some large cloth rags to dry themselves. They shivered as they dried themselves as best they could, then draping the cloths around their shoulders.

When the tank was drained, they went back inside and started scraping down the loose scale and rust. The tank had originally been coated in a cement-wash, and a lot of the scale was this old material. The tank bottom became littered with it, and it had to be removed. They filled empty five gallon paint drums with the scale, and these were hauled up by rope, by the sailor and one of his watch mates. The scale was then taken up to the poop deck and dumped over the side.

After completing this stage, the three Apprentices climbed out of the tank covered in dirt and sweat. They looked rather like the stokers you saw in films, after shoveling coal into a ship's boiler. After a short break, they hosed the tank down with fresh water and this, in turn, was pumped out to sea. All that remained was to coat the tank with a new cement wash.

It was lunch time; on deck they hosed each other down and put on dry work clothes. On this occasion, they were allowed to have their lunch outside the galley, sat on the bollards on the poop deck. This was very unusual, as they normally had to get cleaned up, put on their uniforms, and eat in the dining room. This procedure was common, or rather more of a rule in Shell, and in many cases it seemed ridiculous to the apprentices. It was obviously there to keep up the image of the apprentices as future Navigation Officers. Considering the things that they presently had to do, this notion seemed even more ridiculous. One advantage of eating on the poop deck and being so close to the galley was that when they finished the meal they were given, they were given another plate full. The three of them looked like Oliver 'asking for more' but in this case they got more. It turned out to be a common thing for apprentices - you just could not give them enough to eat!

After eating they prepared for their decent once more back into the 'hell hole'. Armed with six inch 'white wash' brushes and the cement wash prepared by the storekeeper, they descended into the tank. It was a noxious, dirty job and they went at it like maniacs, splashing cement wash everywhere as they completely coated the inside of the tank; agreeing to get the job done quickly so that they didn't, as Doug put it so succinctly, "have to do this shit again tomorrow". Finally getting the bottom of the tank evenly coated, they climbed out once more to get hosed down on the deck.

"Holy shit, I hope there's no more of these to do," voiced Edward. "I joined up to see the world, not do this crap," he laughed good-naturedly. Actually, he had rather enjoyed the hard physical labor; it was good for the soul.

One thing was for sure; the three of them were hard muscled, lean, tough youngsters, and as a team, were a force not to be taken lightly.

Crew members would certainly tease them, but because they were so close and because of their uncomplaining work ethic, they were held in the highest regard. They certainly were not envied for the things they had to do!

They got themselves showered and changed and, all spruced up, reported to the Captain to continue with their theoretical learning. They were all doing well, and in the evenings practiced their memorizing on each other. Edward learned by picturing where the chapters and paragraphs were on the page and pictured the words as he turned pages in his mind while reciting.

An extractor fan had been put over the entrance to the fresh water tank, and had been running all night. The cement wash had dried, and all that remained to do was a light wash down with fresh water, to remove any loose residue. Then the tank was drained once more and left to dry, and that was it. Thankfully, the apprentices never saw the inside of the tank again; another job well done.

....

Their time off every night and on weekends was enjoyable. After dinner, and the occasional hour's studying, they usually congregated in the officer's smoke room aft, playing darts, checkers, or cards. The most popular card game was solo, closely followed by cribbage, which they usually played for matchsticks, but on occasion got serious and played for cigarettes. Some studious pairs played chess, but this was too involved and slow for Edward. His favorite games pastime was definitely darts. Sometimes everyone just sat around talking, drinking beer and cracking jokes. Whatever it was, it was always fun.

Edward was also an avid reader and would often sit and read in his cabin, enjoying the quiet isolation. Favorite authors were Alistair McLean, Hammond Innes, Denis Wheatley, Zane Grey, Agatha Christie, Sir Arthur Conan Doyle with Sherlock Holmes, Mickey Spillane with Mike Hammer and his constant smoking of 'Luckies' and, of course, Ian Fleming and 007.

There was also a host of short, quick read novels, authors forgotten. They were mostly westerns, the plots of which were invariably the same; save the damsel in distress, defeat the greedy cattle baron and avenge a loved one, the hero always being the fastest draw in the west. They were all paperbacks, and were usually left by all the crew in the small hospital room amidships where anyone was welcome to find their next adventure in print. Sometimes the pickings were slim and you read what there was. Most had loose pages, and some were missing; evidence of their widespread use.

Edward discovered that a library, two crates of hard backs, was available to ships through The Missions to Seamen, but for some reason the Combia did not have one! Shell introduced movies; usually three movies to a box that were on large twelve inch reels. The projector and film splicing equipment supplied, together with the playing of the movie was usually the responsibility of the apprentices. These books and movies could be exchanged in most ports of call, and were occasionally exchanged with other Shell Tankers when in port together.

Decks of playing cards were hilarious; they got so well used that they were like dealing a loaf of bread. When new, thin shiny decks were obtained usually through the companies supplying the cases of beer, they often-as-not ended up all over the deck, as shuffling them was so difficult, but they too soon got worn-in.

All activities onboard were subject to the constant steady roll of the ship, which after a while was not even noticed by the sailors. Sometimes it was funny when playing darts; most players were quite accurate in their throws, but on occasion a dart would stick into the woodwork of the board's cabinet. When this first happened to Edward he could not believe he had missed the board. It was explained that once you threw the dart it was no longer attached to the ship, and on a sudden roll, or pitch for that matter, the board would move away from the approaching dart, hence the miss. Landlubbers should try playing darts when the wall on which the board is mounted is moving, along with the floor!

37

Another week passed and they were in the region of the Mid Atlantic Ridge, at the Tropic of Cancer; that imaginary line of latitude that runs around the world at 23.5 degrees north and in this part of the world runs between the southern tip of Florida, and Cuba. It's counterpart in the same latitude south being the Tropic of Capricorn, it was simple not to get the two mixed up by simply remembering Capricorn was south the same as Cape Horn, they rymed. Orders were given by the Captain to 'change to whites'; a change from the blue uniforms to tropical gear. So for the first time, Edward got to put on his whites; short sleeved shirt with epaulettes, shorts, knee length socks, and white canvas-upper shoes. There was also a white cap cover. First time wearing these Edward felt rather self conscious; mainly he thought, because the new gear was stiff and creased; never mind the white legs.

Hell, will I ever learn, he thought, *I should have dhobied* (washed) *this lot before I wore it for the first time.* He had two sets of whites and two sets of khakis. The khakis were worn as an everyday thing, but whites had to be worn if on the Bridge, or in the dining room. After dinner he washed one set of each and hung them up to dry, after which he ironed and folded them neatly. Wearing one of the newly washed set he promptly washed the other two sets, feeling a whole lot better with the much more comfortable uniforms.

On all ships, there was usually one of the crew that was the barber. Some were good; others questionable. On the Combia, it was one of the daytime (did not keep watches) ABs. The three deck apprentices had heard some comments made about their long hair so, on a Saturday morning, they trooped down to the poop deck and the AB gave each of them a 'short-back-and-sides'. The fee was two cans of beer each.

Edward smiled thinking about home, as his hair quickly fell to the deck. His Father referred to it as 'getting your wool cut'. In Yorkshire it was 'getting your lugs (ears) lowered'. The AB was a good barber and they all smiled at each other as they bent forward, scrubbing their scalps vigorously to remove the loose hair.

"Now we look more like Officers and Gentlemen," remarked Doug.

"Yea right!" was John's retort. Laughing, they made their way to the smoke room to play some darts.

As they steamed on their southwesterly course, southwesterly being 225 degrees, towards the West Indies the weather got nasty. The sea was being whipped up by strong northwesterly winds; the direction that the wind was coming from. In contrast the direction of a sea current is indicated by the direction in which it is going – a northwesterly current, therefore, is running to that direction. Waves were crashing against the ship's starboard side sending spray whipping across the decks, making good timing imperative for a dash down the flying bridge. The only shelter between the midships accommodation and aft was behind the main mast, and was often used standing sideways, shoulders crunched up and arms straight down, to afford as small a target as possible to the stinging spray. It reminded Edward of hiding behind a tree in Bradley Woods, back in his home town, hiding from his friends, and then jumping out and scaring the living crap out of them.

The reason for this bad weather was a relatively weak hurricane originating on the West African coast. As it crossed the North Atlantic, it tracked on a path towards the eastern seaboard of America. It had already passed ahead of the Combia, so the eye of the storm was moving away from them, and was now on their starboard quarter about one hundred miles away. They were on the outer extremities of the storm system, but it was enough to result in considerable discomfort for the crew. Its anti-clockwise rotation was causing very strong winds, and waves over twenty feet high that were cresting before they reached the ship; always a bad sign. There was also a considerable swell making the ship roll heavily, as well as pitching down into the deep troughs. Her bows crashed into the rising seas then rose shuddering to shake off the water before diving back in once more. Rolling and pitching together is known as cork-screwing, and is very uncomfortable for ship and sailor alike. The hurricane's path would eventually curve northwest; away from the U.S. coastline, and slam into the Canadian East Coast.

....

Edward loved to watch this perpetual crashing of the bows into the oncoming seas and also the Storm Petrels; these sea birds were amazing as they skimmed along the heaving surface, up the walls of water, then curving round at the crest and zoomed back down into the trough just inches from the rolling sea.

....

Twenty four hours later, the wind had dropped to a stiff breeze and the waves subsided. They did still have the aftermath to contend with, the swell, which lasted for a couple of days more. Edward often stood at the rail, just marveling at the incredible power that nature displayed, always reminded, that man traveled the world's oceans at the mercy of Mother Sea and that every now and then she would re-emphasize her power, lest you forget, and that she would not be tamed. If you were in her favor, she would let you pass.

They finally approached the Guadeloupe Channel, between the island of Guadeloupe in the south and Montserrat and Antigua to the north and, thankfully, the passage through was calm, and a welcome relief. The scenery was certainly a welcome change, and many of the crew stood at the rail to admire the view, while being enveloped in the wonderful fragrance of the land. Their landfall was on the island of Antigua, whose capital is St John's on its northern shore. The port they saw on the south side was Falmouth. (Named after the town in Cornwall, England, that sat in one of the most beautiful natural harbors in the UK). Four hours later they passed Montserrat and its port of Plymouth, another name from the south of England. This was part of the Leeward Islands which, together with the Windward Islands to the south, formed the Lesser Antilles. Included in this category was Curacao and Aruba; the Greater Antilles being Cuba, Jamaica, Puerto Rico, and Hispaniola (the latter now being Haiti and the Dominican Republic).

The sea was calm and a beautiful turquoise blue, the light breeze was warm, or balmy might be a better word.

Standing at the rail, Edward watched the soaring and swooping antics of the Frigate Bird. They were distinguished by their large, six foot wingspan and forked tails, and the height at which they soared. In contrast, pelicans flew in formation, skimming just above the surface of the calm blue sea. In flight, the pelicans held their heads proudly back, and always looked, to Edward, rather like pre-historic Pterodactyls.

Edward was thrilled with being in the Caribbean; his thoughts going back to the days of the pirates that had been the scourge of these waters, as well as those to the north off the Carolina coast.

Names like Edward Teach, better known as Blackbeard; Henry Morgan, the greatest of the buccaneers, who became the Lieutenant Governor of Jamaica; and of course, the famous Captain Kidd; and Bartholomew Roberts. Even Sir Walter Raleigh, who named Virginia after his queen – Elizabeth I, was referred to as a pirate by the Spanish, because of the Spanish ships he plundered. Probably though, the most famous pirate; also dubbed so by the Spanish, was Sir Francis Drake. Although he was not a pirate in the sense that Blackbeard, Kidd, and Bartholomew were, he committed numerous acts of what the Spanish considered to be piracy. He plundered Spanish ships and ports on the Spanish Main; that stretch of the South American coast in the Caribbean. He also plundered Spanish ships in the Pacific, along the coasts of Chile, Peru and Ecuador, all in the name of his Queen. He became notorious for raiding Spanish treasure ships, and took a fortune in gold, silver, and jewels back to England, where he was knighted in recognition of his exploits. His ship, the Pelican, was renamed the Golden Hind, and it was in this ship that he later circumnavigated the globe, on a voyage that took almost three years.

Edward contentedly basked in the sun, soaking up its rays and the history of his surroundings. His skin had gone from a pale, fish belly white, to a healthy looking sun tan, from constantly working on deck.

Curacao was about 600 miles distant, so there was still two and a half days steaming left. It was hot; certainly the hottest weather Edward had ever experienced, and he loved it. It was the first week of June. His Mum's birthday was later in the month, and he would send the letter that he was still writing to her in a birthday card from Curacao, and hope that she would get it in time. He had also been writing to his sister, Eva.

"How do you like this weather?' Doug asked him one afternoon as they sweated like dogs, painting the forward bulkhead of the fo'c'sle.

"I was born to be a hot-house flower," was his laughing response. "This is what I came to sea for." Edward continued with a sweeping motion of his arms, indicating the beautiful blue sea surrounding them.

Laughter was the chorused response from his two companions. They continued their painting enjoying the moment.

38

The following morning at 1000hrs, the Captain took advantage of the good weather, and ordered a fire drill. This entailed connecting six canvas fire hoses to the fire hydrants under the flying bridge; two on each side of the main deck, and one on each side of the fore deck. Each was manned by two crewmen at the nozzle, and one crewman per two valves. All the valves were opened, and the jets of sea water were aimed over the side. The idea was to ensure that the engine room could maintain high enough water pressure, when all six hoses were in use; which they did. Six long jets of water shot out over the side. They looked like a fire boat in New York harbor welcoming an in-coming passenger vessel at the completion of a maiden voyage, or record 'blue ribbon' crossing of the North Atlantic.

Edward, standing by with the other two apprentices on the main deck near the midships accommodation, thought of pirates again; *these would come in handy for repelling boarders,* he smiled to himself.

The apprentices each had a large canister fire extinguisher, and on orders from the First Mate, who was overseeing the whole fire drill, turned them upside down with an index finger over the small nozzle, and shook them as hard as they could to mix the foam activator. Removing their fingers, they aimed the shooting foam at the bulkhead about three feet above the deck. The foam ran down the bulkhead and along the deck towards them in a thick carpet of white froth. The theory was that any fire would be smothered by the spreading foam. After the fire drill the mess was hosed away over the side, using one of the fire hoses. The hoses were rolled up to empty them, and stowed back into their respective boxes. These boxes were assigned to specific crew members, so in case of the real thing, there was no confusion as to who went where. The apprentices' job was to re-charge the fire extinguishers they had discharged. Edward watched as his two companions refilled the extinguishers noting how they were careful to keep the extinguishers upright when re-stowing them in their bulkhead brackets, as the foam activator was in a small, but heavy, loose capped container inside the top of the canister; it was the action of turning the canister upside down and shaking it, that allowed the components to mix and create the foam.

The apprentices' lessons with the Captain were now on Monday, Wednesday, and Friday at 1500 hrs. Apart from the invaluable knowledge they were gaining, they all enjoyed this time as it took them away from their labors on deck; or below it, as the case may be! They all showered before meeting with the Captain, and took it in turns on these days to go aft, to pump up the water to the midships holding tank, to ensure that there was plenty of water for the Second Mate when he came off watch. On normal working days they had resolved to do this before and after they got showered. There was nothing worse than hearing your surname being screamed out from the officer's shower room when the water had run out, while said officer was covered in soap.

Another routine that all on board had to prepare for was the Sunday morning inspection of the ship by the Captain. Accompanied by The Mate for the amidships accommodation; The Chief Engineer for the Engineers and engine room personnel; the Bosun for the deck personnel; and the Chief Steward for the Galley and provision stores, including the freezers. All stores and accommodations were inspected to ensure that everything was clean and ship-shape.

The apprentice's cabins appeared to be a particularly favorite target, and the white gloved hands of The Captain would be run across the top of wardrobes and cupboards, sills under the ports, and ledges around the hand basin. Any dirt brought harsh words, and the cabin had to be re-cleaned and later inspected again by The Mate. They usually did a thorough job the first time, right down to the polishing of the linoleum tiles on the deck, so that they could see their own reflections in them. Of course, the bunks had to be made properly and be clean.

"All good fun," as John sarcastically put it.

They arrived at Curacao during the 4-8 morning watch, having passed to the southeast of Bonaire, the island of white flamingos. The apprentices were back on their respective watches. When Edward went up to the bridge at 0800, he was all excited about the prospects of going ashore on a tropical island. A Dutch pilot was onboard, and they were steaming up and down the coast waiting to enter the narrow channel that ran through Willemstad, the capital of Curacao, and on to the Shell refinery at Emmerstad. There was a reason for the ship steaming up and down the coast; the water off Curacao is too deep to anchor.

When they finally got the all-clear, they headed for the narrow channel at half ahead; a speed designed to counteract the strong current that ran along the coast of this small island. It actually looked like they were going to miss the entrance; no job for a novice, this one. Tugs stationed themselves on either side of the ship, and when the Combia entered the channel and had slowed down to a crawl, they took towing lines from the ship and stayed on-station until she was berthed.

When they passed through the centre of the Willemstad, there had been a pontoon bridge spanning the channel to connect the two sides of the town. The bridge had been swung to one side, and tied up alongside the shore. To Edward, it had looked like a row of large rowing boats with a road running over the top of them.

It was a beautiful place, and Edward drank in the sights, scents and colors as he stood at his post, making his entries into the Movement Book. There was a large passenger ship tied up beyond the town. The pilot turned to the Captain with a big smile.

"Watch the prices in town Captain; the American cruise ship in port means that all prices will be American dollars, not guilders."

The Captain, with a wry smile, nodded to the pilot. Edward made a mental note of this valuable information.

They tied up port-side-to to one of the many wharfs at the refinery in Emmerstad. The tall gantry towered above them, with its many hoses for different grades of refined and crude oil products hanging by wires, ready to be lowered down for connection to the ship's manifolds. They put the gangway ashore, and started the familiar routine of getting ready for loading their cargo. In the meantime, the sea valves in the pumprooms had been opened and they were running out the ballast; letting gravity do its work before the pumps were started to complete the job.

First, however, was the number one priority for all the sailors; the mail had come onboard. The Chief Steward sorted it from the large canvas bag, and put the letters in piles. The Bosun took all the deck personnel, the Engineer Storekeeper took the Firemen's and Oilers' letters etc. Edward had five letters from his sister, Eva, and one from his mum.

Mail was always read avidly; it was the connection to family back home. Letters came from family, wives, girlfriends, sweethearts or friends. Some were perfumed; attested to by sailors affectionately lifting them with eyes closed, inhaling their fragrance. Some had capital letters written on the back across the seal, like the most popular S.W.A.L.K. – Sealed With A Loving Kiss; B.U.R.M.A. which believe it or not meant Be Undressed and Ready My Angel; and other codes known only to the recipient. These letters from home, over the course of the trip to the next port, would be read and re-read. For some, not receiving a letter from those back home was very disconcerting. Some never received letters, as they simply had no one back home. Edward thought how very sad this was. He had once asked the Third Mate, whilst on watch one night, why it was that sailors got married. It didn't seem to make much sense to him, with being away for such long periods; up to a year at a time.

The Third Mate's reply had been very insightful; "It so there's someone to share in what it is that you do. To have someone who knows that you actually exist, and looks forward to having you back. There are parents, but they will not be there over the long haul. It's someone to have kids with, and therefore a family to go back to, a place to go when not on a ship; a place to grow roots."

Edward thought about this for some time, and although his youth dictated a flippant attitude towards just about everything, the Third Mate's wisdom stayed with him.

"Do you have a sweetheart back home, Paige?" the Third Mate asked.

"I can hardly afford one Third Mate," he replied solemnly.

The Third Mate laughed saying, "Money has nothing to do with it when you love someone, Paige."

"What is love, anyway?" he asked with a smile.

"What do you think it is?"

"I read somewhere that it is when the happiness and wellbeing of another person is as important to you as your own," Edward replied.

"Wow," the Third Mate replied, thinking about this for a moment, "That's as good a definition as I have heard; and to the point." he responded.

39

Discharge of ballast was completed, and they began loading their cargo of gasoline, kerosene and gas oil, to be delivered to Buenos Aires in Argentina. Edward could not have been more excited at the prospect of this long voyage deep into the South Atlantic Ocean, which entailed his crossing 'The Line' (the Equator) for the first time.

On the following morning's watch, the Third Mate asked Edward,

"So what do you think about going down to Buenos Aires?"

"Better than working down the fish docks!" he replied as he thought about his friends back in Grimsby. "This is all absolutely fabulous." he concluded opening his arms out to the shore.

"Yes it is," the Third Mate smiled.

After lunch Edward , Sparky, Chippy, and Doug all went ashore together, into Emmerstad. Edward's three companions had all been there before; it was a regular stop, as it was a Shell refinery here. Their destination was a bar just outside the gates of the refinery, known as The Mad House.

"Why is it called the mad house?" Edward asked

"Because it can get pretty wild inside when crews from all different ships have had a few drinks," was Sparky's reply, "but don't worry, there will be lots of our crew there."

Edward did not understand this last comment at the time, until he and Doug were surrounded at the bar by sailors from another ship. They were just getting drinks, but there was a lot of pushing going on, and they were crushed up against the bar. There was more pushing and shoving, and suddenly Doug and Edward were surrounded by sailors from their own ship.

They stood there for a while then George, the AB from Edward's watch suggested, "A table away from the bar would be a little safer." They took his advice, and were joined by Sparky and Chippy.

"What was all that about?" asked Edward.

"Shipmates protecting their own," was Doug's proud reply. "If you ever get in trouble ashore, ship mates will protect ship mates, even if they don't like you on the ship."

"Good to know," was all Edward could muster as he gulped some of his beer down.

Above the clamor of voices, a plinking of notes could be heard from the piano that stood near the bar. They turned to see Bill, one of the sailors from their ship, sitting at the piano. He was one of the older members of the crew; tall, wrinkled, and weather beaten. He sat looking at the piano keys, and was opening and closing his long, knurled fingers, much to the amusement of those watching. He then interlocked his fingers, and turned his hands palms out, at arm's length. Onlookers were now openly laughing at the display of finger exercises, but it stopped instantly when those same gnarled fingers lit upon the keys, and began playing beautiful classical music. It was awe inspiring, and everyone sat and watched. He finished playing and sat looking at the keys, his head shaking slightly, as if unsatisfied. Sailors from all over the bar walked over and, without saying a word, placed drinks on the top of the piano forming a long row. The old sailor nodded and continued playing. He was left to it as everyone continued with their conversations. The beautiful, unexpected, musical backdrop was much appreciated though, and the row of drinks was not allowed to diminish in length.

"If he drinks that lot he'll have to be carried back to the ship," laughed Sparky. They all nodded in agreement.

After a couple of drinks they decided to go into Willemstad, to do some shopping. They grabbed a cab outside and were on their way. Edward sat on the front of his seat looking out the window, hardly able to contain his excitement as they were whisked away in the hot afternoon sun. The countryside was dry and sparse, the road ahead of them looking like it was wet and shiny, as a result of the mirage effect on it. He pointed this out and the others smiled at his enthusiasm for what they hardly noticed anymore.

They were dropped off outside a row of shops facing the waterway and the pontoon bridge. It was a gorgeous day, and Edward wanted to buy presents for his parents and two sisters. He eagerly looked into the shops with their wide open doors. He bought a Kimono top, and a gold and silver filigree bracelet for his sisters; a silk scarf for his Mum; and a book about the Spanish Main, in the days of Sir Francis Drake and his raids, for his Dad. For himself he had bought two pairs of cheap working shoes, one pair being canvas topped with rope soles, the other with leather soles, and his first pair of flip-flops, for casual wear around the ship. He also bought and posted a birthday card for his Mum. All letters written to home were collected before arrival in port, and placed in a mail sack, which was mailed to the UK by the ship's agent.

On his first purchase he was quoted American Dollars. "I'm not from the passenger ship, I'm from a Shell tanker," he had informed the shop keeper, who smiled and changed over to guilders; about half the price! Edward found that amusing, and loved this tropical island. The only thing that disturbed the tranquility of it all was the squealing of car tires. The taxis were especially bad, as they rounded the right angle bend at the end of the row of shops; it was a constant screeching noise, along with the incessant blowing of cars horns. He just couldn't understand the reason for it.

Edward could have wandered around for hours, but Doug had to be back onboard at 1600 for his watch, so the four of them hopped a cab and went back to The Mad House. From there, Doug walked back to the ship, while The Three Musketeers went back into the bar. The piano was now silent, and they hoped that Bill had got back to the ship alright after all his drinks. The room was quieter, and they went to the bar and ordered beers. They paid for their drinks, and the change was slapped down on the bar that was running with beer and cockroaches. Lifting up the notes and shaking them, they turned and took their drinks to a table, where they relaxed for a while before returning to the ship for dinner.

Women were conspicuous by their absence in this bar. There were none at all; the same as earlier in the day. There were, however, quite a few sailors drinking, laughing and talking loudly among themselves. Edward could hear their conversations and suddenly realized, looking back at conversations on the ship, that sailors talked mostly about men, not women! They tended to discuss the various characters that they had sailed with, good and bad; it was quite a surprising revelation!

When they returned to the ship, Edward stowed away the gifts he had bought, got a quick wash to freshen up, changed into his uniform, and went for dinner. It was a little after 1800 when he returned to his cabin. He had not seen John, who had gone ashore right after his watch. Edward decided to have a nap before his own watch at 2000hrs.

While on watch, Edward asked the Third Mate about some strange looking Shell tankers unloading at jetties close by. They were small 'coasters', with canvas awnings over and around the accommodations. These ships, the Third Mate explained, were the mosquito fleet. They ran constantly between Lake Maracaibo in Venezuela, and Curacao, carrying crude oil to the refinery from places like Cabimas and Miranda. Their shallow draft allowed them to get into the lake, where a light, highly volatile Tijuana Crude was loaded. They also traded from Punta Cardon in the Gulf of Venezuela, which is the gulf leading to the entrance to Lake Maracaibo.

"That is one hard working fleet." the Third Mate informed Edward. "They usually keep you on those for no longer than three months; any longer than that and you'd wind up losing your mind. You'd probably have to be locked up. For those ships it's like 12 hours from Cardon to here. It's a non-stop loading and unloading ordeal. Horrible!" he concluded.

Hope I never get put on one of those, Edward thought. The trips around the UK coast from the Thames to the Mersey had been hard enough, but nothing like the time-line of the mosquito fleet. Apart from that he just loved being at sea, plowing through an ocean swell.

40

L oading was completed, and they were singled-up and ready to leave after being alongside for two days. Edward was sorry to be leaving, as he had enjoyed Curacao. He had not been into town again, since his funds were pretty limited, but he had wandered around outside the refinery, and had enjoyed the heat of the arid island. There is not much natural shade on Curacao, and Edward was fascinated by a tree whose branches grew horizontally in a fan shape. He later learnt that this was the Divi-Divi tree, and afforded just about the only natural shade on the island. The same was true on the neighboring island of Aruba. The trees are bent into this shape by the constant prevailing winds. Another remarkable plant was a large towering cactus that flowered, apparently, every hundred years. It was aptly named The Century Plant.

Edward was longing to get back to sea for the long voyage south, and wondering what surprises and adventures might be in store for him in Buenos Aires.

As the Combia passed back through Willemstad, Edward noticed the shops where he had bought his gifts. Some people stood at the water's edge and waved to them as they went by. He could still hear the blasting of car horns and the squeal of tires on the nearby road.

They steamed out of the channel and let go of the tugs, one of them staying alongside to pick up the departing pilot. The course was set, and they were on their way once more.

Their first leg to depart the Caribbean took them off the southern coast of Bonaire, north of the Las Aves Islands, north of Blanquilla Island, and then on to the passage between Trinidad and Tobago. This was some 550 miles distant, so they still had over five days to enjoy the Caribbean. Edward was in heaven. The apprentices were to stay on watches until they cleared Trinidad, working on deck in the daylight hours and on the Bridge at night. That suited Edward fine, as he would be able to brush-up on his stars, and on his Morse code with the Third Mate. The latter was done by calling passing ships on the Aldis lamp; a hand held lamp with a sight on top which was aimed at a passing ship. Once the other vessel replied with a steady light, the message sent was usually 'what ship?' They would reply with their ship's name, last port of call, and their destination. You then replied back with your own information, ending with Bon Voyage.

This was usually the extent of the exchange, and a record was kept of the ships contacted, in a notebook in the chart room. If it was a known ship with a known person onboard, usually another Shell tanker, conversations could ensue. This was easier when there were two people, as one could write down the letters as they were read out loud. Edward could read a lot of the Morse, but had trouble putting it all together as words when complete, so someone writing it down as he called out the letters was a big help. At that time, he found it a lot easier to send than to receive. If the sender on the other ship was slow and steady it was manageable. If the sender was fast with his Morse, Edward couldn't keep up, novice that he was.

The stars were now completely different and Edward had trouble finding them, as Orion was no longer visible and had been his reference point for locating the stars he had learnt. To the north, he did find The Big Dipper with its long curved handle pointing to Arcturus, which was incredibly bright and almost overhead. The North Star was almost 'middle sky'. The Third Mate pointed out some new stars to Edward. To the East, ahead of them, over on the port bow at the top of the Northern Cross, was Deneb. It was actually easier to locate on the curve of a large D, which also helped in remembering its name. Above that and further towards the bow, at the bottom of a small V, was the very bright Vega. To the South was Antares, a reddish star at the centre of a line of three and slightly offset; and Spica, found by following the top line of what looked like a ship's sail; a Spanker or Mizen, the same as that found on a fishing trawler. Astern of them, to the west, the Third Mate pointed out The Sickle, with the bright star at the bottom of the handle being Regulas. Further round near the horizon, were two familiar stars that Edward would never have found and named; the twins, Pollux and Castor.

Just after sunset an incredibly bright 'star' was visible low in the western sky that set after the sun. This was the planet Venus, just about the Earths twin in size, and was referred to as 'the evening star' at this time of year; even though it was a planet. Earlier in the year this planet could be seen in the eastern sky before sunrise and was then referred to as 'the morning star'. It disappeared from the naked eye with the rise of the sun but if you knew where to look it could be seen through the telescope on the sextant. All this information came from the Third Mate.

"What is the difference between a star and a planet?" asked Edward

"A star, like our sun, produces its own light. A planet reflects light, just like a moon does and, believe it or not, a star does twinkle and a planets reflected light does not." was the Third Mates informative response.

Two days out, Edward was looking at the small scale chart of the Caribbean and noticed the island of Tortuga, a hundred miles to their south. Yet again his thoughts went to pirates. He had a rather romantic notion of the life of the buccaneers, but deep down knew that it was anything but. It was a hard life, and for most a short one. This Tortuga was not, however, the one of pirate fame; that Tortuga was the small island off the northwest coast of Hispaniola; or off the north coast of what is now Haiti.

Edward's five night watches heading east in the Caribbean were a joy, and his knowledge of stars and Morse being put to the test each night. The Third Mate had Edward take a bearing of a different star each night, and along with star tables, checked the accuracy of the gyro compass, entering the result in the appropriate logbook. It was a beautiful peaceful time with a waning moon shining brightly in the southern sky.

A darts tournament was organized, and everyone who wanted to participate entered their name on a list posted on the notice board in the Officer's smoke room. Names were then drawn to determine who played whom. Matches were played in the evenings where possible, all depending on watches, of course. Twelve officers and apprentices signed up from the deck and engine room, and each put in fifty cigarettes, so the winning prize was six hundred cigarettes; just about enough to smoke yourself to death!

When Deck was playing Engine Room, each supported their own and a friendly rivalry ensued. It got down to two Deck in the final, The Chief Officer (The First Mate), and unbelievably, Edward, who was understandably nervous.

It seemed everyone had shown up for the final, putting Edward even more on edge. They were playing 301, starting and ending on a double, best out of three games. The first game was about to start.

"If you win this you'll be on field days for the rest of the trip," the Mate quipped in a loud voice, while looking at Edward with a wry smile. Everyone laughed loudly. The Chief Engineer slapped Edward on the back.

"Don't let him bully you, son."

For Edward, field days meant that if on watch, he would be working every afternoon; and if on day work, he would be working every Saturday. Not a very happy prospect. Edward figured that The Mate was probably just kidding anyway, and no matter what, he was going to do his best to win. Either way, attempted intimidation did not go down well with Edward, so it made him more determined to win no matter what the consequences. A bit stupid maybe, but he didn't think The Mate could be that petty.

The Mate won the first game; *false sense of security,* thought Edward, who won the second game. Now it was really on, and it was the Engineers present that were shouting their support for Edward; probably the old oil and water never mixing outlook. It was nerve racking for Edward as he tried to calm himself. Here he was, a first trip apprentice going up against, certainly as far as Edward was concerned, the most powerful man on the ship. It was a close game, and with his last throw Edward put his dart into the middle of the required double. The room erupted! He had won the match and hence, the tournament!

The Mate, standing close by, patted Edward on the shoulder. "Good lad!" was all he said. Edward did not show his absolute elation, and he was still a little apprehensive.

"Here, have a beer son," said the Chief Engineer, handing him a cold can of Amstel. "Well done."

There were no repercussions over his win. It turned out The Mate was a lot bigger than that. In fact, it probably made Edward a little safer against any nasty assignments for fear of being called a bad loser! *No,* he thought, *the Mate wouldn't shy away from assigning a necessary task, for the very same reasons that I didn't shy away from doing my best to win.*

Edward shared his winnings with his fellow apprentices so they had two hundred each. Some were in packets of twenty, English and American, some tins of fifty's mainly the brand 555 and Players, others were loose. All-in-all it had been an exciting time and his win, and rightfully so agreed Edward, had been put down to luck.

41

A few days later they were passing through the channel between Tobago and Trinidad. Edward smiled when he looked at the large scale chart of the passage and saw the name of Tobago's principal town was Scarborough; also the name of a Yorkshire seaside resort. This island was to become Princess Margaret's (the younger sister of Queen Elizabeth II) favorite vacation island.

On their starboard side was Trinidad. It was this beautiful island that had a Pitch Lake, used by sailors for hundreds of years to re-caulk their ship's wooden decks. Sir Walter Raleigh and Sir Francis Drake were among those known to have taken advantage of this natural gift to the sailing man.

Rounding Galera Point, the northeastern tip of Trinidad, they set their southeasterly course, for the next 800 miles or so, to five degrees north latitude, off Cayenne in French Guyana. Then it was to be right round the Brazilian Coast. *How could life get better than this?* Edward thought. Clear of land, the apprentices went back on day work; wonderful.

The cyclonic weather pattern put the sea and swells abaft the port beam, making life very pleasant. In England it's said that, if it were not for the weather, people would have nothing to talk about. At sea the weather dictates everything. The degree of severity and its direction, dictates course and speed. It also dictates ship maintenance in the constant battle between salt and steel. This weather was great, and a Chief Officer's delight for maintenance.

As the apprentices were back on day work, their afternoon lessons, three days a week were resumed. Day work also meant that they worked on Saturday mornings cleaning the wheelhouse, the first tripper having the privilege of cleaning all the brass work. This included the dogs and rims of side portholes in the wheelhouse as well as the chart room, handles and locking catches on the wheelhouse windows, and the biggy; the compass binnacle cover, and the long brass cylinder holding the Flinders Bar (a soft iron correcting bar) on the front of the binnacle. It was a dirty job, and the Brasso was awful to get off hands afterwards. Doug cleaned the outside of the windows by lowering one down, and leaning out to clean the window on either side. Their usual banter when working together was non-existent; it was not appreciated on The Bridge.

Afterwards, while cleaning up for lunch, Edward hand scrubbed the chamois leather used by Doug to clean the windows, in hot soapy water. This not only cleaned the leather, but also helped to get the Brasso out of his hands. Edward also learnt a useful trick here from Doug. After cleaning the chamois, the soap was left in to stop it from drying out like a piece of wood. Maintenance continued on the ship and she was getting to look quite spruce.

John and Edward were given the job of covering the wire hand rails of the Companion Ladder; the gangway that ran at an angle down the side of the ship. It was usually put out when at anchor, and in ballast, for easier access by Pilots and other shore personnel. Edward was to follow Johns lead here. They first removed the wires from their vertical supports and stretched the first of them tight between tank lid guard rails, about three feet above the deck. They then cleaned the wire off with vegetable oil using old rags, first covering the deck below the wire with rags to catch the oil drippings. The wire was then 'wormed', Edward watched John as he filled the spaces between the strands of wire with spun-yarn to make it smooth. His contribution was to pass the ball of yarn around the wire as John continued down its length. After completion they greased and 'parceled' the length of wire. Parceling was simply covering over the worming with strips of old duck canvas that was secured at regular intervals with pieces of yarn. They then 'served', again with spun yarn over the canvas. Serving entailed wrapping turns of yarn tightly around the parceled wire at right angles to its length, and against the lay of the wire. All this activity was first demonstrated by John and then Edward just followed along. The whole length of the wire was served, with no gaps in between, completely covering the canvas. A tool they used was a 'serving mallet'. This looks like a small wooden mallet, except that the head has a groove on one side to fit over the wire. John started the serving for a couple of turns by hand, and then Edward watched as he wrapped the yarn around the mallet, which he then turned round and round the canvas covered wire, applying the 'service' very tightly. The small pieces of securing yarn were removed, by Edward, as they progressed down the wire. Edward stood further down the wire, and passed the ball of yarn around the wire, in unison with John turning the mallet. Half way down the wire they changed places and Edward took over the 'serving'; after observing John's technique very carefully, and finished this first wire. They strung the second wire up further down the deck and repeated the process.

Upon completion they had stronger, smoother, thicker rails that were a lot easier to grip. They can be left as is or painted. John and Edward painted them, first dampening with water to lay down the fibers, and then the paint was applied. When dry they sand-papered the whole length to remove any sharp fibers, and then re-painted to a wonderful smooth finish. The end result was quite satisfying. Edward had seen a similar process used, by one of the day-time sailors after a mooring wire had been spliced. When the strands of the splice were cut along the splice they left sharp pieces of wire jutting out. These were covered in old canvas and then served in much the same way as they had just done, but without the mallet, in order to smooth out the splice and protect a sailor's hands.

After a couple of days they altered course slightly off Cayenne to take them off the northeasterly tip of Brazil near the town of Natal; about six days away. This small alteration at 5 degrees north latitude brought them into the area known as 'The Doldrums' that stretched around the Equator between about 5 degrees north and south latitudes. The Doldrums is an area of mostly calm weather, but is known to have short, sharp squalls. Any breezes are usually light, and from all over the place. The area was most disliked by sailing ship crews, as they could be becalmed here for days on end.

The following afternoon the three apprentices and the day work crew were on deck, when the ship was hit by a sudden quick squall. Because they were fully loaded, the smaller freeboard made it seem worse than it really was. One minute it was calm, and the next there were swirling winds and spray, throwing dust and dirt all over the wet paint on the pumprooms and the midships forward bulkhead. Where the heck did dust and dirt come from?! It was like a mischievous dust devil he'd read about in his paperback westerns; looking to make trouble, a hit-and-run.

One of the crew summed it up best when, with paint brush in hand he called out, "What the fuck was that?"

Looking around, they could see 'the little devil' scampering off towards land as if looking for someone else to startle.

It was time to start thinking about crossing 'the line'. Neither Edward nor John had crossed the Equator before, so Doug had given them a heads-up that there would be an initiation to mark their crossing. There were also the three Engineer Apprentices, the deck boy, and a couple of sailors to be initiated. Edward was not sure what was going to happen, but was told by Doug that he could hide if he wanted to, but when found - 'because they will find you' - initiation would be that much worse.

A day away from the Equator they were steaming through a large arc of discolored water. This turned out to be the effluent from the mighty Amazon River, which entered the ocean some 200 miles southwest of them.

42

It was mid afternoon and the weather was calm as they crossed the Equator. Everyone available appeared to participate, including The Old Man, The Mate, and the Chief Engineer. One of the sailors, Bill, the piano virtuoso, played the role of King Neptune, with a long blond wig and a grass skirt; both made with rope yarns. He had a trident in one hand, and sat on a throne set up on the main deck. His court, a sailor and a fireman, stood at his side, also wearing grass skirts, and armed with soft soogy brooms and a five gallon drum of Teepol; that slimy soap concoction made by Shell, and a cut-down 40 gallon drum filled with sea water. Water hoses were also set up from the fire hydrants, the Engineers thankfully keeping the pressure low.

As the victims were 'caught' they were brought before the court and stripped of all their clothes. Buckets of sea water, which was surprisingly cold, were thrown over them, and they were daubed from head to foot with Teepol. The long handled brooms being first dipped in water, then the Teepol, then each body was scrubbed mercilessly until covered with thick soapy bubbles, their hair matted down with the thick, slimy soap solution. They were made to stand before Neptune who, with paper in-hand, loudly extolled;

"I hereby sanction and affirm that Our Most Noble Cross of the Equator be bestowed on these individuals, who but mere Mortals have this day accepted in good grace and humour, the most rigorous Initiation into our Aquatic Court, before these witnesses."

Then, amongst the cheering of all those in attendance, the initiates were all mercilessly hosed down with, what seemed like freezing cold sea water, each of them cupping their genitals to protect them from the stinging hose, and turning sideways as if to shoulder off the onslaught. It was a great day!

They were then allowed to leave the deck and go their separate ways to get showered and cleaned up. Although they were already as clean as they would ever be, the shower got off the salt, and the sticky mess of Teepol still thick in their hair. John showered first and as he dried himself off Edward stepped in,

"Hell, I've never been so clean when I got into a shower before," Edward yelled over at John as he stood under the lovely warm spray from the showerheads.

"I'm glad that's over with," replied John, "it could have been an awful lot worse from what I've heard."

After getting dressed, Edward volunteered to go and pump the water up, as they had probably just about emptied the tank.

Later they were all given a certificate, dated and signed by the Captain, proclaiming their initiation. Edward, looking at his certificate saw the date, 19th June. It was his Mum's birthday, and here he was at the Equator heading into the South Atlantic.

Edward lifted the can of beer he was drinking, "Happy Birthday Mum, it's a great day!"

Over the next couple of days, along with the routine of maintenance, they had a lifeboat drill, and a fire drill. They made their way southeast towards Natal, which they reached on the third day, then on to Recife, which they passed the following morning.

It was off Recife that they hit some bad weather coming in from the southeast. They had altered course to a south-southwesterly direction. This was enough to start shipping seas on the main deck and solid spray onto the boat decks. Edward had been sent to the portside boatdeck amidships to check the security of the lifeboat retaining wires. It was blowing quite hard and as he pulled on the wires, held tight by bottle screws (turnbuckles), the ship rolled to port and a wave actually broke on the boatdeck. Fortunately, Edward was well protected by the lifeboat, and the fact that he had hold of one of the wires with both hands as he pulled on it, kept him on his feet.

As the water receded, a silver fish flopping on the deck caught his eye. He ran over and grabbed this gift from the ocean. It was a flying fish, and a good sized one, over a foot in length with approximately the same wing span. He took it up to the bridge to show the Third Mate.

"That's a beauty," the Third Mate exclaimed "they're good eating, take it to the cook and he'll cook it up for you."

Edward took his prize aft to the galley and presented it to the cook, who gave Edward a big smile. "I'll cook it for your lunch; they're a bit boney, kind of like a herring, but they're good eating," he exclaimed. "I'll send it midships with Ray."

"Could I have the wings?" Edward asked. The cook cut these off and handed them over. He later spread and dried the wings, actually the pectoral fins, then varnished and mounted them on a piece of plywood and hung his trophy in his cabin. He'd still have them many, many years later.

The cook was right about them being good eating. Edward realized as he ate that it had been a long time since he'd had fresh fish, and you sure couldn't get any fresher than this. He later took the cook two cans of beer as a thank you; they were accepted with grace.

The following day the storm had passed but the swell remained, making the Combia roll and pitch, but it was not uncomfortable. Unlike the North Atlantic, the South Atlantic does not have hurricanes, but the weather can get nasty. Luckily though, they had more days of good weather than bad.

Edward went onto the bridge one evening to ask about the new stars to the south. He was introduced to the Southern Cross, with its brightest star, Rigel Kent. The Third Mate informed him that this was the closest star to Earth, other than our Sun, and was four and a half light years away.

"Imagine," he said, "travelling at the speed of light, which is 186,000 miles per second, or close to 670 *million* miles per hour; for four and a half years just to reach that star! Put another way, it takes the light from Rigel Kent four and a half years to reach us; that just boggles the mind. That means if it were extinguished now, we would not see it go out for another four and a half years. To put that into perspective; our Sun is about 95 million miles away, it takes the light from the Sun about eight and a half *minutes* to reach Earth!" He paused to let this sink in then continued, "What you see up there, Paige, is history. What you see up there now, may no longer be there." Again he paused for effect and then concluded, "By the way, the star Regulas, that you now know, is about 1,000 light years away!" Edward said nothing, trying to absorb the enormity of space. He'd try again, many times in the future, but always found it too difficult to comprehend.

....

The run down the Brazilian coast brought them off Cabo Frio (Cold Cape). Rio de Janeiro was a hundred and fifty miles to the west. They were also just north of the Tropic of Capricorn. It was here that Edward entered into the realm of the immortal. He was to see the Albatross! He'd read the expression, loved it, and repeated it to himself; *I am among the immortal, for I have seen the Albatross.* Edward learnt that Cabo Frio is about as far north as the Albatross comes, as they need constant wind; further north the wind is unreliable. So it was here, at 23.5 degrees south latitude that the great Wandering Albatross picked up the next ship going south, in this case, by their good fortune, it was the Combia.

There were usually two or three of them that followed the ship south, hardly moving their wings that had spans of six to eight feet. They were gorgeous, and Edward could watch them for hours. They would come up alongside the ship below mast height, then swoop down under the flare of the bow to gain momentum, arch back astern, and then turn and 'come up onto the ship' (approach) once more. They were absolutely tireless. Edward also learnt that these birds were thought to circumnavigate the globe south of Cape Horn, in the stormy latitudes known as 'the roaring sixties' a latitude uninterrupted by land.

In all the years that followed in his life at sea, Edward would never tire of watching these wandering giants of the southern oceans. Some said they were old Bosuns lost at sea; a romantic notion.

43

Cabo Frio was well named, as once south of there it started to get colder. The Captain gave the word for all personnel to revert back to blues. They also assumed a more southwesterly course, heading for the entrance to the Rio de la Plata; the River Plate. The name itself instilled excitement in Edward, as it had been the scene, in late 1939, of the Battle of the River Plate. The battle was between the magnificent German battleship, Admiral Graf Spee and the British ships, Ajax, Achilles, and Exeter. The battle was well known to Edward, as he had read an account of it in one of his father's books. All four ships took a pounding in this battle, and according to the story, the British ships had received the worst of it. It was the Graf Spee, however, that finally took refuge at Montevideo; a neutral port. By law, under this neutrality, she could only be made seaworthy, meaning that armament could not be repaired.

The Royal Navy sent out bogus messages that all available naval vessels, including the Prince of Wales, were to converge on the River Plate to ensure that the Graf Spee would not escape. In actual fact, it was only the three original vessels that were to lie in wait, and no help was on the way at all. They were bracing themselves for the coming battle.

The Graf Spee, along with her sister ships the Admiral Scheer, and the Deutschland, were known as pocket battleships – surface raiders. They had the high speed of a Cruiser, with the fire power of a Battleship; six, 11inch guns. They were not large vessels, just over 10,000 tons displacement, which was not much bigger than the Combia. They were designed to catch and sink inferior vessels, and run and escape from larger, more powerful ones. The Graf Spee had earlier been in the Indian Ocean where she sank the small Shell tanker, Africa Shell, off East Africa. Altogether, she sank nine British freighters before the Battle of the River Plate. First though, Captain Hans Langsdorff of the Graf Spee had removed the crews of each ship, resulting in no lives lost. Captain Patrick Dove and his crew from the Africa Shell were later released in neutral Uruguay. Captain Dove reported that Langsdorff was a gentleman of the 'old school', and had treated his crew very well during the month that they'd been on board his ship.

Whilst in Montevideo, Captain Langsdorff was given orders to scuttle his ship as it was thought that half the British Navy was now waiting for him, and they did not want the Graf Spee to fall into enemy hands. He protested, wanting to go out and fight, but the admiralty was unrelenting. It was hard for Edward to understand the logic of this. Anyway, thankfully for the three partially crippled British ships waiting in the mouth of the river, the Graf Spee did not make for sea.

The ship was scuttled just off Montevideo harbor, after Captain Langsdorff put ashore the majority of his crew; his primary concern. After a huge explosion rocked the ship, the Captain and his demolition team motored back to shore in the ship's launch. Sadly, Captain Langsdorff later shot himself in his hotel room in Montevideo, for the 'shame of it all'. In Montevideo and Buenos Aires there is, to this day, a large population of people of German descent, many of them being descendants of the crew of the Graf Spee, that never did return to the homeland.

Upon arrival at the River Plate, the Combia rounded Punta del Este, and approached Montevideo. The apprentices went back on watches, and the log that had been merrily spinning away astern since their departure from Curacao was brought in and stowed. The wind was from the northwest, blowing the water out of the massive river. As a result, they had to anchor outside the port; and there she was. The superstructure of the Graf Spee was still reaching defiantly above the surface, between the Combia and the shore. Edward stood at the rail staring at the wreck, trying to imagine what it had been like in those few days of hell just over seventeen years ago; his present age! Three ships were bent on destroying one, and the one had almost destroyed the three! The three did win in the end, however, albeit not by their hand, but just by their presence.

The mouth of the River Plate is more like a bay; an estuary, being approximately a hundred and forty miles across from Punta del Este to Punta Norte to the southwest. At Montevideo, the river it is still over fifty miles across, hence the water depth problem when the winds are from the northwest; it literally just blows the water out of the river. It's not a very deep river in the first place. So they sat at anchor, waiting for the wind to change, and the water to rise. The companionway with Edward and John's handiwork was put over the side, for use by the Pilot and other shore personnel that would visit the ship; customs, immigration, and the like. The Captain left the bridge to go to his cabin below, his parting comment making those on the bridge laugh nervously.

"Hope we don't see that bastard ship that ran into us in the Channel."

Of course, realized Edward, *that ship was registered here in Buenos Aires!* Fortunately, the Argon was nowhere to be seen! (No information was ever received with regard to the outcome of that collision although it was obvious that the Argentine ship was totally at fault. This probably confirmed by the fact that after Edwards initial appearance, at a tribunal in London, along with all others present on the bridge at that time, for an inquest into what had happened, they were never summoned again).

There is a buoyed channel that runs down the center of the river to Buenos Aires. The seaward end of the channel was marked by a First World War dreadnaught being used as a light ship. It was a strange looking vessel, whose bows stretch forward beneath the waterline, rather than the usual rake astern. Like their ancient Greek and Carthage counterparts, they were designed for ramming the enemy, thereby holing them below the waterline.

On the dreadnaught was a light tower that flashed to indicate the rise of water in the channel; one quick flash for ten centimeters rise, one long flash for one meter rise. They lay at anchor for two days, watching the light alternate between one and and two quick flashes. Finally the wind changed to a southeasterly one, and the light began emitting a single long flash. A pilot came onboard and advised the Captain to standby. As they weighed anchor, at the Pilot's request, the light was giving out three long flashes; almost a ten foot rise of the river's water level. Unbelievable! The companionway was heaved up so that it lay level with the deck, then swung inboard and stowed. The Argentine flag - the courtesy flag - was hoisted up on the foremast starboard yardarm. Edward remembered that the last time he had seen this pale blue and white flag, it had been flying from the stern of the Argon in the Dover Strait!

As they made their way up the channel they did touch bottom, on a number of occasions. Although the river bottom was only mud, the sound was remarkable; it sounded like someone dragging heavy chains across the steel deck, and through the center castle under the midships accommodation. Notations were made in the Movement Book of these 'touched bottom' incidents.

"Why don't you dredge this channel?" the Captain asked the Pilot.

"What for Captain?" he smilingly replied. "Your ships come through here all the time and do it for us."

They both laughed, but it really didn't seem funny to Edward. The Engineers had been informed of the shallow approach, so the deep water intakes had been closed, and the shallower intakes were being used. This drastically reduced the amount of mud and debris that might be sucked in, which could potentially disrupt engine and condenser cooling.

Their destination in Buenos Aires was Doc Sud - South Dock. As they approached the dock, Edward, who was on the poop deck with the Second Mate, was staring at a number of strange looking ships with large open sterns, tied up alongside; some alongside each other. They were rusty and neglected.

"Are they whalers?" he asked the Second Mate, remembering films he had seen at the cinemas back home.

"They're whaling factory ships," he replied, "owned by Onassis. They're all laid-up because of the decline in the whaling industry, although there are still ships out there in the trade, including his."

"Onassis? The Olympic ship owner like the Olympic Flame we saw in Ellesmere Port?"

"That's the one," the Second Mate answered.

Edward later learnt that Onassis, in his youth, had been a desk clerk at a hotel in Buenos Aires. Talk about rags to riches!

Doc Sud was in a dirty industrial area. The water had, in fact, more chemicals in it than water. Edward heard a story that one of Shell's ships, an H class, had visited this dock. - Different types of ships had letter designations, and their names began with this letter, to simplify categorization. - This particular H class ship had come into the dock with green algae and growth on her sides, between the light and load water lines. After completion of unloading the cargo, her sides were 'as clean as a whistle' – burnt off by the chemicals. The water also stank to high heaven, and Edward shuddered to think that they'd later be pumping the stuff into their tanks for ballast.

44

Moored alongside, they started the process of discharging their cargo of gasoline, kerosene and gas oil, which in this case was slower than usual.

At 1730hrs, after having dinner, Edward, John, Sparky, and Chippy made their way ashore. Their destination was a small bar close to the dock that Chippy had been to before. Its name was Tanker Joe's; a watering hole. The owner was a staunch Eagle Oil man, and had a wonderful collection of models of Eagle Oil tankers in glass display cabinets throughout the bar. Years later, when Shell took over all these 'Eagle Boats', as they were known, Joe remained a staunch Eagle Man, and scoffed at the Shell guys for taking them over. All the Eagle Boats had names beginning with San, for example San Gasper, San Flaviano etc so they were often referred to as the San boats.

Tanker Joe's was renowned for its steak sandwiches. Although they had all recently eaten, the four ordered the specialty of the house. Edward, it seemed, could never get enough to eat anyway. When the sandwich came Edward just stared. He had never seen anything like it! The meat was nearly an inch thick, and had to weigh close to a pound. It stuck out of the bread bun on all sides. Edward had been a Butcher's Boy while at school, and had delivered meat to households on Tuesdays and Saturdays. He had delivered smaller pieces of meat that were destined to feed an entire family, some for a week!

They all bit into their sandwiches like they hadn't eaten for days. It was the most succulent sandwich Edward had ever had, and its cost was just one dollar US. Together with a glass of beer it was a fabulous meal.

"Now this is certainly something to write home about!" he exclaimed; which he did. They stayed in Tanker Joe's until Edward had to return for his watch. John walked back to the ship with him, to get some sleep before midnight came around. Sparky and Chippy stayed-on for more drinks.

Edward found out that Shell had a standing order for their ships visiting Argentina, and that was to fill the freezers to capacity with the fabulous beef, which was famous for its quality and low cost. They'd continue to enjoy it long after they left Argentine waters.

The following morning Edward was approached by Sparky, who said he and Chippy were going into town that evening and wondered if he wanted to get John or Doug to do his watch for him, so he could go with them. Edward was not familiar with such arrangements, and asked Doug about it. It was simple really; one of them would do an eight hour watch, and then Edward would return the favor. This meant that when he came off watch at noon, he would be clear until 0800hrs the following morning. Sounded good!

The First Mate had to approve the exchange, and he did. John agreed to do his watch that evening, so he would be on deck from 2000 to 0400hrs, then when Edward went on watch at 0800 the following morning he would stay on until 1600 doing John's watch, leaving him clear until midnight. This turned out to be a common arrangement, not just among apprentices, but by all watches. Even The Third and Second Mates would often do this, in the interest of quality time ashore; especially in ports like Buenos Aires. Edward still wasn't sure why it had been suggested that he do this though.

After lunch, Edward went ashore with Sparky and Chippy, just for a change. It's interesting to note that it was frowned upon for apprentices and officers alike to socialize with members of the crew. Some officers didn't even like you talking to the crew. A ridiculous situation for apprentices, seeing that half the time on a ship they were working alongside the crew, shoulder to shoulder in some cases, and were given the most menial tasks while doing so. It was understandable though; officer/crew member relationships were frowned on, and in most cases they would not want to socialize with each other anyway. Sparky, of course, was an officer and had all the rights as an officer onboard ship. Chippy however, although he could be classed as a Petty Officer, was not an officer in the sense that Sparky was and was a member of the deck crew and his cabin was in the crew quarters.

The subject of Sparky, Chippy, and Edward always going ashore together was never mentioned by Edward's superiors. Looking back on this friendship years later, he concluded that it was probably Sparky's presence that saved the day, although Chippy was a fine upstanding young man who was respected by all onboard. After this ship Edward would not see either of them again, but would never forget the two of them, and the security they gave him on his trips ashore as a total novice; they really looked after him.

45

The Musketeers were bundled up in the back of a taxi, speeding towards the city of Buenos Aires. Edward couldn't believe how lucky he was to have chosen a life at sea. How could it get better than this? He was ashore with his two good friends and he was not due back on watch until 0800 the following day!

Buenos Aires was a busy, bustling, noisy capital, although it would get noisier as the day wore on. They were dropped off at the city centre, a large open area with different colored paving stones. It was breezy, and paper was blowing and swirling around. He had liked football back home where there were certainly some avid fans, and a few football hooligans, but they were tame compared to this place. There was the white and pale blue of the Argentine flag everywhere. People were pushing and shouting and waving pieces of paper. Some buildings were boarded up and covered in posters advertising an up-coming game, as were the lampposts and every other available space; it was absolute bedlam.

They were near the football stadium and were able to look inside and see the playing field. See it you could, but the section they could see was through two high wire-mesh fences about twenty feet apart with a hollow, rather like a shallow moat, between them. The stadium was referred to as The Bear Pit, and you could see why. The fences were there to protect the players, especially the visiting team, and the Referee and Linesmen. Apparently the locals were prone to throwing beer bottles and other missiles in order to show their displeasure. *Wasn't this supposed to be a sport?*

"Holy God," Edward spoke out loud, "I sure wouldn't want to be in there during a game." Chippy and Sparky agreed.

"Let's move on somewhere else." pleaded Sparky as they pushed their way through the crowd.

They finally found a quieter area, and a small bistro type café with wrought iron tables and chairs outside. A few brave souls sat drinking coffee in the cool afternoon. They found a table and did the same, sitting and enjoying the sights and sounds around them.

"This is more like it." Sparky sighed, leaning back in his seat.

Leaving the café they just wandered around enjoying the walk, especially the square and the Spanish architecture that surrounded them. One building was particularly impressive. It had grey stone pillared structures with arched terraces at the second level, with a balcony at its center. A long flight of stone steps led to large wooden double doors, which were the entrance to the first level. This was the home of the famous, or should that be infamous, Juan Peron, and the site of his revolution. It had also been home to the much loved, and in some circles, much hated - especially by the British whom she had kicked out - Eva Peron. She'd had the unconditional love of the common people though, and had died here just four years earlier, in 1952. This little insight into the past all came from Sparky as they took in the sights.

They decided to eat before finding a place to drink and have a good time. They found a café that was quite large but not very busy, not usually a good sign.

"Don't worry," piped up Sparky, who seemed to have become their guide, "the locals don't eat until much later."

The menu was in both Spanish and English, the latter seeming to be the international language for tourists. Edward ordered a steak with all the trimmings. It was a large meal that he ate ravenously, the steak again being spectacular.

Chippy looked at Sparky, "He must have hollow legs," he commented. They both laughed as they were still only halfway through their meals. Edward was a little embarrassed at having eaten so quickly. When all were finished, they had strong black espresso; *strong enough to pull your fillings out,* thought Edward. Sparky decided against his pipe, thank goodness, and they all smoked cigarettes and relaxed.

Later in the evening, they found a place with a large bar, lots of tables, good music, and a dance floor, and the place was busy. Excellent! They found a table near the dance floor, Edward ordered beer, Sparky and Chippy decided to share a bottle of wine. They sat and watched the dancers. Edward was enthralled by the women - they were of all ages and danced with a rare passion and sensuality; they exuded a smouldering, exotic beauty!

It was actually hard to tell the ages of these women, especially from behind. Some had long flowing hair, some shoulder length, and others had their hair tied aggressively in a bun above the neck. Medium height strong heeled shoes accentuated shapely legs. The slim waists, and small round bottoms encased in tight skirts, below the knee length, and their passionate dancing belied the age of many. As the evening wore on, one particular dancer caught Edward's eye; a young raven haired beauty that did not dance with the same guy all the time. Her long dark hair swept from side to side as she danced, flowing below her shoulders, full, faintly colored lips in a beautiful smile, except when doing the Tango. Then, she was very serious, and danced with an erotic passion, her dark eyes flashing as she and her partner twisted, spun, and abruptly changed direction.

Edward could not take his eyes off her and as she passed by their table Chippy and Sparky noticed, and exchanged a look. Edward missed the quick lift of the eyebrows by Sparky. The girl had also noticed his fascination with her, and on occasion their eyes would lock; hers a dark brown, his pale blue, but he always looked away. *Chicken shit!*

Edward's heart almost stopped beating when, in between dances, this raven haired beauty came over to the table and looked him straight in the eyes.

"Do you dance?" she asked simply, nothing timid about Argentine women.

Edward, giving a short sharp cough so he could speak, replied, "Not that dance," referring to the Tango. She just laughed, and held out her hand.

"Would you like to learn?"

Edward stood up, his legs feeling a little wobbly, took her hand, which was small, warm and smooth, and she led him to the dance floor. There was a 'breather dance' on, a waltz. She held him close as they went round the floor. She was strong and led him through the dance. As the saying goes; 'she swept him off his feet'. He was about half a head taller than her, and she snuggled in close putting her cheek on his shoulder. He could smell the fragrance of her hair, and was in heaven.

The waltz, or whatever it was they had just done, ended. *Damn it!* Tango music came back on. Edward had been watching many of these dances, so had a rudimentary idea of the steps and movements, but it looked very difficult. The men and women around him danced with a confident, serious passion.

They had stood apart for a second, then, looking at him with an open hand placed above her ample breasts, she simply said, "Maria".

He replied in the same manner, touching his chest, "Edward". She smiled, nodded, and stepped in once more, pulling him close to her. She pushed his elbows high and spun him round, stepped forward and pushed him back. Spun him round once more and stopped.

"You have to dance this Argentine Tango with passion. As if you wanted to make love to me right here on the dance floor", then pressing her loins against his she added, "It feels like you have that part covered."

Before he could say anything; well, anything that didn't sound like gibberish, she swept him across the floor to the incredibley sensuous music, turning abruptly, pausing, and going back the same way. It was really a slow dance, but along the way there were these fast back kicks that she did, that he did not dare to attempt, where her heel was flipped up between his knees and then down, then half-spins, and crossing feet; all very technical. He felt wonderful, but thought he must look like a clumsy ox compared to those dancing around him. No one seemed to notice though; they were too absorbed in the passion of their own dancing. He let the music and the beautiful woman in his arms take him over. The music ended, close to the table where Spark and Chippy sat watching.

"You're a natural," she lied politely, gave him a little nod and left, walking towards the bar.

Edward slumped down into his chair looking at his two companions, who sat smiling at him with eyebrows raised. He mockingly put his tongue between his teeth, his chin dropping towards his chest.

"Well?" asked the two of them.

"That was the most incredible thing I have ever done," Edward said excitedly. His companions laughed.

"Well it sure looked good to me," said Chippy. "Is she coming back?"

"I only wish," he replied looking around towards the bar while taking a gulp of his flat beer. "The night is young."

She did come back; standing away from the table she held out her hand. "Come," she said simply. He lurched to his feet, took her hand, and once more was swept away. This time he thought it was a foxtrot, but who knew? Her hair was newly brushed and shiny and he pressed his face into it. Her perfume was a little stronger but not overpoweringly so. His right hand in the small of her back held her close and tight. They twirled around the floor like they had danced together for eternity. She still, however, controlled most of the dance.

The dance finished, Maria and Edward walked back to the table. This time she sat down with them. Edward asked if she would like a drink, and held his hand up to attract the attention of their passing waitress. She brought back a gin and tonic and placed it in front of Maria, who took a quick sip.

The four of them chatted, answering the usual questions; where are you from, why are you here, what do you do, how long will you be staying, etc. Maria was a secretary/typist in the nearby public building. The chatter was light with lots of soft laughter. Edward excused himself and went off to find the bathroom. Upon his return, the three were still chatting away, but ceased as he approached.

Tango music came back on and this time it was Edward who stood and held his hand out to Maria. Standing, she laughed, swished her hair from side to side and took his hand. This time Edward felt more comfortable, but still let her lead him, knowing it would be a long time before he was proficient enough to lead her, or anyone else for that matter, in this type of dance. He had to learn to relax and go with the flow.

Short of breath, they returned to the table. Maria looked at Sparky and then

Chippy.

"So, you are going to wait for your friend?"

"Yes," they both said.

Edward was a little puzzled then Maria grabbed his coat off the back of the chair and pushed it to his chest, "Come with me." She took his hand and led him towards the bar, where she picked up her own coat, and then headed for the door. Edward, still holding her hand, could feel his heart thumping in his chest. At the door they let go hands, slipped on and fastened their coats, and stepped out into the cool night. She slipped her arm through his, simply pointed their direction, and they set off into the darkness.

46

They slowed at a two storey grey stone building. A flight of steps led to double doors with etched glass in the top halves. Climbing the steps, Maria opened one of the doors and they stepped into a small vestibule, to another set of double doors, one of which she unlocked with a key taken from her pocket. Inside was a large, ceramic tiled foyer. Stone stairs curved up to the second level with wrought iron railings. Apartment doors were visible in the dim light on both levels. They climbed the stairs and Maria opened the second door on the landing, entered, and beckoned him inside.

The dimly lit apartment was clean, tidy and smelt faintly of a flowery scent, and looked very cozy. In the left corner of the sitting room was a small kitchenette, to the right a slightly open door revealed a bedroom, again dimly lit by a small bedside lamp. A narrow hallway led off to the right.

"Your coat," Maria asked smiling, snapping him out of his daze. He handed it to her and she draped it over the back of an arm chair. "Would you like a drink?"

"No, thank you." was all he could manage.

Smiling, she took his hand and led him, without preamble, to the bedroom. The double bed was neat, flat, and wrinkle free. Over in the corner Edward noticed a chest of drawers with a large bowl and pitcher sitting on the top.

Maria kicked off her shoes, unbuttoned her cotton blouse, and let it fall from her shoulders, revealing an amply filled black lace bra that barely covered half of her breasts. She was watching him all the time and said softly, "Don't forget to breathe Edward."

He had been holding his breath and let it out with a sigh, at which they both laughed, relieving the tension. Edward showed his relief by kicking off his shoes and pulling off his socks, throwing them to one side Maria then unclasped the skirt from her narrow waist and let it fall to the floor. Brief panties matched the bra.

"You are absolutely beautiful." Edward choked.

She moved close to him, smiling, and unbuttoned his shirt. Reaching up, shorter now without her shoes, she slipped it off his shoulders, her breasts pressed against his chest. He gasped audibly; they were both enjoying the moment. Unbuckling his belt and unfastening his trousers she let them fall to the floor and he kicked them to one side. Stepping back slightly she ran her hands over his shoulders and down his chest then across his hard, flat, rippled stomach. Looking further down and then back up she looked into his eyes, and then tapped his flat stomach with the back of her hand.

"You're pretty beautiful yourself," she said softly.

She unclasped her bra, shrugged her shoulders and let the bra fall to the floor, her breasts springing forward as if thankful for their release. She slid her panties down and stepped out of them, and he dropped his under shorts, kicking them away.

Stepping close, they held each other tightly then fell onto the bed. Her soft full lips were pressed against his as they rolled on the bed, her hard nipples poking against his chest. She pulled him on top of her and wrapped her strong legs around him and, arching her back, pulled him inside her. The sensation of the warm smoothness was too much; they made fast animalistic love and, understandably for Edward, it was over in minutes. He was young and it didn't even slow him down. They continued their lovemaking as she rolled on top of him. They explored each other's bodies and made love again, much slower this time, savoring each moment. Edward buried his face in her beautiful breasts before taking each hard nipple into his mouth, rolling his tongue around and grating his teeth over them. Maria gasped, arched her back pressing even harder against him and then sighing, slumped down on top of him as his body arched and shuddered.

They lay side by side exhausted, covered in lovemaking's glorious sweat. Maria pulled the bedding round over the top of them and snuggled in close. Edward was in absolute heaven.

They dozed and snuggled for some time and made love once more. Finally Maria rose and put on a dressing gown, saying softly to Edward,

"You have to go, your friends are waiting." Edward nodded, got up and dressed, and they made their way to the door.

"You can find your way back to your friends alright, Edward?"

"Yes," he replied sadly as he turned and wrapped his arms around her. Kissing her hair softly, he said, "Have a wonderful life Maria."

"You too." she replied softly.

Tears welled up in his eyes as he left.

As he walked back to the dance hall the cold air brought him back to reality, unfortunately, and he rubbed his eyes dry. Re-living what had just happened to him, it was far more than he had ever dreamt it would be. Probably, he thought, the most delightful thing that would ever happen to him, and he shook his head as the tears came back. He wanted to turn and run back, but resisted the almost overpowering impulse. He smiled, the vision of Maria strong in his mind, then he turned and looked back.

"Good night Maria, I will remember you forever." he whispered.

Entering the dance hall he spotted his friends, walked over and slid into his chair. They both looked at him, saying nothing. It was Edward who broke the silence.

"I think I need a beer."

His two friends laughed and summoned the waitress, who put the large cold drink down in front of him. He lifted it in salute, and nodding to his friends drained the glass. It was immediately replaced, but this one he sipped.

"Well?" Sparky and Chippy said in unison, looking at him intently.

"Absolutely, absolutely wonderful, fabulous, marvelous!" he answered.

To which they both rose and slapped his shoulders, then each other's. They had clearly had enough to drink.

"She sure was gorgeous," Chippy said, "not like my first one." He shuddered his shoulders twitching, and pulled a face.

"Well you know us sailors," Sparky countered, "never went to bed with an ugly woman," he paused and then continued, "woke up with a few though." They all laughed, but the frivolity could not take away from Edward the vision that was Maria.

It was Chippy that finally got up and said, "Come on let's go home. It's after two o'clock."

They paid the bill and hurried outside and jumped into a waiting taxi. As they were whisked back to the ship, Edward reflected on all that had happened to him since waving goodbye to his parents. It seemed an eternity ago, and yet, like yesterday. Almost everything he had done and seen, on a daily basis, was for the first time. He marveled again at the life he had chosen, and 'first times' he knew, would continue for a while to come. His thoughts were interrupted by a slap on his knee, and the laughter of his two friends as they said something about him 'no longer being a virgin, that now he really was a man'. Edward smiled at his two friend's frivolity, but made no comment.

They clambered up the gangway, said their goodbyes and went their separate ways. It had been 12 hours since they had gone ashore. John was on deck and they waved to each other. Edward made his way to his cabin, undressed and collapsed onto his bunk, pulling the covers up to his face. With the scent of Maria still lingering on his body he fell into a deep, peaceful sleep.

47

He slept unmoving until Doug called his name at 0715hrs. Sliding out of his bunk he wrapped a towel around his waist and hurried round to the shower room. After washing himself down he stood for a few moments with the water on cool, sad in some way that he had washed off Maria's scent. He needed, however, to be awake for his next 8 hours on deck. Back in the cabin he dressed quickly, being careful not to disturb John, who was snoring quietly in his bunk, and went to the dining room to eat breakfast. He was absolutely starving and after finishing his plate, asked the steward, Ray, if there were any spares. He was given another plate of bacon and egg, which he just about inhaled, *probably Sparky's* he smiled to himself, doubting that Sparky would be up for breakfast.

Once in his working gear he relieved Doug on deck, and got the lowdown on the progress of unloading. It was going to be a long day, with doing John's afternoon watch as well as his own. Smiling to himself, something he seemed to be doing quite a lot of lately, he turned towards midships. *Thanks John, this one will be a pleasure.* Maria's beautiful smiling face framed by her long raven hair was still fresh and clear in his mind.

Get to work Edward and keep your mind on the task ahead, he admonished himself.

John had left a note to be called for lunch, after which he went ashore to enjoy his time off until midnight. Watching him going down the gangway, Edward hoped that he would have as good a time as he'd had; but he doubted that possibility very much.

Discharge of cargo was going well and Edward enjoyed the afternoon watch with the Second Mate, a knowledgeable and pleasant officer. They were kept busy, and 1600hrs soon came around, when Doug came out on deck to relieve him.

Edward showered; washing the strong smell of gasoline from his body. Quite different to the last shower he'd had when it was the fragrance of Maria he had reluctantly washed away.

Sparky was in the dining room, looking like he had just got up. They exchanged pleasantries, but no mention was made of their trip ashore. After dinner the two of them walked aft to the Officer's Smoke Room, which was currently sealed tight from the outside air, to have a cigarette. Edward thanked Sparky for the fabulous trip ashore.

The reply was a hearty smack on the back with, "The pleasure was all ours."

After finishing his cigarette, Edward excused himself and went back amidships to get a couple of hours sleep before going on watch again at 2000hrs. *The price we pay for pleasure!*

Again, he relieved Doug on deck; it seemed like only five minutes ago that it had been the other way round. It was going to be a busy one, as two sets of tanks were very low and would have to be stripped ashore. It was as this watch started, that his two friends, Sparky and Chippy, waved to him as they made their way ashore once more heading for the big city.

Gluttons for punishment smiled Edward, feeling no regret for not being with them. For reasons he would find hard to explain, he did not want to go back to the city. Maybe he didn't want to burst the bubble; his visit there couldn't possibly have been any better! He didn't want to risk tarnishing the memory.

48

By noon the following day, discharge of cargo was almost complete. Edward posted the 'end of shore leave' board at the top of the gangway; ETD (Expected Time of Departure) 1800 hrs. Cleaned up once more, he skipped lunch and walked ashore to Tanker Joe's for a steak sandwich. Afterwards, he just sat by a window sipping on a cold beer, reflecting on a fabulous trip to Buenos Aires. Waving goodbye to Joe, who was standing behind the bar chatting, Edward made his way back to the ship, deciding to have a nap before dinner and stand-by for departure.

After dinner they were ready to leave, the various department heads reporting that everyone was onboard. Ballasting was minimal, just enough to put the propeller blades under water. The First Mate wanted as little of the stinking Doc Sud water in the ship as possible; less to get rid of when they dumped it.

Tugs were alongside and the Pilot came onboard. The gangway was taken in and they were ready to go. It was 1900 by the time they singled-up and finally left the dock. Edward was told to go on the bridge for departure, as Doug, already in working gear, went forward and John went aft. Edward would then remain on the bridge for his watch. As they quietly slipped away from the dock, Edward looked around, wondering if he would ever come back here. He sure hoped so.

At midnight they approached the town of La Plata on their starboard side. They were in the buoyed channel, and Montevideo lay a hundred and fifty miles ahead. From there, it was round the Uruguay coast, and head once more for Cabo Frio. Edward thrilled at the prospect of the ocean voyage ahead.

Their first priority was to clean and gas-free the ship while dumping the ballast they had onboard and replacing it with clean sea water. This done, they were to make their way to the Amazon River, where they would dump all sea water ballast, and load a complete cargo of fresh water from the river, for Curacao.

Holy God, now I'm going up the Amazon, thought Edward. Pictures of natives with bones through their noses, blow pipes and poison darts, dugout canoes, and piranhas, flashed through his mind.

They were off Montevideo and Edward was standing at the ships rail watching the city go by. Not much to see, no tall buildings to speak of just a stretch of buildings along the coast, but still thrilling to see, and of course the Graf Spee lying quiet and mostly forgotten. Day work and tank cleaning started, and to Edward's delight they picked up two albatross to accompany them on their northerly trek to Cabo Frio.

They were surprised to note, however, that they had picked up something else! The three apprentices were on deck, cleaning tanks, when they observed a man walking along the flying bridge toward amidships.

"Who the hell is that?" Doug asked the other two, whose responses were the same. "No idea".

They had a stowaway onboard and he was on his way to give himself up to the First Mate. It was rather funny really, as he was a sailor from an Eagle Oil tanker. He had, apparently, got drunk while ashore, passed out in a brothel, and missed his ship. Instead of reporting to the authorities, this Scotsman had decided to hang around Tanker Joe's and wait for an appropriate ship.

The Combia turned out to be the 'appropriate ship', and he had obviously been helped by one, or more, of their crew. As they were three days out, there was not much that could be done, so The Captain signed him on the Ship's Articles as a DBS; a Distressed British Seaman. This could have been done more legally through the British Consulate, but no harm done, the result would have been the same. Shell Head Office was, of course, notified so that all the appropriate people could be informed. The sailor, Jimmy, turned out to be a good worker and was well liked by all, although he was teased mercilessly about being from 'The Enemy – Eagle Oil!'

Once the tank cleaning and gas-freeing was complete, and clean ballast was loaded once more, they started the awful task of de-scaling the bottom of the empty tanks. The scale this time was loose rust that falls from the tank bulkheads. The cargo of gasoline had really stripped it off, and it was this that they had to remove. The three apprentices, of course, were part of this, along with the watch and day-work deck crew. There was a surprising amount of scale in the bottom of the tanks, considering it was not that long since it was last done, as one sailor put it, "I think the old girl is falling apart". With a sailor standing at the open tank lid ready to heave out the buckets of scale, and to keep an eye on everyone's safety, the muck digging started.

Edward was surprised at the amount of fumes that were disturbed as they shoveled up the scale. The loaded buckets were heaved up onto the deck and were then dumped over the side. They took a break every hour when they all went up on deck coughing and spitting, and gasping for breath. Although they had the portable gas-freeing canvas ventilators blowing fresh air into the tanks, it still got quite noxious down there as the scale was disturbed. They carried on for a number of days until all the scale was removed. The tank bottoms were then flushed with sea water, and that in turn pumped back out to sea.

One day, in the middle of the afternoon, one of the sailors was overcome by fumes. He started wandering around the bottom of the tank muttering to himself, and staggering about as if he was drunk. They tried to get him to go up the ladder to the deck but he wouldn't go. One of the sailors tied a heaving line round his chest and with one guy pulling from the top and another pushing him up the ladder from below, they finally got him out.

The rescued deck hand collapsed on the deck, unconscious, and one of the AB's quickly took charge. Thank goodness he knew what he was doing. He rolled him over on his stomach and, making sure his tongue was clear of the back of his throat, gave him artificial respiration. He used the Holga - Neilson method, putting the victim's head onto his overlapped hands with elbows sticking out at right angles to his body. The AB, with one knee on the deck close to the deckhand's head, pressed down on his back then slid his hands along the deckhand's arms, grabbing the elbows and pulling them away from the deck, then back to press on the centre of his back, and so on. This was an exhale, inhale sequence that the AB did to the rhythm of his own breathing. After six or seven sequences, the deckhand coughed and spluttered and, looking around confused, sat up to re-orientate himself.

The AB was congratulated for his quick action and a few days later given the task of teaching everyone this method of resuscitation. He made clear that it was not a method that could be used if the victim had chest injuries. Mouth to mouth resuscitation was unheard of at the time.

After all tank de-scaling the crew were always given a tot of rum. It was thought at the time that this would help neutralize the effects of the gas fumes from the tanks. Whether this was true or not didn't really matter, it was something they looked forward to and small price to pay by Shell for the work that was done. Strangely enough though, this tot was never offered to the apprentices,

"I guess apprentices don't get gas inside their lungs" Doug quipped from behind the line of sailors. The Chief Steward, who was dishing out the tots, looked up at Doug,

"You guys see me afterwards." he said nodding at the three apprentices. They did so later round at his cabin, and he gave each of them a tot of the strong dark liquid. All of them shuddering and gasping as they knocked it back in one gulp, much to the Chief Stewards amusement, knowing he was not supposed to give the rum to them.

The Mate decided it was time to finish getting the loose sticky coating of PF4 off the decks, clean off the rust, and recoat them. During the tank cleaning process, Edward had been standing at one of the tanks in the rope-soled shoes he had bought in Curacao. On walking away, he found that the soles of his feet were bare. The canvas tops were still on his feet, but the rope soles were stuck to the deck where he had been standing. He walked back, peeled them off the sticky PF4 and, much to the delight of the sailors on deck, pulled the canvas tops off his feet and threw the lot over the side. He walked bare foot back midships, to the accompaniment of laughter, including his own, and put on the leather soled shoes he had bought at the same time. Whether ripping this old stuff up and replacing it with new would make any difference remained to be seen. At least they would get rid of some rust, and after his shoe incident Edward would be pleased to see the old stuff gone.

At Cabo Frio, and hence the Tropic of Capricorn, Edward's friends the albatross turned, and with hardly a movement of their large wings, again headed south, looking for another ship to escort to the south. The weather was good, and they went back to wearing tropical gear; *ah, shorts again at last.*

49

The trip around the Brazilian coast was busy but uneventful. They were approaching the Equator and also one of the mouths of the mighty Amazon; the Rio do Para. Their destination was about 100 miles upriver, just above Belem. A pilot boarded to take them to their anchorage, where they would load the river water. The idea being to get upriver from Belem, and the pollution dumped into the river by this city.

So this is the Amazon thought Edward, thrilled at being here and even more thrilled to be able to tell people that he had been here. But it was a little disappointing. The water was brown and appeared calm but had a strong seaward flow. He saw a few dug-out canoes closer to the shore. The light breeze brought the fragrance of the jungle, sometimes fresh and other times musty and humid. But no Pigmies, poison darts or piranhas. Edward smiled at his original thoughts of this river, *still great to be here though.*

As far as Belem was concerned; from the river, it was very unassuming. They were in mid-river, which was about 20 miles across, so not much could be seen. Looking at a small scale chart, Edward noted that fifty miles upriver from them, another river, the Tocantins, flowed into the Para. This river flows from the south for some 1200 miles; greater than the length of Britain, observed Edward, in awe at the vastness of his surroundings.

First they ran-out their salt water ballast, which would soon make its way back to the sea, and then started the pumps. Once free of her ballast, the ship rode high in the water on a taut anchor chain. They started to pump in the fresh river water.

Curacao, Edward was told, had no naturally occurring fresh water; it was completely dry. Drinking water was obtained through desalination plants that had been built on the island. In the not too distant future, in fact, Curacao would build the largest desalination plant in the world; closely followed by their neighbor Aruba, an island with the same problem. The fresh water they were taking back was for use in the refinery for cooling purposes; salt water, because of the salt, being of no use for this.

The companionway had been put out over the port side for shore personnel to come onboard; Edward noting how smart the two new top hand rails looked; with the ship completely empty it was quite a stretch for it to reach the water line. The ship's agent from Belem came onboard bringing mail that Shell, bless them, had forwarded. He also took a bag of mail to be sent to the UK. Edward had written a long letter to his sister, who still lived at home, so everyone got to read it, and he received two from her. He eagerly read the news from home and, like all the letters he received, they would be read many times over.

Loading was now complete, this was the lowest Edward had seen the ship riding in the water. She was loaded down to the deepest draft allowed, down to the Fresh Water mark on the Plimsoll Line. This was, of course, because the ship was floating in fresh water, which Edward thought funny because they were loaded with fresh water! The Fresh Water Allowance (FWA) on the Combia was 6 inches, so once out into the ocean, she would rise by that amount due to the density of salt water. The pilot was onboard and they weighed anchor, and were on their way down river to the sea.

When Edward had been at school he collected sets of cigarette cards; these approximately 1"x 2.5"cards had originated in packets of cigarettes, hence their name. They had pictures on one side and written information on the back about the picture. They covered all sorts of subjects from dogs, horses, flowers, jockeys, ships and airplanes and were collected in sets, trading 'doubles' of these cards with fellow students, being a constant activity to make up the sets. Curiously enough, he'd had a passion for the set on airplanes. He prided himself on being able to recognize them and knowing all their names. He was thrilled when, passing Belem, he heard a loud roaring noise, and on turning, watched as a Sunderland Flying Boat landed on the river not far from them, going to the city. He was informed by the ship's pilot that these airplanes traded up and down the rivers in this part of the world, being perfect for the job and the large rivers being perfect landing strips. In fact, they were the only contact with the outside world for some of the more remote areas. This one had come in from Manaus, about 1,000 miles up the Amazon.

Leaving the river they headed northwesterly and re-crossed the Equator. Edward remembered their previous crossing on the way south, *who would ever forget that?*

John spoke for both of them when he said, "I'm glad we don't have to go through that again!"

They were once more heading for Trinidad – Tobago and then on to Curacao about ten days away. Presently they were in the Doldrums; the sea was glassy calm and the air hot. Thankfully, the speed of the ship gave a good breeze, but it did not cool things off much.

50

A few days out, after being on deck all day, Edward was ordered by the First Mate to, 'keep a shirt on your back'. He had quite a good suntan, but on this particular day he overdid it in the sun, and got his back badly burnt. The Chief Steward put chamomile lotion on the burn which soothed it, but that night it hurt like hell. *Won't do that again in a hurry* he promised himself. It certainly proved that getting sun-burnt is not a good idea; he peeled like a snake shedding its skin; very uncomfortable.

One morning as they were getting ready to go to breakfast John asked, "By the way, who is Maria?"

Startled, Edward asked, "Why do you ask?"

"You said the name a few times during the night." John replied, looking at Edward questioningly. Edward had never spoken about Maria and Buenos Aires, but now told John.

After listening to the story, John's only comment was, "She sounds wonderful, congratulations Edward." The simplicity of the comment was just what Edward needed.

The only break in the everyday routines came when, about 300 miles out from Trinidad, they had a 'scavenge fire' in the engine room. It was explained to Edward; the Scavenge is that part of the cylinder, of an internal combustion engine, that removes the burnt gases after each power stroke. The fire, apparently not an uncommon occurrence, forced the shut down of the engines while the Engineers, God Bless them, did repairs. It was so hot in the engine room that the hand rails of the steel-grated steps could not be touched with bare hands. The stoppage also eliminated the little breeze that they'd had, and the heat was stifling.

Two black canvas balls were hoisted onto the yardarm on the monkey island. These 24" diameter black balls, about ten feet apart, were displayed as a warning to passing ships that they were 'not under command'. They drifted for twenty-four hours, the Engineers having to 'pull the piston'. They worked like dogs and, as Engineers will do, fixed the problem in an environment that made the air on deck seem positively balmy. Once more under way the induced breeze was a welcome relief to all. Edward thought that this was probably what it felt like in the days of sail, after a ship had been becalmed in these waters for days, and then finally a breeze comes along and they were able, once more, to get under-way.

By the time they got to Curacao the ship was looking very good with new paint shining everywhere. Even the deck looked good. Good thing; it was Edward's part in recoating this that had given him the burnt back. Steaming up and down once more off Willemstad, the Dutch courtesy flag flying from the fore starboard yardarm; it was hard to believe, for Edward, that it was almost two months since they were here last.

Alongside, more welcome mail was received, and they commenced discharge of their precious cargo to the thirsty tanks ashore. As always, of course, fresh stores and produce were received; vegetables, salads, fresh milk - a lovely change from the powdered stuff - Dutch butter, Dutch beer - Amstel and Heineken, meat, (no beef though the ship could have probably supplied the shore with that)! Funnily enough, they also took on fresh drinking water and, naturally, bunker fuel. The latter was, apparently, free in exchange for the cargo of fresh water they had delivered.

Unloading complete, all cargo tanks were inspected and, unsurprisingly, they were to load a cargo of Avtur - Aviation Turbine Fuel. It was no surprise because the tanks were so clean, and no pollutants were present. All cargo lines were drained of their last dregs of water, into the after-most centre tank, which in turn was stripped ashore. Any remaining puddles of water in the tanks were then mopped up manually by the deck hands. Unbelievably, the apprentices were not involved with this. When that was finished, they changed the discharge hoses to shore, then commenced loading of samples into the bottom of the tanks. Once each tank's samples were checked and passed by the shore-side laboratories as being free of pollutants, loading of cargo commenced once more.

The cargo was for Dundee, in Scotland. On hearing the news, Doug remarked, "That is unbelievable; we have a stowaway onboard and he's from Scotland! Do you think he knew something the rest of us didn't? Talk about picking the right ship."

Like he said, it was unbelievable. The stowaway, Jimmy, was very happy, especially when The Old Man agreed to keep him on and literally take him home. As far as Edward was concerned, he was just looking forward to another great ocean voyage to another country he had never been, Scotland.

Trips ashore for Edward were to buy necessary toiletries etc. and to send a birthday card to his eldest sister, whose birthday was in August. He did, however, see some really good quality dress pants that he liked. He bought them, together with a leather belt, dress shirt and shoes. For him, they were a lot of money but he reasoned, *there is no point in being poor* and *looking poor*!

He wandered around town just to enjoy the sights, sounds, and aromas. Sitting at a table outside a small bistro on the water front in Willemstad, he sipped a cold beer and yes, watched the ships go by. It was a great way to relax, especially when two familiar voices made him turn to see, much to his delight, his two buddies flopping down at the table to join him. They had come ashore together that morning while he had been on watch.

After a light meal of savory rice, shrimps and salad, and just generally lazing around, they made their way back to the ship for Edward's watch. They stopped at The Mad House on the way, for a final drink. They didn't know it at the time but sadly, this would be their final trip ashore together.

Loading complete, the ship prepared for departure, once more this entailed cleaning the ullage tapes and topping-up sticks, battening down all tanks, and mopping up any spilled oil from the decks. The pilot came onboard and made for the bridge and the gangway was pulled in. The ship was singled up, and with tugs in attendance these mooring lines were let go and they slid away from their berth. They slowly made their way down the channel through Willemstad and out to Mother Sea; ready once more for whatever she decided to dish out.

Clear of the entrance, they dropped off the pilot and this time turned to starboard, to make their way around the westerly side of the island. They would then take a northerly course up to the Mona Passage, between Hispaniola and Puerto Rico, about four hundred miles distant. From there, it is a clear run to Scotland, bypassing the Azores, which they would not see this time as they would be too far west. It was 3rd August, and their trip to Pentland Firth, the passage north of John o'Groats, would take about three weeks. From there, it was less than a day's run to Dundee; expected day of arrival (EDA) on the 26th. The weather as they rounded Curacao was calm, hot, and with beautiful, turquoise seas.

51

The transit through the Mona Passage was gorgeous. Edward stood at the rail, taking in the land and seascapes, and the tropical smells that wafted over the ship. There were sea birds everywhere; herring gulls vying for a perch on the top of the masts and screeching out their protest as others knocked them off. Edward loved the screeching of the gulls, even though he knew that it had sent many a fisherman to shouting hysterically at them to shut-up; or words to that effect. They swarmed around fishing vessels waiting for hand-outs as the men gutted their catch and threw the guts over the side, to be pounced on immediately by these screeching hoards. To Edward, it was like high pitched laughter.

Groups of pelicans skimmed the glassy sea, as if in transit from one island to another, unwavering from their course, and dozens of frigate birds displayed their now familiar soaring. Much to Edward's delight, a school of porpoise darted, jumped and swerved around the bows, and effortlessly shot ahead of them. Edward perched himself on the bow looking directly down at these amazing creatures who seemed to be smiling and really enjoying themselves, as if they were escorting the ship.

Clear of the Mona Passage, bearings were taken of landmarks, to fix the ship's position. Getting distances from the radar, their northeasterly course was set for their long passage across the North Atlantic. This would be the last land they would see until making landfall on the Outer Hebrides about twenty days away.

As they plowed their way northwards, a long lazy swell greeted them. Their bows dipped into the oncoming sea sending water and spray over the bows and decks. *Now this is more like it,* thought Edward. He loved the calm seas and the steady ship that they brought, but there was something exhilarating, for him at least, about plowing your way through an ocean swell.

Just one day out, they passed over the Milwaukee Deep section of the Puerto Rico Trench, its depth at over 28,000 feet, or 5.3 miles (8.5 kilometers). This makes it the deepest point in the Atlantic. *That's a lot of water down there!* Edward thought, *more than five miles deep!*

They moved on into the Sargasso Sea, that stretch of the Atlantic known for its floating seaweed. They passed through large patches of this long weed and on a number of occasions had to haul in the log, the rotor having become fouled by the weed, this was unceremoniously pulled off and thrown back into the sea, and then the log re-streamed. This weed was also known to have stopped sailing ships in their tracks, the weed fouling the bows and getting caught on barnacle encrusted hulls.

They passed over the Nares Deep, approximately 22,000 feet deep. These depths pale in comparison, however, to the Challenger Deep of the Mariana Trench in the Pacific Ocean, the deepest spot known, at nearly 36,000 feet; 6.8 miles, or 11 kilometers!

Their course took them along the Mid Atlantic Ridge, and they also had the Gulf Stream in their favor. This, in turn, became the North Atlantic Drift that flowed over the top of Scotland. It was this that kept the UK relatively warm in winter, which it is considering the latitude. Hard to believe when huddled against a North Sea wind in the dead of winter, but that statement was qualified as '*relatively*' warm.

Despite the heavy swells they made good headway. They also went from tropical gear back to blues.

While at sea, many sailors grow beards and this ship was no exception. One morning while the three apprentices were working together, a stranger walked past them. Doug turned to the others.

"Who the hell was that?" he asked.

"No idea!" was the response from the other two. They asked the Bosun if there'd been another stowaway. He laughingly told them it was one of the daytime ABs. He had shaved off his beard, and was totally unrecognizable with his white face, and it seemed that his chin had disappeared. There were two others the same; it was hilarious. They had shaved off their beards because they were soon going on leave; the goal was to get some color back into their faces where the beard had been, before going home to family. One of these sailors was asked, by one of the others, "What is the second thing you going to do when you get home to your wife!" His response, "Put my suitcase down!" Another remarked, "Hope the wife's not in the bath when I get home." "Why" he was asked. "I'll ruin my best suit."

As they got further north the swell diminished, and made life a little easier onboard especially for food preparation in the galley. For Ray, it also made serving meals a lot easier, but table cloths were still kept damp to stop plates of food sliding all over the place. They were still enjoying the Argentine beef, especially the steaks. On one occasion the cook made a large steak pie which was really good. Edward smiled as he recalled the comic book 'Dandy', that he had read as a kid. The front page of which was taken up by the character 'Desperate Dan', who regularly consumed a cow pie with horns sticking out of the pastry crust. On the ship, the only thing missing from the pie was the cow horns.

The ship would still occasionally give an unexpected lurch into a deep trough, catching everyone off guard. She'd dip her bows into the wall of water ahead, and come up shuddering, throwing her bows into the air and defiantly shaking off the offending water. It was a wonderful thing to watch and thrilled Edward, proud to be a seafarer.

One of these occasions, however, was not such a thrill. Edward was on deck with George, the AB from his watch, and they were on their way forward to get some rope that they were going to splice. Walking along the deck in the shelter of the flying bridge, they figured that they were safer there, than actually on the flying bridge, where they would've had to go onto the fo'c'sle and then down to the fore deck to the fo'c'sle entrance. A wave shipped onboard and ripped across the deck. Edward, walking on the outside of the AB was caught off guard. Unable to grab onto anything, he was swept off his feet. George was able to grab hold of one of the flying bridge supports with one hand, and had reached out with the other to grab Edward, but missed.

Edward was swept across the deck on his side like a rag doll, ending up at the side railings on the ship's starboard side. On the way across, he had hit a rail at a tank lid, an ullage plug, and some piping, but had been unable to grab onto anything. With the breath knocked out of him he hit a stanchion of the side rails, grabbed it, and hung on for dear life, literally. His legs were dragged under the bottom rail as the sea poured back over the side. The ship then rolled to port, away from the sea on his side and he pulled his legs back inboard.

He was about to get up when he heard George yell, "Hang on!" The roll to port shipped another wave that was now racing across the deck towards him. Edward held a rail with his left hand and wrapped his right arm around the stanchion and grabbed onto the left shoulder of his jacket. He swung his legs up wrapping them round the rail, interlocking his ankles and feet. He looked wide-eyed at the water hissing across the deck towards him, took a deep breath, closed his eyes, tucked in his chin, and held on with all his strength.

As the water enveloped him he remembered thinking, *Oh, come on Mother, it's far too soon for it all to end like this,* and at the same time terrified that he would not be able to hang on.

The water subsided and was gone, and George was by his side yelling, "Let go Edward!" as he slapped his hands that held the rail and his shoulder, locked into position by his fear. With some difficulty he relaxed his fingers, and George pulled him free of the rail. Wrapping his arm around Edward's waist, he hauled him to the safety of the amidships accommodation and its shelter.

Sat on a storm step on the after end of the accomodation, Edward caught his breath. Looking up, he simply said. "Thanks George."

"Fuck!" was all George could manage.

Edward looked down, noticing with a start that his feet were bare. "Hey! I lost my shoes and socks!"

George, laughing nervously, knelt down beside him and put an arm around his shoulder, "Thank fuck that's all you lost Edward." he said seriously, giving him a squeeze.

Edward winced. Reality started to set in and he started to shake. It was only now that he started to feel the results of his slide across the deck. He noticed that Stores and the Bosun were also there, looking concerned.

The First Mate arrived, "You alright Paige?" he asked.

"Yes Sir, I'm fine, just got knocked over by a wave."

"Come on." he ordered.

Edward got up and involuntary winced.

"Let's go take a look at you!" the Mate said.

Inside the ship's office Edward stripped to his under-shorts and found that bruises were already showing on his legs, arms, and chest. The Mate determined that nothing was broken.

"You'll be alright Paige, just a bit sore for the next few days." Then looking him in the eyes he added sincerely, "Thankfully, it would appear, you are very lucky, son".

The Second Mate, on watch on the Bridge at the time, had witnessed everything, and had immediately altered course to starboard to swing the stern away from Edward, who, he said afterwards, he was certain had gone over the side. He had also released the life buoy from the starboard wing. This is that round float that has the ships name painted on it. There is one on either wing of the bridge and they are stowed in a wooden slanted frame and held into position by a large wooden pin that goes through a hole in the steel bulwark through the hole in the lifebuoy and then through the wooden frame, simply pulling this pin out releases the buoy into the sea. Attached to these buoys is a light that is stowed upside down in a clamp and is pulled out with the buoy. Once in the water the light floats upright and activates a mercury switch that in turn activates a flashing light. This was now floating away in the rough Atlantic, fortunately not marking the spot of Edward in the water. "Holy shit, Paige, you scared the crap out of me!" the Second Mate said later. "I thought you had gone over the side for sure. Thank God you're safe."

Edward smiled, "Thank you, Second Mate. Hopefully the sea is not going to claim me that easy."

The Second Mate just smiled sadly, exhaling sharply through his nose, and shook his head from side to side.

"I was getting ready to sound man-over-board, it was hard to believe, when the sea subsided, that you were still there clinging to the rail. Thank God!" he added sincerely.

The man-over-board signal is three long blasts on the ships whistle; the letter O in the Morse code and also O in the international code of flags – when hoisted on a yardarm on its own, simply means man-over-board. Sounding this on the ships whistle would have brought a lot of people out on deck. Edward was reminded of his father who, although spending 20 years at sea in trawlers, could not swim a stroke. When Edward had asked him why, his reply was simple. "There is no sense in prolonging the agony, if you go over-the-side in a storm, once the skipper has turned the ship around, it's like looking for a football, your head, bobbing up and down in the storm tossed sea. They just wouldn't find you!" was his fatalistic conclusion. Edward reasoned though that from a low lying trawler disappearing down into the deep troughs of the ocean the latter comment was likely true. From the vantage point of the bridge wing, on this ship some 25 feet above the surface, would be a different story. *I don't think I would have given up that easily* thought Edward. *After all, hope lies eternal in the human sole, when hope is lost, all is lost.*

Many onboard, when they learnt what had happened, voiced much the same concern and thankfulness. The Captains comment though pulled at Edward's heart strings when he simply said, "Mrs. Landry would never have forgiven me if I had lost you Paige. Just be more careful out there!"

The incident was never mentioned again.

52

One morning, Doug had made his usual trip to the Bridge before breakfast, to see the First Mate for the work orders of the day. When he excitedly returned, he gave Edward and John some unexpected news; the three of them were to be relieved in Dundee, to go on leave. This really was a surprise, as both Edward and John had expected to do closer to one year onboard, which Doug was actually close to. The news delighted both Doug and John, and Edward was thrilled at the prospect of seeing his Mum, Dad and sisters. For some strange reason though, he was sad about the thought of leaving the ship and his comrades, and the friends that he had made.

One thing Edward did smile at was, that on his next ship he would no longer be a first tripper! However, he would never forget that he had been very close to being only that.

As they approached the narrowest part of the Atlantic, west of Scotland, many trawlers - fishing boats, appeared. This really piqued Edward's interest, and he went up to the bridge to look through binoculars at them; watching as they totally disappeared from sight into the deep troughs of the rolling ocean. Thoughts of his father filled his mind; of when he had plied these waters on his way to the Newfoundland Banks, to fill the holds with cod.

Over the next few days Edward saw more of the trawlers fighting their way westward. They not only fought the sea and weather, but also the current that was against them on their outward journey. All bore large identification numbers and letters painted on their bow and stern; Gy for Grimsby, H for Hull, Lt for Lowestoft and An for Aberdeen; he saw them all. As they made their way east, some of these could be seen heading northwesterly to the fishing grounds off Iceland.

They made their landfall at the Butt of Lewis, the northern tip of the Isle of Lewis in the Outer Hebrides. The craggy barren-looking land, filled with sea birds, was a welcome sight after their long ocean trek. From there it was Easterly to Cape Wrath, on the northwest Scottish mainland, and then on to Pentland Firth.

Edward knew, from his father's books, that it was north of here in 1939, not long after the Second World War had started, that the Royal Navy's flagship, HMS Hood, was sunk by the German battleship Bismarck, she had sunk so fast that there had been a loss of over 1,200 men; news that stunned the British Nation into disbelief. This event set up the largest sea hunt of all time by the Royal Navy. Their orders had been simple - find and sink the Bismarck. They eventually did, although it had been no easy task.

....

Through the Pentland Firth they headed down into the North Sea, Edward's 'home sea', away from land once more, as they crossed the bay that leads down into Moray Firth. The seas were short and choppy, with a cool Arctic wind from the northeast. Landfall was once more made, and they rounded Rattray Head to begin their final run down to the Firth of Tay and Dundee. The weather was now on their stern so they were making good time, putting the final run down this part of the Scottish coast at about eight hours. They would arrive the following morning.

The apprentices got their suitcases and trunks out of storage and started packing. Edward, his gear having been new when he last packed, had a devil of a job getting the now used gear - well, used except for those white number tens - back into the same space; plus he now had the things that he had purchased. From duty free, he had bought a carton of 200 Senior Service cigarettes for himself. Nobody else in his family smoked, and neither would he when in the house. He also had a bottle of Cutty Sark Scotch for his Dad.

Now alongside in Dundee the Customs Rummagers came onboard and searched the ship for contraband. Declaration forms had to be completed for all articles purchased abroad. Edward completed his form declaring everything and their true cost. They then had to line up to see the customs officer and pay any duty that was due. The officer, looking at Edward as it became his turn, asked what he did on the ship. After hearing that he was a first trip apprentice, he reduced the value of all Edward's purchases by so much that he ended up paying just a few shillings duty. Nice guy!

Edward did his morning watch, then showered and changed into the new gear he had bought in Curacao. It was mid-afternoon when his relief came onboard, a young lad named Peter, from Aberdeen. God Bless him, he was a first tripper, who Edward left in the charge of Doug. In the meantime, he had searched out Chippy and Sparky and said his goodbyes; shaking hands and giving a big hug to both. He thanked them for looking after him; friends and shipmates that he would never forget.

Together with John and Doug, he said his goodbyes to Captain Landy who, being a true gentleman, had taught them so much, and whose parting words were, "Keep up the studies boys."

They also said their goodbyes to the First, Second and Third Mates, just incase they missed them when it came time to actually leave. Edward signed off the ship, and received his papers and pay owed him to that date.

Incidentally, Shell had obtained Jimmy the stowaway's papers, Discharge Book etc. and they were delivered to the ship. He went ashore with the ship's agent to do whatever paperwork had to be done, and from there returned home to Glasgow.

Edward was ready to leave and said his farewells to Doug and John, who were leaving a little later when their relief's turned up. He wished all the very best to Peter, the First Tripper. He took his bags ashore to the waiting taxi, supplied by Shell. The taxi would take him to the station, where he'd catch a train to Grimsby. Going back onboard he again said goodbye to his cabin mate John, and they shook hands warmly.

He had been onboard the ship for almost nine months and smiled as he thought about it. His experiences over those nine months, an appropriate number, made him feel that he had been re-born.

At the top of the gangway he took a final look around the ship on which he had learnt so much. Then, looking beyond, he stared at the white crested sea in the distance.

"I have to go," he said softly to the sea.

"I have to go away for a while, but I'll be home again soon."

LaVergne, TN USA
14 December 2010
208597LV00001B/43/P